N. G. OSBORNE

RESILIENCE

N. G. Osborne grew up in Angus, Scotland and graduated in 1995 from Oxford University with a B.A. in Politics, Philosophy & Economics. At the age of eighteen, Osborne spent twelve months as a volunteer for Project Trust working in a school and the Afghan refugee camps of Peshawar, Pakistan. This experience was the inspiration for his novel Refuge. Resilience is the second book in the trilogy.

Resilience

The Second Book of Refuge

A Novel by

N. G. Osborne

Cranham & Keith Books

FIRST EDITION, NOVEMBER 2013

Copyright © 2013 by N. G. Osborne

ISBN-13: 978-0-6159028-0-7

For my parents

James and Georgie Osborne

Human beings have enormous resilience.

Mohammad Yunus

PART I

entry

ONE

Riyadh, Saudi Arabia

April 1992

NOOR TAKES IN the vast entrance hall and feels as if she's passed through the gates of hell. The mahogany doors and antique furniture, the upside down forest of crystal chandeliers and the profusion of Ming era vases and gold ornaments all seem placed there to incinerate her soul. At the far end, twenty Indonesian and Filipino maids, dressed in black dresses and white pinafores, stand in a line. They seem to Noor like a brigade of the devil's minions. Despite the fact that her niqab and abaya cover her from head to toe, Noor shrinks under their collective, neutral gaze.

"What do you think of your new home?" the perfectly coiffured woman says.

"It's incredible," Badia says.

"And you, Noor?"

Noor doesn't reply. Rather she has become transfixed by a fleck of dirt on the otherwise shining marble floor. It seems so out of place, so subversive.

"Malaya," the woman says, "please relieve Princess Noor of her outer garments."

An elderly maid at the far end of the line approaches. She offers Noor a gentle, grandmotherly smile.

"Your Highness," Malaya says.

Noor shakes her head. Malaya looks over at the woman.

"If her Highness wishes to remain covered that is her choice," the woman says.

"You can take mine," Badia says.

Badia unwraps the niqab from around her head and wrestles free from her abaya. She hands them to Malaya and shakes her hair loose like a dog that's just been let out of its kennel.

"Let me show you the rest of the palace," the woman says.

The woman strides across the marble floor, the click clack of her four-inch heels breaking the otherwise perfect silence. Badia scurries to catch up. They make an incongruous pair. Badia's finest shalwar kameez looks tawdry in comparison to the woman's exquisite get up. In her perfectly tailored jacket and knee length skirt the woman resembles a high-powered business executive. When she walks her jet black hair undulates like waves on a sun dappled ocean. It's only when the woman looks back that Badia outshines her for Badia is not only twenty years younger but also far better looking. However masterful her make-up job, the woman cannot mask the fact that nothing about her face quite fits; her nose is too large, her lips too thin and her cheekbones too flat.

"Come on, Noor," the woman says.

They pass through a series of carpeted reception rooms, each grander than the last, before arriving at a sunlit courtyard. It has gravel paths lined with lemon and orange trees, alcoves with couches and gurgling fountains, a manicured lawn and rose bushes of every conceivable color and scent. The woman points proudly at the glass roof and remarks that it was modeled on the one in her own palace.

"On cooler days it can be retracted," she says before indicating an aviary over in one corner.

Badia asks a never-ending litany of questions in broken Arabic. Noor only picks up a fraction of the woman's answers not because her own Arabic is deficient but because, right now, it requires all her concentration just to stay on her feet.

Beyond the courtyard is a dining room, its table set for twenty with solid gold cutlery and plates, a succession of sitting rooms, a television room with five huge TVs, and an indoor swimming pool with an azure tiled bottom. Noor stares at its languid depths and wishes she could be down there and never disturbed again.

The woman breaks Noor's trance by saying she'll have to show them the outdoor pool and gardens another time. It's too hot right now. Instead they make their way along another wing of the palace. Here there's a mosque which could fit thirty but which is purely for Noor's use. There is a nursery with a gilded crib awaiting a yet unborn child, and then a never ending series of guest bedrooms. To Badia's delight, the woman tells her that she can choose whichever one she wants. They come to a smaller hall. Two mahogany doors lead off it. The woman points at the one on the left.

"Through there are the only rooms in the palace you must never enter," the woman says. "They're where the Prince receives guests when staying here. And through here, are your private quarters."

The woman guides them into a suite that consists of a small dining room, another sitting room, and finally Noor's bedroom. It's the size of a tennis court. Noor stares at its four-poster bed and wants nothing more than to lie down. The woman, however, insists on showing Noor her closet. It's almost as large as the bedroom and is already outfitted with a vast selection of clothes and shoes. The bathroom is only slightly smaller.

"Look, Noor," Badia shrieks. "Tariq wasn't lying. The taps really are made of gold."

Noor feels the room begin to spin.

"I must rest," she says.

They're the first words she's spoken since they landed in Riyadh.

"Of course," the woman says, "but before you do, you must allow me to look at you."

Noor doesn't have the energy to object. The woman walks up to her and delicately removes the niqab from her face. The woman gazes at Noor like she is a work of fine art.

"You're even more beautiful than your considerable reputation led me to believe."

"It's my curse," Noor says.

A tear winds its way down Noor's cheek. The woman wipes it away with the tip of a perfectly manicured finger.

"No, you're mistaken. Allah is ever merciful and beneficent. Your beauty is a gift from Him."

Noor's legs go from underneath her, and she collapses onto the floor. Malaya and another maid appear by her side and carry her to the bed. Noor feels a hand on her cheek and opens her eyes. The woman is leaning over her.

"I'm sorry," Noor says, "but I've forgotten your name."

"I am Princess Hadiya, the Prince's first wife. I will come by tomorrow and check on you."

"Thank you, but that won't be necessary."

Princess Hadiya frowns.

"For if Allah is truly merciful," Noor says, "I will surely be dead by then."

TWO

THE CAR DROPS down into the gloom of the Midtown Tunnel. Charlie's father breaks the silence.

"Natalie and the twins are dying to see you. But I still think it's best if we go straight over to Lennox Hill."

Charlie looks over at his father. The passing fluorescent lights make his complexion seem sickly and pale.

"Don't worry, we won't have to wait around," his father says. "Doctor Young called this morning and secured you a bed."

"I'm not going to the hospital, Dad."

"You have a fractured skull and a broken arm, Charlie, and God knows how many other injuries."

"I don't have time. I've got to get to Saudi Arabia."

"And how do you intend on doing that?"

"I'll get a visa."

"Doing what?"

"A tourist visa."

"There's no such thing. If you don't have a job they don't let you in."

"How do you know?"

"Last year half my clients were Saudis. Iraqi invasion had them buying U.S securities like they were going out of style."

Charlie spots the end of the tunnel approaching and, for the first time in his life, his heart doesn't beat faster upon approaching Manhattan.

"I'll get a job," Charlie says.

"Doing what?"

"Demining. The Iraqis laid millions of them along the border."

"And who's your reference going to be? Your last job? The one you were fired from for having an inappropriate relationship with a local. That'll certainly go down well with the Saudis."

The car bursts out into the bright light. Charlie's head throbs and he closes his eyes, the cacophony of midtown Manhattan jackhammering his skull. They stop behind a line of cars.

"Look, I'm sorry if I sound like a prick," his father says. "I don't mean to, but Noor's gone, Charlie, married to a man, wealthier and more powerful than you, me and nearly every other living soul on this planet. Now if there was a way I could help, I would, but there's nothing I can do, hell there's nothing the U.S. Government can do. Somehow, some way, you have to move on."

Charlie opens his eyes. Up ahead the light turns green and the cars start to pull away.

"See, Dad, that's the difference between you and me," he says. "I've never been good at that."

Charlie grabs his duffel bag. The driver behind them leans on his horn.

"What are you doing?" his father says.

Charlie pulls on his handle and kicks the door open. He practically tumbles out of the car.

"Thanks for picking me up," he says.

Charlie edges around the front of the car and hobbles across the other lane of traffic. A yellow cab screeches to a halt. The driver screams at him. Charlie reaches the sidewalk and looks back. His stricken father has gotten out. He stands by his car's open door.

"Charlie, please," he shouts. "Don't do this."

Charlie gives him a final wave and continues down Third Avenue.

THREE

IN THE GARDEN back in Peshawar, Noor and Charlie sit side by side on the oak tree's highest bough. Up through the canopy they can make out a million stars, while down below is the veranda with its seductive rocking chairs. Their hands entwine. There is no need for words for it's as if their minds are one. Baba calls out to them. They scramble down the trunk to join him, Bushra and Wali for dinner. At the table Baba expounds on the latest V. S. Naipaul novel he's read. Charlie proposes a toast and they all lift their glasses.

"To life," Charlie says, and they all repeat it.

Noor looks down the table to find her father staring at her, his eyes glassy with pride and love.

"You are going to have an amazing one, my love," he says.

Noor smiles.

Yes I am, she thinks.

She feels Charlie squeeze her shoulder as if in confirmation.

"Noor ... Noor," a voice says.

It's a woman's voice. It feels so out of place. She turns towards Charlie but he's no longer there. Her chair begins to rock as if she's in the midst of an earthquake.

"Noor ... Noor."

She looks back down the table only to discover that Baba has disappeared also.

"Noor."

She opens her eyes to find a shadowy figure shaking her. She screams, and instinctively the person retreats.

"Please Noor," Badia says, "you must get up. At least have something to drink."

"Get out," Noor screams. "Get out! Get out!"

Badia squeals and sprints from the room. Noor closes her eyes, yearning for the happy memories to return. However they don't, for Noor is now awake, and when she's awake she is racked with nothing but nightmares, nightmares that are all too real.

Hours of wakeful horror pass. She recalls her father on his knees on the lawn, asking Allah to pardon his sins only for Tariq to shoot him dead. She imagines Charlie being dragged into a freezing courtyard where a group of mujahideen encircles him, each with a large stone in hand. The first is thrown. It strikes Charlie at the base of his skull. Charlie topples forward, blood oozes from the wound, and soon after the other stones rain down on him. His body jerks under the barrage until finally it moves no more, the very life beaten out of him.

"Let me die, Allah," Noor whispers. "I beg you let me die, for what purpose do I have anymore?"

Despite her parched throat and cracked lips, Noor can still cry and cry she does. Tears pour down her cheeks as she calls out to Charlie and her father, begging them to intercede with God so that she might join them. She hears the door open and she screams at Badia to leave her alone. But it isn't Badia, it's Princess Hadiya. Malaya and three other maids come creeping in behind her. The Princess sits down on the bed beside Noor.

"Please get out. Please. Leave me in peace," Noor says.

"That's not possible, my dear," Princess Hadiya says. "We need to get you cleaned up."

Princess Hadiya nods at the maids. They attempt to remove Noor's urine soaked abaya. Noor lashes out, kicking her legs and swinging her arms, but she is too weak to resist for long. She closes her eyes and weeps once more as her clothes are removed.

Perhaps I'm mistaken, she thinks, *perhaps I'm already dead and they're preparing me for my funeral.*

They carry her naked body across the room and place it in a warm bath. She feels washcloths soap her limbs, her breasts, her face. Someone comes up behind her and washes her hair.

Yes, that's it, I'm dead.

They lift her out of the bath and back to the bed. The sheets feel clean and crisp. She assumes this is her *kafan,* her burial shroud. They dress her in a gown. Noor waits for them to wrap the *kafan* around her. Instead a pillow is placed underneath her head. Noor opens her eyes to find Princess Hadiya perched by her bed. She sobs once more. Her fantasy is over. Princess Hadiya strokes Noor's hair and after a while her efforts have an effect. Noor quiets. Princess Hadiya raises a china cup to Noor's lips. Noor shakes her head and the Princess takes the cup away. A minute later she brings it back up again and Noor shakes her head once more. The Princess retreats but she never gives up. Finally Noor's lips part and a sweet, syrupy tea trickles down her throat. She descends into another bout of tears.

I've failed, she tells herself.

She accepts a second cup and then a third, and when Princess Hadiya offers her a plate of dates and bread she consumes those too.

"I assume you're not happy about this marriage," Princess Hadiya says.

Noor doesn't respond.

"It's all right, you wouldn't be the first woman in the Kingdom to feel this way."

Princess Hadiya nods at Malaya who opens the curtains. Noor shields her eyes from the bright light.

"How long have I been here?" Noor asks.

"Four days," Princess Hadiya says. "I have to say, of all the Prince's wives, past and present, that's a record."

"How many has he had?"

"You will be his eighth."

"But you were his first?"

Princess Hadiya smiles.

"He can't divorce me, my father is much too important."

Princess Hadiya looks at her watch and stands.

"Everyone is so eager to meet you, and on most days we, ladies, meet at four. Now you don't have to come today, you don't even have to come this week, but I won't let you mope forever. At some point you need to embrace your new life, Noor, however hard that might seem right now."

Noor bites her lip. Tears form once more in her eyes.

"Does he beat you?" she says.

A flicker of despair passes over Princess Hadiya's otherwise serene face, but only a flicker.

"The Prince is my husband," she says. "As a righteous woman I am devoutly obedient to him. It will be best if you are too."

Princess Hadiya exits the room, leaving Noor alone once more.

FOUR

CHARLIE SITS IN the doctor's office and scans the pamphlet he brought with him. It contains the latest Saudi job listings. Financial analyst, drilling foreman, machine engineer, geologist, energy systems specialist, IT consultant, cardiologist, clinical nurse specialist, hematologist, paramedic, radiology technician, ultrasound technician, HR systems analyst, commercial development consultant, teacher ...

He pauses on teacher and reads the description: 'Candidates must have a Masters degree with specialization appropriate to subject assigned, a North American teaching credential and at least six years full-time experience.'

I'm not remotely qualified, he thinks.

The only thing he is qualified for is demining, yet when he'd looked into demining jobs he'd discovered that all of those operations were based out of Kuwait. It made sense; the Iraqis never laid mines across the Saudi border.

God damn it, he thinks. *There's nothing.*

A technician wanders into the waiting room.

"Charlie Matthews," he says.

Charlie stands and a searing pain envelops his left foot. He limps as best he can into the x-ray room and sits on the table. The technician takes in Charlie's plastered right arm, the yellowed bruises on his face, his shorn and bandaged head.

"Car accident?" the technician says.

"If only," Charlie says.

"Ah, I see. So how many were there?"

"I'm sorry."

"Only other explanation is that you got beat up."

Charlie gives the technician a grim smile.

"Honestly I don't remember," he says. "A few I think."

"And now your foot's bothering you?"

"I was stupid enough to sublet a seventh floor walk up in the East Village."

"Yeah that's generally not a good idea even when you're healthy."

The technician asks Charlie to take off his left shoe and sock, and places a lead gown over Charlie's torso. He then places an x-ray plate underneath Charlie's foot.

"How long you been doing this?" Charlie says.

"A few years now," the technician says.

"You enjoy it?"

"Pays well. Hours are decent."

The technician pulls the x-ray tube down and focuses its ray on the center of Charlie's foot.

"How long did it take you to get qualified?" Charlie says.

"Couple of years."

"Guess it's complicated."

The technician takes an image and removes the plate.

"Not really, these technical colleges like to suck as much money out of you as they can."

"So you think I could learn it quicker than that if I wanted?"

"Sure. There are accelerated programs out there where you can graduate in a year. Longer hours but if you're in a hurry ..."

I'm in more than a hurry, Charlie thinks.

The technician has Charlie turn his leg on its side. He takes another image. He grabs both plates and disappears into a darkroom.

Charlie retrieves the job listings from his jacket pocket and finds the postings for radiology technicians. He looks at the requirements. 'A.R.R.T. certification in radiography. Graduate of a 2 year A.M.A. approved School of Radiologic Technology. Minimum of five years experience in Radiologic Technology.'

There's no way I can fulfill these requirements, he says to himself.

The technician returns with the developed x-rays and stuffs them in a folder. Charlie stares at him.

Not if you apply as yourself.

"That's my part done," the technician says.

The technician heads for the door. Charlie jerks out of his daze.

"Mind if I ask you a question?" Charlie says.

"Not at all," the technician says.

"Would you ever consider working in Saudi Arabia?"

The technician laughs.

"Why? You recruiting?"

"Just curious."

The technician shakes his head.

"Nah, it's not for me. From what I hear you can't drink over there, do anything fun for that matter."

"What if it was only for two years, say at twice your present salary."

The technician thinks.

"No, not even then. But I'm sure there's a bunch of fools who could be persuaded."

There's got to be.

The technician exits, and Charlie focuses once more on the listings. One stands out. It's at the King's Hospital in Riyadh.

Riyadh. Where Noor is.

The doctor ambles in, his nose stuck in the x-rays.

"You're in luck," he says. "Seems like it's merely a sprain."
Charlie couldn't care less. He's already working on a plan.

FIVE

NOOR WALKS UP to the edge of the indoor swimming pool and stares at its crystal clear waters. A couple of weeks ago, when she first arrived, the thought of sinking to the bottom, would have been too tempting. But now ...

What's stopping me? she wonders.

She slips off her sandals and sits down. She dips her feet below the surface. The water is warm and seductive. She senses a presence and turns. Malaya is standing by the far door. Noor's certain that Hadiya has instructed Malaya to keep a close eye on her. She's everywhere Noor goes.

"It's fine, Malaya," Noor says, "I don't require anything."

"I'm most happy to stay, your Highness," Malaya says in perfect English.

"That's kind of you, but right now I'd prefer some privacy."

Malaya seems torn. Noor has given her a direct order, and what Noor's learned is that when she gives one the servants respond immediately. A few days ago when she had first left her bedroom and begun roaming the house, she'd noticed that the maids would stop their work and stare at her when she entered a room. It had made her feel so uncomfortable that on next seeing Malaya she'd asked that they not do this.

The next day, to her great shame, whenever she entered a room the maids would look away, some even going to the trouble of turning their backs on her, and despite rescinding the order, the maids had continued to avert their gaze whenever she passed by. Noor suspects they'll do so forever now.

I have never been more alone, she thinks, and she finds herself once more fighting back tears.

Her grief has come in waves. There have been times when she's been so overcome that she's collapsed on the ground and descended into self-perpetuating bouts of sobbing. At certain points she would sense the presence of others - Malaya, Badia, Princess Hadiya - but they were no more than garbled blurs, her grief so all consuming that her capacity to focus and hear had seemingly vanished.

At other times when her mind has been clearer she has called out to Charlie and begged him to come back. When he didn't she would scold Allah, calling Him all sorts of vicious slurs, only to then reverse course and beg for His mercy. After all wasn't it true that only He, the Almighty, had the power to raise the dead?

Why, oh why, couldn't He do that for me now?

She senses someone close by and looks towards the door. Malaya isn't there.

"It's going to be all right, Noor," she hears Charlie say.

Noor freezes. Charlie sits down, his feet caressing the water beside her.

"How do you know?" she says.

"Do you trust me?" he says.

"Of course."

"Then there's no need to ask. Just believe."

All Noor wants to do is turn in Charlie's direction and hold his face in her hands. However she doesn't. She daren't. For some time they sit there luxuriating in each other's presence. He rises.

"Don't go," she says.

"For now I must," Charlie says.

"You don't understand, I can't live without you."

"You did once and you can again."

Her chest heaves. Charlie places a hand on her shoulder.

"Shhh," he says. "You must be strong, Noor. Promise you'll be strong for me."

Noor nods.

"I love you," he says. "I always will."

Noor twists around, but it's too late. Charlie's gone. Noor lets out a pained wail.

"Your Highness."

Noor turns to discover Malaya back by the door.

"Can I be of assistance?" Malaya says.

Noor shakes her head. She stands and staggers down the corridor. A maid sees her coming and scurries off in the opposite direction. Noor passes the prayer room and stops. She finds herself unable to resist its pull. By the far wall is a silver basin. She turns on its gold tap and holds her hands underneath its cool stream.

The gift of clean water, she thinks.

She remembers when they had first stayed at Charlie's house. She had been so entranced by the water pouring from his shower. She washes herself then takes a rug and places it in the center of the room. It is the first time she has properly prayed since the day the Prince told her Charlie was dead. She raises her hands to her ears.

"Allah Akbar," she says. "Allah Akbar."

She brings her hands down and places her right arm over her left as if she were cradling a child.

"Subhanakalla humma wa bihamdik, wa tabarakas-muka, wa ta'ala jadduk, wa La Illaha Ghayruk."

Glory be to You, O Allah, and Yours is the praise and blessed is your Name, and exalted is Your Majesty, and there is no god besides You.

"Audhu billahi minash shaytanir rajeem."

I seek refuge of Allah from the condemned Satan.

Refuge, she thinks, *once I sought it from Charlie, but now, O God, only You can provide it.*

She finishes and, for the first time in weeks, she feels God's presence and a veil lifted from her heart.

It's time to put my trust in Allah again, she tells herself. *He will show me the true purpose of my life.*

SIX

IT IS EIGHT o'clock at night, and Charlie sits on the scuffed, wooden floor of his barren seventh floor walk-up. He studies a radiography textbook. Through the floor the thumping beat of a Wu Tang Clan song reverberates while through the wall come the grunts and moans of a couple having boisterous sex.

The phone rings. Charlie dares not pick it up. He can't risk anyone on the other end hearing the babel that's pervading his apartment. The answering machine beeps and his recorded message plays.

"Hi, this is Tony Daniels at Saudi Recruiting Specialists USA. I'm sorry I'm unable to take your call at this time, but please leave a message and I'll be sure to return it as soon as possible."

The answering machine beeps. He waits for someone to leave a message. They don't.

Shit.

For the last two weeks he has divided his weekdays in two. In the morning he attends New York City College of Technology where he's enrolled in an "Introduction to Radiology" course, while in the afternoon, he shadows Brad, the technician who took the images of his foot. When he had first approached Brad with his proposal, Brad had turned him down. Charlie had then slipped him five hundred dollars, and Brad's reticence had melted away. As far as everyone at the radiology center is concerned Charlie is Brad's cousin getting a feel for the field. As far as Charlie's concerned it's a way to learn more advanced techniques and gain intelligence. On his second day, he'd managed to download a directory of all the parent company's technicians along with their home phone numbers. From there it had just been a question of calling the male ones at night and making his pitch. No one had bitten, but a couple had said they'd think about it. That must have been one of them. He hadn't given his phone number to anyone else.

Next door, the guy groans like someone's stepped on his balls, and the girl lets out one final orgasmic screech.

Thank God that's over.

He focuses on his textbook only for the phone to ring. Charlie scrambles over to it.

"Tony Daniels speaking," he says.

"Hi, this is Joe Stapinski. I thought I'd try again in case—"

"How you doing Joe?"

"Good, thanks ..."

There's a pause. Charlie waits.

Don't come across as too eager.

"Reason I'm calling," Joe says, "is I've been thinking about your job offer, and I've got to say it's tempting, I mean the salary at least."

"Don't forget the country club membership and the free car," Charlie says.

"I haven't ... I guess I was wondering if the position's still open."

"Give me a minute to pull it up on my computer?"

"Sure."

Charlie puts down the phone and pretends to type on the floor.

Make him wait, he tells himself. *Build the anticipation.*

Down below, the Wu Tang song finishes, only to be re-placed by a rap song with an even more thumping bass line. Charlie picks up the phone.

"Hey Joe, I'm sorry about that noise in the background. It's Steve, my co-worker. Idiot likes to crank up his computer speakers once everyone else's left the office."

"So is it still available?" Joe says.

Good, Charlie thinks. *You're eager.*

"Actually it is," Charlie says.

"So what would be the next step?"

"Well first I've got to get all your documents. The Saudis are very strict about that stuff. Won't even schedule an interview until they're sure they're in order."

"What documents you talking about?"

Charlie picks up the list he'd jotted down when he'd called about the job.

"Just the usual. Your medical certificates, diploma, a cou-ple of letters of reference, a letter of employment verification from your employer and, oh yeah, your passport."

Joe goes quiet.

Shit, Charlie thinks. *He doesn't have a passport.*

"I'm not sure if I can do that," Joe says. "I don't want my employer knowing I'm looking for a job."

Charlie relaxes.

"That's okay, totally understand. As long as you can get me the rest, we can hold off on the letter of employment for now. So when do you think you could have them ready?"

"I don't know. A week?"

"Can you do it quicker? Hate for you to lose out because someone slipped ahead of you."

"Well I suppose I could have them ready by Thursday."

"Great. I'm going to be in your part of town that day. How about I pop by and pick them up first thing. Nice and discreet."

"That could work."

Charlie hears a low but steadily rising set of moans emanate from next door.

Oh Jesus, not again.

"Mr. Daniels, I have one more question."

Shit.

The headboard starts thumping against the wall.

"People, they enjoy working in Saudi Arabia, right?"

"Joe, it's like living in a five star resort. I'm telling you, when your year's up, you're not going to want to leave."

Charlie hangs up and takes a deep breath.

You can do this, he tells himself. *All you got to do is continue to believe.*

SEVEN

NOOR SITS ON her bed. She wears a simple long sleeved Chanel dress that comes down to her knees. She would far rather have worn a shalwar kameez but she couldn't find any in her closet, not even the one she had arrived in. She suspects Princess Hadiya had it burned.

At least the dress is black, she thinks. *For mourning.*

She hears a knock.

"Come in," she says.

Malaya enters with a gentle smile on her face.

"I told you, you don't need to knock, Malaya," she says.

"I understand, your Highness, but the Prince prefers that I do."

Noor can't help but shiver. The very thought of his return fills her with dread.

"I wish you would allow me to make up your face," Malaya says.

"Are you worried 'the ladies' are going to eat me alive?" Noor says.

"No, I'm worried that you want them to."

Noor can't help but smile. Noor stands.

"I should be going," she says

"Aren't you forgetting something?" Malaya says.

Malaya goes to the closet and returns with a black abaya and niqab.

"Of course," Noor says.

Noor allows Malaya to place the abaya over her head. Malaya pulls it down until it hangs but a millimeter from the floor. She then wraps the niqab around Noor's face and hair. Finally Malaya pulls a pair of black silk gloves onto Noor's hands. The only thing anyone can now see of Noor are her eyes and the bridge of her nose.

They head through the house and out the main door. Noor wavers. The air is so dry and hot her lungs feel as if they're being scorched. A rotund Bangladeshi man in a thobe and checkered head dress waits beside a shining black Range Rover. Sweat is swathed across his brow. On seeing Noor he bows and opens the back door. Noor climbs into the freezing interior. The Range Rover pulls away and rolls through the palace compound. The compound is vast and lush, dotted with a myriad of sand colored buildings, expansive lawns, marble fountains and burgeoning flower beds. Noor imagines that many people might mistake it for heaven. They pull up outside Princess Hadiya's marble palace. It looks very similar to her own, and Noor wonders if the Prince had four of them built at the same time to house his eventual wives.

The passenger door opens and the driver indicates a set of carved wooden doors. On cue they swing open and Noor walks into a vast entrance hall. Noor realizes her presumption was correct. It is no different than her own. A maid awaits her.

"May I take your outer garments, your Highness," the maid says.

"Of course," Noor says.

The doors slam shut. Noor startles.

Now you're truly in the lion's den.

The maid takes great care removing Noor's abaya, niqab and gloves, and hands them to a subordinate.

"If you would, follow me," she says.

Noor's legs wobble. She chastises herself.

What are you scared of? The worst thing they can do is kill you.

They head down a long, carpeted corridor and as they approach another set of doors the hum of female voices gets ever louder. Once more the doors seem to magically open. The conversation halts. Seven perfectly made-up women stare up at her.

Back in Peshawar, when Noor had worked at Dutch Aid, the headmistress had given her the task of going through a box of books sent by some well meaning women from Atlanta. Beyond a plethora of out of date textbooks, there were a few titles that had excited Noor, Anne of Green Gables being one of them, and a few she'd considered downright peculiar. The most bizarre of all was a photo book featuring the cast of a TV show called Dynasty. Noor remembers staring at the book and wondering who these women were with their extravagant and shimmering gowns, plunging bodices, pearl draped necks and diamond laden earlobes.

In what world do creatures like this exist? she'd asked herself.

Now she finally has her answer for apart from the tone of their skins these women could have been plucked from those very pages.

Princess Hadiya, wearing a pink strapless gown, rises from her satin sofa and glides over to Noor.

"Salaam alaikum," she says.

She rubs her lips across each of Noor's cheeks.

"As-salaam alaikum," Noor says.

"I am so glad you came. Please let me introduce you around."

Hadiya takes Noor by the hand and escorts her over to the room's oldest inhabitant, a walrus of a woman in a ruffled gold gown. She sits beached in a love seat that's meant for two but which can barely contain her gargantuan backside.

The woman screws up her fleshy eyes and looks Noor up and down. Noor shivers. It reminds her of the way the Prince had first looked at her from the window of his S.U.V.

"Noor, this is Princess Fadilah. The Prince's mother," Hadiya says.

"Salaam alaikum," Noor says.

The woman doesn't respond but rather holds out a flabby hand. Noor thinks the woman is showing off the grape sized diamond ring on her index finger, but Hadiya soon disabuses her of that notion.

"You should kiss Princess Fadilah's hand," Hadiya whispers.

Noor leans in only for Princess Fadilah to clasp hold of her chin. Noor gasps. Princess Fadilah pulls Noor's face closer and examines her, her fetid, garlic breath enveloping the space between them. Princess Fadilah lets go but before Noor can straighten she grabs a hold of Noor's breasts and gives each of them a pinch. Princess Fadilah snorts.

"Her skin's so dusky, she might as well be a monkey, " Princess Fadilah says in Arabic. "But I see why he likes her. She's his type. Emaciated, no breasts, barely any hips. Cut her hair off and you'd mistake her for a boy."

"A boy monkey," one of the other women says.

A number of the women laugh. Princess Fadilah waves her hand at Noor as if she were shooing away a pesky animal.

"Suppose it'd be foolish to expect anything more knowing she's a whore from the slums," she says.

Noor maintains a neutral expression. Hadiya leans in.

"Princess Fadilah says you are a woman of remarkable beauty," Hadiya says in English.

Noor realizes no one in the room thinks she understands Arabic.

Why would I? After all I'm a whore from the slums.

Hadiya takes Noor's arm and guides her over to a chaise lounge on which a woman lies. She has pinched anorexic features and a barely concealed scowl.

And the mother had the audacity to call me thin.

"This is Princess Bahira, the Prince's second wife," Hadiya says.

"Salaam alaikum," Noor says.

Princess Bahira nods.

The next two women, Princess Mysha and Princess Ismah, sit side by side on a satin white couch. Their multiple chins look like rolls of dough, their pudgy jowls like the udders of a pregnant cow, and in front of them on an antique coffee table is what seems like a cafe's worth of French pastries. Hadiya mentions they are two of the Prince's sisters. Noor is unsurprised.

Like mother, like daughter.

Noor proffers salaams to the both of them but once again her greetings fall on deaf ears. Princess Hadiya moves Noor on and they approach a young woman in a slim, white, floor length dress. She wears heavy make-up and has her long hair done up in such a way that she looks like a Grecian oracle.

"Of course, you know Badia," Hadiya says.

Noor does a double take. Badia has so transformed her appearance that she didn't recognize her.

"Salaam alaikum," Noor says.

"Wa-alaikum salaam," Badia says before switching to Pashtu. "Are you better now?"

"I am," Noor says. "I apologize if I was cruel to you in any way."

"I forgive you," Badia says. "You've been through a lot. Even I found the transition hard."

Not from the looks of it, Noor thinks.

"I haven't seen you around the palace these last few days," Noor says.

Badia blushes.

"Princess Fadilah kindly offered me a room in her own palace," she says.

Before the conversation can progress further, Princess Hadiya intervenes.

"Enough with the secret conversation," Hadiya says, taking Noor once more by the arm. She guides her over to the final woman.

"This is Princess Asra, the Prince's third wife."

From her soft complexion Noor guesses that Asra is not much older than she. She is plump, though not nearly in the same weight class as the Prince's mother and sisters, and pretty with a mane of jet black hair and long eyelashes. It is her gregarious grin, however, that is her most striking quality. She jumps up from her couch and gives Noor a traditional kiss on both cheeks.

"Salaam alaikum," she says.

"Wa-alaikum salaam," Noor says.

"Oh, I can't tell you how good it is to have you here," Asra says switching to English. "You kept us waiting so long I thought the suspense might kill me."

"That's the last thing I'd wish."

Asra pats the cushion beside her.

"Well come sit. Are you hungry?"

"A little I suppose."

Asra snaps her fingers and a couple of servants materialize out of nowhere. One pours Noor a glass of tea as another offers an assortment of pastries and sweets from a silver tray. There is such a selection that Noor finds herself unable to choose. A flock of servants scurry about attending to the women's most basic needs while Princess Hadiya walks around wafting sweet smelling incense from a silver urn into the faces of the women.

"It's all right to have more than one," Asra whispers.

Noor picks up a pink fudge and pops it in her mouth. Its sweet yet salty taste transports her back to that night in Charlie's house when they had gorged themselves on Mukhtar's feast and drunk endless cups of tea as they talked grandly about their futures. Her throat constricts and tears rise in her eyes. Noor tries to breathe but it seems impossible.

It's all gone, she thinks. *They're all gone. Forever.*

Someone clasps her hand and she looks over to see Asra smiling at her.

"It's the incense, isn't it?" she says. "It's irritating your eyes."

Noor manages to nod, and Asra relays this explanation to the rest of the room.

"Come," Asra says, "You can wash them out in the bathroom."

Taking Noor by the arm, Asra guides her out of the room and down a corridor to a bathroom whose opulence already feels unremarkable. Noor sits down on the toilet seat and cries, so lost in her misery that when she finally sees Asra kneeling in front of her, she has no concept of how long she's been there.

"I detest him as much as you do," Asra says. "His mother even more if that's possible."

Asra's directness is enough to stop Noor's tears.

"She called you 'a whore from the slums', can you believe that?"

"It doesn't surprise me."

Asra holds out her hand. Noor allows Asra to pull her up. She guides Noor over to a make-up table where she uses foundation to disguise Noor's tear ravaged cheeks.

"She was right about one thing though," Asra says. "You are his type. Tall, thin, small tits."

"I guess I hit the trifecta," Noor says.

Asra frowns.

"It's a gambling term," Noor says.

"You've gambled?" Asra says.

She looks genuinely shocked.

"No, but someone not so long ago taught me the expression."

"A man?"

The greatest man who ever lived.

Princess Bahira enters the bathroom and glares at the two of them. Asra reddens like a guilty schoolgirl.

"We should go back in," Asra says.

On their return the remaining women turn their direction.

"What took you so long?" Princess Fadilah asks.

"She had something in her eye," Asra says. "It was almost impossible to get out."

"Well tell her I have some questions for her. About her background."

Noor patiently waits for Asra to translate what she already understands.

"Princess Fadilah wants to know more about you."

"Tell her she can ask me anything."

Asra translates, and Princess Fadilah comes back with her first question.

"She wants to know how long you were a refugee?" Asra says.

"Eleven years."

"And for that whole time you lived in a camp?"

"Yes, my father, sister, and my brother, at least for the first few years, lived in a mud hut no larger than that rug."

The women stare at the eight by six rug in incredulity.

"All of you?" Asra says.

"Yes. We had no running water, no toilet. I possessed only two sets of clothes and only a single pair of shoes."

The final detail draws gasps from the two sisters.

"You must feel very fortunate that my son plucked you from such an environment," Princess Fadilah says.

Asra translates.

"In my opinion she who sacrifices freedom for wealth deserves neither," Noor says.

Asra hesitates.

"What did she say?" Princess Fadilah says.

Asra has no choice but to translate Noor's remark. Princess Fadilah frowns.

"I don't understand," she says. "Is that a hadith? Something the Holy Prophet, peace be upon him, said?"

"No it's from Benjamin Franklin. Though if I'm not mistaken he said 'security' rather than 'wealth'."

Asra is about to translate when a speaker on the wall starts playing a recording of a muezzin calling the faithful to prayer. From a side door, a host of maids enter with silver bowls filled with warm water. They approach each of the women and, without any of the women lifting a finger, the maids wash their hands, face, arms and feet. Another set of maids lay seven prayer rugs on the floor. Two maids grasp one of Princess Fadilah's hands and pull her up from the love seat. The Princess takes her place on the prayer rug directly in front of everyone else's and leads the other women in prayer. When she drops to her knees the floor shakes and whenever she's required to stand the two maids rush over and raise her by the elbows.

Noor can't help but notice that none of the women want to get there before Princess Fadilah. They remain crouched over, knees bent, like sprinters on their starting blocks, until Princess Fadilah wobbles into position. Noor tries her best to concentrate on Allah but eventually she realizes it's impossible. She is too eager to get out of there.

Once the prayer is over, Princess Fadilah returns to her love seat with her head held high, as if she were the holiest woman in the Muslim world. Noor intercepts Princess Hadiya.

"I must be going," Noor says.

"We never even had a chance to talk," Hadiya says.

"I think it's best," Noor says.

Hadiya nods. Noor says goodbye to the other women and everyone, but Asra, seems relieved to see her go. Asra kisses Noor on both cheeks.

"Can I come by tomorrow?" she whispers.

"Of course. It's not as if I have anything else to do."

Noor walks out of the room and the doors close behind her.

Now they can truly gossip about me, she thinks.

EIGHT

CHARLIE SITS IN the rear of the ramshackle jewelry store, his friend, Rob, beside him. The Hasidic store owner squints at Charlie and strokes his long, salt and pepper beard. Charlie feels as if he's being examined with as much care as the diamonds.

"How do you know him?" the owner says.

"We were in the Gulf War," Rob says.

"You boys did good over there, but you should have kept after that bastard, Saddam. Sent him and those no good sons to hell."

"Wasn't up to us," Charlie says.

"No, I suppose it wasn't. Well go on then, show me what you need."

Charlie hands the owner the documents he received from Joe Stapinski that morning. The owner peers through his horn-rimmed glasses at the diplomas and medical certificates.

"A child could forge these," he says.

He picks up Stapinski's passport.

"But this, this is expensive."

He points with his stubby finger at Stapinski's passport photo. Stapinski and Charlie look nothing alike, Stapinski being bald, bespectacled and pale.

"Once I remove the photo," the owner says, "and replace it with one of yours, I must get the imprint to match exactly. See."

"I'm sorry, you misunderstood," Charlie says. "I have to return this. I need my photo and his information put into a copy."

The owner grabs a hold of the braid dangling below his right ear and twirls it around his finger.

"Oh, then that is even more expensive."

"How much?" Rob says.

"Three thousand dollars."

"That's a lot," Charlie says.

The owner tosses the passport back at him.

"Then go find someone else to do it."

There isn't anyone else. The only way Charlie had gotten to the jeweler was because one of Rob's side businesses was providing high end fake IDs to Upper East Side kids.

"Maybe we could do a package deal," Charlie says.

The owner drums his fingers on the desk.

"I need three more passports. A Turkish and an American one for her."

Charlie hands the owner the passport photo he took of Noor back in Peshawar.

"And a Turkish one for me. I've written it all down here. The names, the dates of birth."

The owner stares at Noor's photo.

"She's beautiful," he says.

He drags his attention back to Charlie.

"So why three?"

Charlie glances at Rob. He seems just as eager to know.

"If you don't tell me, young man," the owner says, "I can be of no assistance to you."

"I'm looking to get her out of Saudi Arabia. If we travel as a married Turkish couple we're less likely to raise suspicion."

"But then why the additional American passport?"

"Because once we're out, I need to get her into the United States."

The owner pushes his bulky frame out of his chair and lumbers over to a large, cast iron safe. He dials in the code and extracts a black binder. He returns to his desk and leafs through it.

"You seem to have thought of everything," he says.

"A lot of hours down at the library."

"But what about the Saudi entry and exit visa, have you thought about that?"

The owner flips the binder around and points to a photo-copy of an internal passport page with stamps and Arabic writing.

"If the two of you don't have an entry visa they will assume you entered the country illegally and will arrest you. And if you don't have an exit visa, they won't let you leave."

"Are you able to forge those?"

"Of course, anything can be forged. But these visas only have a six month window."

"So I have to choose a start date?"

"Exactly."

In Charlie's conversations with the employment agency, they had made clear that the hospital was hoping to have someone in place within a couple of months. But that all depended on the Saudi embassy in DC processing his visa in a timely manner. The agency said there had been rare instances where they had taken close to a year to approve an application.

"I need a date, sir," the owner says.

Charlie does a calculation in his head. Two to four months to get to Saudi Arabia. From that point who knows how long it would take to find Noor. He is tempted to start the clock towards the end of the year.

But what happens if you find her sooner? You won't be able to get her out. You might lose your one and only chance.

"Start the visa on July first," he says.

"Good," the owner says. "I should have the American passports within a week. The Turkish ones, they'll take longer, at least a month."

"And how much will it all cost?"

"Six thousand for the American passports, and fourteen for the Turkish ones, including the visas."

Charlie tries to look unfazed. He knew the passports would cost a lot but never this much.

"Like I said, I was hoping we could do a package deal," Charlie says.

"We are," the owner smiles. "I'm throwing in the medical certificates for free."

Charlie knows he has no other choice.

"Fifty percent up front," he says.

"As with Rob that is always the case."

Charlie takes out an envelope from his inside pocket and counts out a hundred hundred dollar bills. It comprises every last penny he'd saved in Pakistan.

Where the hell am I going to find the other fifty percent? he thinks.

The owner borrows an eyepiece from the old man next to him and examines a couple of the bills.

"You know if you fail in your endeavor they'll chop your head off," he says. "You must love this woman very much."

"I do," Charlie says. "More than life itself."

NINE

THAT NIGHT, NOOR'S despair returns with a vengeance. Despite praying over an hour, Allah offers her no guidance, no reason for continuing on in this world. She returns to her bed and clings to one of her pillows. She imagines it's Charlie, and they're safe and sound in a place where no one can find them. It's enough to lull her to sleep.

When she awakens it is close to noon. She forces herself out of bed and looks for something to occupy herself. She discovers it's a fruitless task. Her Filipina staff does every ordinary task she can think of. Malaya brings her breakfast and has another maid draw a bath. Whilst in the bath her bed is made, her room is cleaned, and a maid even squirts some toothpaste on her toothbrush.

Noor wanders through the house on a hunt for something to read but finds only fundamentalist, religious texts. In the sitting room she turns on the television and finds its offerings equally bleak. There are three channels in total with the first featuring a documentary on the haj, the second some rant by a long-bearded cleric, and the last a stultifying news item about the Crown Prince opening a new hospital wing. When she asks Malaya if there is a library in the palace, Malaya gapes at her as if she's enquired into the existence of the closest bar.

"When Princess Shafia lived here," Malaya says, "the Prince was most insistent that she not soil her mind with forbidden books."

No wonder Princess Shafia ended up killing herself, Noor thinks. *Beyond the beatings, she must have gone stir crazy.*

"Are you Muslim, Malaya?" Noor asks.

Malaya's eyes flick around the room as if the religious police might be lurking behind the curtains.

"My beliefs should be of no concern, your Highness," she says.

"I'm just curious, I promise, nothing more."

Malaya stands there, her lips pursed.

"Please know," Noor says, "that 'whoever believes in God and does good, shall have their reward from their Lord. And that includes Christians and Jews.'"

"Please, your Highness, I beg you not speak in such a way, especially once the Prince returns. It will only inflame him."

"I don't see why. All I'm doing is quoting from the Holy Quran."

Malaya doesn't seem to believe her and to her evident relief another maid enters and announces that Princess Asra has arrived. Moments later Princess Asra bursts in wearing a pair of cut off shorts and a tight t-shirt.

"You looked shocked," Asra says.

"I didn't realize you could dress that way," Noor says.

"As long as a man never sees you, you can wear whatever you want."

"Even around the Prince?"

"No."

"I thought not."

"He's only interested in seeing us naked."

Noor would laugh if the prospect wasn't so terrible.

"What do you say we go swimming?" Asra says.

"I can't swim," Noor says.

"Then I'll teach you."

"I don't have a bathing suit."

"Trust me you have hundreds."

Asra pulls Noor into her walk-in closet. She opens drawer after drawer and soon enough discovers five that contain nothing but bathing suits.

"Chanel, Dior, Armani," she says tossing the bathing suits onto the floor until she finds a skimpy gold two piece that takes her fancy.

"Ah Versace, perfect."

She strips. Noor stares at her.

"First time you've seen a naked woman?" Asra says grinning.

"In the flesh," Noor says.

"So what do you think? I'm fat, aren't I?"

Asra is a curious mix. Her breasts are small and pert, while her round belly protrudes out over a perfectly waxed groin that's squeezed between two ample thighs. In fact if it weren't for the thin, horizontal scar above her groin Asra could be mistaken for a plump, pre-pubescent child.

"How many children do you have?" Noor asks.

"Two daughters. Four and two. In fact that's all the Prince has. Nine of them in total."

"Never once a son?"

"Hadiya had one but he died when he was only six months old. No one knows why. One morning the nanny found him lying cold in his crib."

"How awful."

"Certainly was for the nanny. Princess Fadilah accused her of killing her grandson, and had the authorities behead her."

"You're joking?"

"Trust me, if Princess Fadilah could, she'd have all our heads chopped off. Not a day goes by when she doesn't rail at us for letting down her son. She claims we haven't produced a boy because we're not devout enough."

"How many sons does she have?"

"Seven."

"So that makes her the most devout woman in Saudi Arabia?"

"Absolutely."

Asra puts her hands on her hips.

"Go on, tell me, do you think I'm fat?"

"I'd say plump. Is that too cruel?"

"No," Asra grins, "I'd go with that any day."

"I promise, you're not even close to the size of your sisters-in-law," Noor says.

Asra laughs and pulls on the bottom half of the set.

"No. That'd be impossible to achieve."

She clasps the top half around her breasts and grabs a white, one piece from the drawer.

"Now your turn," she says.

"Right here," Noor says.

"Trust me, there's nothing you've got that I haven't seen."

Noor feels she has no other choice. She takes off her shirt and dress and stands there in her underwear.

"Come on," Asra says, "I'm freezing."

All Noor can think of is the moment the Prince forced her to undress. She trembles.

"Fine," Asra says, "I'll wait in the bedroom. Just don't take forever."

Asra leaves, and Noor wills herself to keep going. When she enters the bedroom, Asra lets out a low whistle.

"Damn, you really are perfect," Asra says. "Now come on, let's go."

Asra skips ahead, leading the way, her swimsuit bottoms so minuscule that Noor can see most of her jiggling butt. When they arrive at the outdoor pool, they find that misters are already spraying a fine cool haze and the lounge chairs have been positioned under vast umbrellas. Asra takes a running leap into the pool.

"Ah, it's beautiful," she says. "Come on, jump in."

Noor treads down the wide steps until the water comes up to her waist. Asra swims over in long, languid strokes.

"You serious you can't swim?" she says.

"Swimming pools were never a high priority back in the refugee camps."

"I still can't believe that's where you grew up."

"Half the time I couldn't either. Now I'd give anything to go back."

"You dreading his return?"

Noor nods.

"If it's any consolation we all are," Asra says. "You see there's something you've got to understand, Noor. You're not special. He treats us all the same. The only thing you should be thankful for is that you only get him one night out of four."

A maid arrives with iced bottles of Pepsi and a plate with fries and four cheeseburgers on it.

"Ah, at last," Asra says.

She flops out of the pool.

"When I lived in L.A, I loved going to this place on Sunset called Mel's. They had the best burgers in town. I have the patties flown out here frozen once a month."

Another maid hands Asra a towel and she plunks herself down on a lounger. Noor lies down next to her. A maid hands Noor a chilled towelette to cool her face with. Asra begins wolfing a burger down.

"Do we go to him?" Noor says.

"No, he spends the night with us. More often than not he likes to do it around seven before he leaves to eat with the men. If you're lucky that's it."

"And if you're not."

"Round two's at two in the morning. And then for good measure he sometimes throws in a morning session before he heads out for the day. Hell, if there's one thing you can say for the man, it's that he's got stamina."

Asra holds out the plate of burgers to Noor. Noor shakes her head. It's the last thing she feels like at this time.

"Does he always beat you?" Noor says.

"Depends what you mean by beat. Slap, spank, that's pretty routine. But beat, just if he's angry or thinks you've done something wrong. When he does, I'm telling you, you need the next three days just to recover."

Noor feels her throat constrict and realizes she's about to vomit. She jumps up from her chair and runs to the bathroom. She leans over the toilet and throws up her breakfast. She goes to the sink and washes out her mouth. She looks in the mirror. Staring back is a woman she doesn't recognize, in an outfit that seems utterly incongruous.

I'm in the lair of a monster, she thinks.

When she returns, Asra is finishing off the second of her burgers.

"Sorry, I didn't mean to freak you out," Asra says.

"Don't worry, like you said it's scary for all of us."

Asra points at the two remaining burgers.

"You sure you don't want those?"

"No, go ahead. I'm not hungry."

Asra grabs the third and begins stuffing it down.

"I don't know how you've lived your whole life this way," Noor says.

"I haven't," Asra says. "Until I was married, I spent half my time in Europe and the States. My mother and sisters still go there all the time."

"And when you were back in Saudi Arabia?"

"It wasn't so bad. We'd go the mall every day and at home we had satellite. We got all the European channels. M.T.V., Canal Plus, you know the usual shit. We even got wasted from time to time. My father has a thing for Blue Label so he never missed the odd bottle."

"So why marry you to a man like the Prince?"

"Simple. Prestige. And hell if that meant ruining your daughter's life so be it."

"Do you still see them?"

"When they're in town they visit. It's tough though. They still have lives, things to look forward to."

"But you never go and see them?"

"You kidding. There are only two things the Prince allows us out of here for: our weekly shopping trip and visits to the doctor. Other than that we're stuck behind these four walls. Trust me, when I first discovered we only had three channels in this place I wept for days. Eventually I had my sisters slip me some magazines and books, but he found out. How the hell I'm still not sure, but let me tell you something, don't trust anyone around here, especially not the servants. I'm convinced he pays them to spy on us. Either that or he has the whole place wired with hidden cameras."

"What did he do?"

"What do you think? He beat me up so bad I ended up in hospital for a couple of weeks. I suppose the only upside was that it got me out of going to Pakistan. Crazy to think but I was his favorite wife at the time and was meant to go with him. But, by the time I got out of hospital he'd taken Shafia instead."

"And what was she like? Shafia, I mean."

Asra thinks for a moment.

"Like you in some ways. Beautiful, tall, kind. But she was also weak, paralyzed by fear."

"I don't think I've acted so much different."

"No, when I look at you, I think to myself, this girl is strong because she acts as if she has nothing to lose."

I don't, Noor thinks.

And then it comes to Noor. Her purpose. It's so blindingly obvious she can't believe she hadn't thought of it before.

I've been sent here to save these women. I've been sent here to kill the Prince.

Noor becomes so obsessed by the idea that she hardly hears another thing Asra says. After Asra leaves, she returns to her room and starts formulating a plan. She thinks about stabbing the Prince while he is asleep but wonders where she'd get a sharp knife. She could order a steak perhaps and keep the knife, but what if the servants reported it missing.

She gets up and goes to her bathroom. She stares at herself in the mirror.

There must be some other way.

Next to the sink, she spies the single sleeping pill Malaya has been leaving out for her every night. So far she's not taken one.

But what if I pretend to? Won't I soon have enough?

She picks up the pill and hides it in the back of a scarf drawer in her closet. She returns to her bedroom and lies down on her bed. She decides it will be too dangerous to drug the Prince when he first comes to visit her in the evening. He might smell a rat, become woozy and scream for help. No, she'll let him have sex with her, and wait for him to return from dinner. The likelihood of him wanting a second round will be high, especially if she waits for him in French lingerie. She will pour him some orange juice to disguise the taste of the ground up pills, have sex with him one last time and wait for him to doze off. Then she'll place a pillow over his face and smother him to death.

Finally I'll be free of him, she thinks. *And so will the others. I will have done my duty.*

She has no illusions as to her ultimate fate. If Princess Fadilah saw fit to have a maid beheaded for the accidental death of her grandson, she will certainly demand a similar punishment for the woman who murdered her beloved son.

"At last we'll be reunited, my love," Noor says.

She falls asleep with a smile on her lips.

TEN

"HOW MUCH DID you say you need?" his father says.

"Fifteen thousand dollars," Charlie says.

Down the other end of the table, Natalie inhales like she's touched a hot stove.

"I don't know, Charlie," his father says. "A dive shop in Belize. I was hoping you'd go to school."

Natalie nods to indicate she fully concurs with her husband.

"If it doesn't work out, I will," Charlie says, "but I'm not ready, not now. I need to get over Noor, Dad, I mean that's what you told me to do, right? And going to college won't do that. That was Noor's dream, the thing she wanted to do more than anything else in this world. If I go I'll see her everywhere. It will rip me apart and your money will be wasted."

"But why Belize?" Natalie says.

"The opportunity came up. The other three guys already have their money together, they're just looking for a fourth."

"You know nothing about diving," his father says.

"What did I know about demining?"

His father picks the napkin off his lap and dabs his mouth. *Something Natalie, no doubt, taught you,* Charlie thinks.

"How about this?" his father says. "You work to raise the first half of the money and once you have it I'll foot the rest."

"It'll be too late by then," Charlie says.

"It's the best I can do."

Charlie stares at the remains of his peach tart. Back in Pakistan, when he had reached out to his father, he thought he'd detected a desire to put the past aside and start afresh. Now it feels as if his father hasn't changed at all. Charlie glances at his stepmother. She doesn't even pretend to look at him with any respect.

God you really don't like me, do you? he thinks.

From the moment he had come over for dinner, Natalie had treated him as if he were carrying some form of infectious disease, and after dessert she had hurried his half-sisters up to their rooms in case they caught it. And then it strikes him.

Of course. You're the key.

"You're right," he says.

His father smiles with relief. A conflict has been avoided.

"And if it's cool," Charlie says, "maybe I could move home until I've raised it. Better to be saving what I'm earning rather than paying rent. I mean I can't believe how expensive Manhattan's gotten."

His father looks down the table trying to gauge his wife's reaction. She attempts a smile but fails. Charlie pushes back his chair.

"The bathroom's down the hall, right?"

Charlie doesn't wait for a response and heads out of the room. In the restroom, he sits down on the toilet and stares at the blue and white floral wallpaper. He suspects it alone cost more than what he's asking for. He leans forward and listens. He detects a tense, whispered conversation.

Let them stew a while longer, he says to himself.

He sits back and recollects an equally tense conversation from earlier in the day. The one he'd had with Joe Stapinski.

"I don't know what went wrong," Joe had said. "I thought my interview with the guy in Saudi Arabia went great."

It had. So much so that the employment agency had called Charlie later that day and, thinking he was Joe, had offered him the job.

"They really liked you, Joe," he'd said. "I promise. Someone more qualified came along, that's all, someone who'd already worked in Saudi Arabia."

"But now my employer knows. I had him verify my employment and everything."

"I feel terrible, especially since I sought you out. Look, let me make it up to you, the next job that comes along–"

"Fuck that. I don't want to ever hear from you again."

And with that Joe Stapinski had hung up. He was out of Charlie's life or at least as much as someone could be whose name you were about to take, and whose resume you had purloined.

He leans forward again. The conversation has come to an end. He flushes the toilet and heads back to the dining room. He sits and looks down the table. His father has poured himself a port. A good sign.

"So Natalie and I have been talking," his father says, "and she made a lot of sense really. You've been through a lot, made your way these last six years without once asking for money–"

"What your father's saying," Natalie says, "is that we'd like to give you the fifteen thousand dollars. No strings attached."

"In fact let me go get my check book right now."

His father strides out of the room, clearly intent on getting this painful exercise over as quickly as possible.

"Thank you, Natalie," Charlie says. "You don't know how much this means to me."

Natalie forces a smile.

"It's our pleasure, really."

She takes a sip of her wine.

"Do you and your friends have a name for this dive shop of yours," she says.

"We're going to call it 'Rescue.'"

ELEVEN

"IT'S MY UNDERSTANDING," Princess Fadilah says, "that Kabul will fall any day now, and, inshallah, it will be at the hands of my son."

"It will be a most magnificent occasion," Princess Hadiya says.

"The Afghans will greet him with flowers and tears of joy," Badia says.

Noor wants nothing more than to roll her eyes.

What flowers? she thinks. *They've all been scorched.*

But she doesn't.

If I'm going to kill her son, it's best I give her a false sense of security.

It hasn't been easy. As the afternoon has worn on, Noor has found her patience sorely tested. Evidently when one is in Princess Fadilah's gold festooned reception room, one's job is to listen to her verbose speeches and heartily concur with whatever nonsense she spouts. No one has seemed more predisposed to doing this than Badia who sits at Princess Fadilah's feet like a seal sharing the same stretch of sand as a beached whale. At first Asra had felt obliged to translate for Noor, but soon she'd tired of the task, and ever since Noor has stared at the ceiling pretending to be the linguistic idiot that everyone thinks she is.

"You wives," Princess Fadilah says, "you do not understand how blessed you are to have such a man as your
husband. He is Saudi Arabia's noblest warrior; a hero to every
god fearing Muslim; a man whose name will rank in history
alongside that of Saladin and Abdulaziz."

Hadiya, Asra and Bahira all protest that they're more than
aware of their good fortune and that they long for the
Prince's return.

Liars.

Noor suspects they're secretly praying that the Prince
catches a bullet in the final push; one preferably to the brain,
and, bar that, to the groin.

"You must understand before the Prince went to Pakistan
the jihad was lost," Princess Fadilah says. "It was he who
persuaded the King to help fund the mujahideen, he who
inspired his fellow Arabs to join the great fight, and he, who
broke the back of the mighty Soviet empire."

Noor can't help but laugh. The women all look her way,
none with more intent than Princess Fadilah herself.

"Ask her what she means by that snickering?" Princess
Fadilah says to Badia.

Badia arches her long neck in Noor's direction.

"Princess Fadilah wishes to know why you laughed?" Badia says in Pashtu.

"I apologize," Noor says, "I was daydreaming."

Badia translates. Princess Fadilah lowers her chin, dou-
bling up her already doubled up chin, and stares Noor down.
Noor holds her gaze.

"The Afghans," Princess Fadilah says, "and do not take
offense at this, Badia, for it is only the truth, are a savage race,
barely one step removed from the caveman. They live in mud
huts, so I'm informed, not just the refugees but your average
peasant too; like cattle they defecate wherever and whenever
they see fit, and when they were faced by Russian tanks they
ran like children, screaming to be saved by men, like my son."

"That's a lie," Noor says in Arabic.

Everyone but Princess Fadilah gasps. If anything Noor detects the slightest smile grace her dark red lips.

"No, it's the truth," Princess Fadilah says, "for it was told to me by your husband, and as we all know there is no more upright man on this earth."

"It's true," Badia says. "The Prince is praised in Pakistan as much for his honesty as his courage."

"Oh come on, Badia," Noor says in Arabic, "even you don't believe that. Everyone in Peshawar knew the Prince to be a coward, and like every other Saudi out there, he loved to dress up and play mujahid, while leaving the real fighting to the Afghans."

This time the women shriek, and even Princess Fadilah's mouth slackens. Noor turns on her.

"We, Afghans, never needed your money or men to get rid of the Russians. Just like we never needed any help to get rid of the Mughals or the British. In fact all you Saudis have done is poison our society with your fundamentalist teachings. I promise you, if you ask the average Afghan who they hate more, the Russians or the Saudis, they would be hard pressed to choose."

Princess Fadilah's hand claws at her left breast as if she's suffering a heart attack, her face now as red as the rouge on her cheeks.

"Mother," Princess Mysha, her daughter, screams.

"Help me," Princess Fadilah says.

Every woman, bar Noor, scrambles to her side, and soon her massive frame is obscured by the mass of women tending to her.

Dear God, I've killed her, Noor thinks.

She rises to her feet, wondering if it might be best to leave the scene of the crime, but then like a monster rising from the ocean depths, Princess Fadilah emerges from her protective coterie and lumbers in Noor's direction. Noor stands her ground. Princess Fadilah draws back her right hand and delivers an upper cut to Noor's chin. Noor tumbles onto the couch.

"Get out of my house, you monkey whore," Princess Fadilah screams.

Noor staggers to her feet and eyeballs her foaming mother-in-law.

"Get out I said."

Noor looks at Asra and catches the horror in her eyes.

Oh God, she thinks, *what have I done?*

She knows it's too late. All she has left is her honor, so as her mother taught her, she raises her swelling chin and strides out the door.

TWELVE

TARIQ STANDS ON the edge of the balcony and watches the Prince accept the acclaim of the chanting crowd of Afghans below. He has never seen such a broad smile on the man's face.

Everything after this will feel like a let down, he can't help but think.

They aren't at the Presidential Palace. In the end they had decided it was too dangerous to venture there. With Najibullah, the Communist leader scurrying for shelter in the United Nations mission, Massoud's force of twenty thousand had ringed the city as every other mujahideen group fought for control. Hekmatyar's Hezb forces had gone on a rampage, shooting at everyone and everything that was in their path, Rabbani's Jamiat forces had secured the most strategically important offices, including the Presidential Palace, and were trying to repel the Hezb forces, while Sayyaf's Ittihad contingent seemed to be fighting both. No one wanted to concede ground or share power and no one sure as hell gave a damn about the citizens of Kabul.

And we were supposed to be liberating these people.

Fortunately on a hillside on the outskirts of the city was the Darul Aman Palace, the so called 'abode of peace'. With the snow dappled mountains behind it, its two domed towers and its neo-classical design made it look like a chateau in the French Alps.

This is a much better place to celebrate. It has grandeur and scope.

Multiple Saudi camera crews are capturing the moment, and after their edited footage is transmitted back to Saudi Arabia no one will be any the wiser. The Prince will look like a conquering hero, the palace will look Presidential, and the local Afghans, who'd been herded into the courtyard, will look appropriately joyous (for unbeknownst to any viewer, and the Prince for that matter, they had been bribed with five dollar bills). Green and white Saudi flags hang not only from the balcony but are also being waved from open windows by the Prince's mujahideen. The Prince's promise to the King that he would be the first to enter Kabul will seemingly have been fulfilled, and once and for all it will be cemented that the Arabs won this jihad.

Tariq's ears prick up as he hears a tell tale whine. Moments later there's an earth shaking thud outside the palace walls. Down below the locals start making for the exits. Even for a people so impoverished, five dollars will only buy so much. Tariq edges up to the Prince.

"We should go, your Highness."

The Prince doesn't reply, reluctant for the moment to end.

"I beg you, your Highness."

Tariq grips the Prince's arm and guides him into a gutted reception room.

"You are too cautious, Tariq," the Prince says. "It was nothing but a stray rocket."

There is a loud boom. Tariq and the Prince are thrown to the floor. Tariq looks back through a gathering cloud of dust. The balcony and the mujahideen who were standing on it are no more. The Prince looks over at him with the eyes of a petrified child.

"Come on," Tariq says.

He takes the Prince's hand and together they stagger down a long corridor, the sound of exploding rockets and whizzing bullets a now permanent accompaniment.

"Who the hell do you think it is?" the Prince says.

"Hekmatyar," Tariq says. "His men have gone berserk."

"Barbarians," the Prince says. "Screw them. We did what we were supposed to. Now it's time to go home."

Despite the now constant bombardment, Tariq feels a visceral thrill. How long has he been waiting for the Prince to say those words?

With the Prince's elite guard surrounding them, they rush down a winding Italianate staircase and reach a domed hall littered with shattered glass. There a group of wild-eyed Arab mujahideen wait. At their feet are a bruised and beaten couple. Their drab Russian clothes are soiled with dirt and blood.

"Who are they?" the Prince says.

"The deputy justice minister and his wife," a mujahid says.

"The ex deputy justice minister, you mean."

The man crawls over the glass toward the Prince.

"Please, your Highness, I beg you, do what you wish with me but spare my wife."

The Prince looks the stocky, plain woman up and down. Blood dribbles from a rude gash on her forehead.

"This woman isn't your wife," the Prince says. "You're Communists. You didn't have an Islamic ceremony so you're nothing more than adulterers."

The man is rendered speechless by the Prince's twisted logic. Another rocket rocks the Palace.

"What should we do with them?" the mujahid says.

"Castrate him," the Prince says, "and then tie the two of them to the back of a truck and drag them out of here."

The man attempts to grab a hold of the Prince's trouser leg only to receive a rifle butt to the jaw. Lying prostrate on the marble floor, he is powerless as a couple of mujahideen pull down his pants while another saws his testicles off with a blunt knife. His howls have a screeching, ungodly quality to them.

The Prince studies the growing pool of blood on the tiled floor and carries on. Tariq makes sure to remain right at his side. They burst outside and make their way down a wide set of steps. The Prince's armor plated S.U.V. awaits. A guard opens the back door and they climb into its plush, leather interior. Through the open door Tariq watches the mujahideen drag the screaming couple towards a truck. A set of chains are already tied to its bumper.

A guard slams the door shut and the S.U.V. speeds away. Tariq forgets about the couple and closes his eyes. He smiles.

Saudi Arabia. Here I come.

THIRTEEN

"SURELY IT'S SUICIDAL for you to come and see me?" Noor says.

"It's probably not the smartest decision," Asra grins, "but if Fadilah asks I'll say I came by to beg you to apologize. Which is true because you should."

"Never," Noor says. "Not in a million years."

Asra makes a gesture with her hand and a maid brings over a fresh glass of Pepsi. Asra waits until the maid has retreated to the other side of the sitting room.

"What are you hoping to achieve, Noor? To be so offensive that the Prince ends up divorcing you?"

Noor shrugs. She daren't disclose her true plans if for no other reason than to shield Asra from the maelstrom that will surely follow.

"Well the way you're going about it won't work," Asra says. "Least not the way you hope. Fadilah had a daughter as bat shit crazy as you. Wafah. Beautiful, intelligent, tough minded, all the things you are. She and Fadilah fought all the time, and when Wafah turned eighteen, Fadilah, out of spite, betrothed her to her great uncle, this eighty year old tub of lard. Wafah freaked out, told her mother there was no way in hell she was marrying the guy, and, as you can imagine, the two of them went at it for weeks. But then just when it seemed as if they might kill each other, Fadilah called off the wedding, even seemed contrite. No one could work out why. It seemed so unlike Fadilah. Wafah, of course, was ecstatic, and when her mother invited her to dinner she didn't give it a second thought.

"The next morning, Wafah found herself in pitch darkness lying on a cement floor. At first she thought it was a terrible nightmare but it wasn't long before she came to the nauseating conclusion that she was awake. For a moment she thought she'd gone blind, but, if that was the case, why was her bed gone? She crawled around and discovered there wasn't a single thing in the room but a metal bucket. She started to scream and continued to do so for hours. Finally she heard a grating sound and she scrambled over to the other side of the room where she discovered a grate in the wall. In it she found a plastic cup filled with water, a roll of bread, a candle, a matchbox with a single match and a sheet of paper.

"She lit the candle and saw that the piece of paper was a letter from her mother. In it Fadilah explained that Wafah had brought great shame on her family and was now fated to live out the rest of her days in this room. Her example would be a warning to others to never question the word of their parents. Wafah was so distraught she knocked the candle over. It was the last light she ever saw. Within weeks she went mad, crawling around in endless circles, scratching at the walls and floor in the hope she might discover an exit. She never found one, of course, and within a year she was dead. They say when they dragged her out she looked like a ghoul, her hair down to her waist, her nails as long as pencils, her skin translucent, her pupils so large there was no color left in her eyes."

"How do you know all this?" Noor says.

"Everyone knows the story."

"But you tell it as if you were in the room."

"It's called artistic license, Noor."

Noor suspects that by artistic license what Asra really means is fiction.

"No one saw her after the wedding was called off," Asra says. "How do you explain that?"

"Don't you think it's more likely that her mother or brother beat her so badly that she died from her injuries."

"So you want to die, is that what you're saying?"

Oh, Asra, if you only knew.

At that moment Malaya enters carrying a silver tray with Asra's perennial favorites of fries and cheeseburgers on it. She sets it down on the serving table.

"What I'm trying to say is that Wafah should have married her uncle," Asra says. "Three months after she went missing he had a massive heart attack at a banquet and keeled over into his bowl of *kabsa*. Wafah would have been free, a wealthy, respected widow set up in a house of her own."

Malaya brings over a plate for Asra with two burgers on it. Asra waits for Malaya to retreat.

"You got to understand, Noor, there's going to come a point when the Prince tires of you, no matter how beautiful you are, and unless you're Hadiya, he's going to divorce you. The trick is to nudge him in that direction."

Asra takes a massive bite out of one of the burgers, and a dollop of ketchup splatters onto her pearl white blouse.

"Shit."

She looks over at Malaya.

"Come on, do something," she says.

Malaya hurries over with a napkin, and, as Noor watches Malaya daub Asra's shirt, she realizes that Asra's had a plan all along.

She's getting fat on purpose. That's why she was so thrilled when I said she was plump. She doesn't need my help at all.

Asra waves Malaya away and holds out a burger to Noor.

"Now come on, you've got to eat. You're skeletal."

All it takes is one whiff of the burger for Noor's throat to constrict. Noor vomits all over the rug. Malaya rushes back over.

"Are you all right, your Highness?"

Noor sits with her head between her knees, the room a blur.

"Here, drink this, your Highness," Malaya says.

Malaya helps Noor sit up and hands her a glass of water. Noor gulps it down. Asra stares at Noor, her mouth agape.

"When was your last period?" Asra says.

"I'm not sure, some time back in Peshawar, I suppose."

"That's two months ago."

Noor feels another wave of nausea hit her.

"Oh shit, girl," Asra says, "you're pregnant."

FOURTEEN

ANOTHER CONTINENT, ANOTHER airport. Once again Charlie finds himself surrounded by Muslim men and women in strange dress speaking in garbled, foreign tongues. But that's where the comparison with Islamabad Airport ends. Instead of there being a pervading, sweat-inducing humidity, King Khalid International Airport is as cold as a meat locker, the frigid air supplied by massive chrome towers that soar from its polished marble floor like missiles in a cavernous silo.

Charlie stands in a long, winding line that contains the non Saudi citizens from his flight and a separate planeload of wide-eyed Bangladeshi laborers. To his right in a separate line, the Saudi citizens make swift progress, the women in their abayas waddling forward like penguins crossing a frozen ice pack. Once they're all through, a group of armed police-men gesture at the Arabs and Westerners in Charlie's line to take the Saudis' place, while any Bangladeshi, who gets the wrong idea, is shoved back.

Charlie isn't thrilled at being placed in a shorter line. Shorter lines mean that the customs officials have more time to do a thorough inspection, and that's the last thing he wants. He's already survived immigration but that was the easy part. As his travel guide warns, it's customs where the real action's at. Supposedly there are no more meticulous custom officials on the planet, their intent not only to find drugs and alcohol but also any video, book, or magazine with a female image in it. Charlie feels a bead of sweat run down his neck.

Act natural, he tells himself.

Yet he doesn't know what natural means. Perhaps being nervous is the natural response in this environment. It certainly seems to be from the way his fellow passengers are shifting their feet and glancing nervously at the long series of tables not far beyond. There bearded custom officials scour through open suitcases, their contents dumped haphazardly to the side. The owners stand paralyzed not daring even to blink. One man watches an official rip up a photo of his wife and daughters while another endures a litany of verbal abuse which ends with his Bible being tossed into a trash can. A third is escorted away, his face so pale you'd think he was being taken to the gallows.

Charlie reaches the front of the line, and a customs official snaps at him to bring his bags forward. Charlie lifts them onto the table and hands over his American passport, the one under Joe Stapinski's name. The official gives it a cursory glance before handing it back.

"Open," the official says.

Charlie unzips both of his suitcases.

"Stand back."

Charlie does as he's told. The customs official inspects each of Charlie's folded clothes, shaking and scrunching them to ensure nothing is hidden within. The shoes come next, the official taking the time to remove the inner sole of each and every one of them. To Charlie's astonishment, he then takes out an electric drill and bores into the heels of his cowboy boots.

Thank God, Charlie thinks.

It's where he'd first thought of hiding the fake passports.

The shoe inspection complete, the official hands the empty case over to a subordinate for an X-ray scan to ensure nothing has been sewn into the case's lining. Once more, Charlie thanks God. That was the second place he'd thought of putting the passports.

The official starts on the second case. Its contents are a mish mash of clothes, toiletries, a Walkman, some cassettes, and a plethora of books. The official makes short work of the clothes and turns his attention to the toiletries. He discovers a bottle of cologne and unscrews the top. The official's nose wrinkles.

"No good," he says. "Alcohol."

"It's for smelling good" Charlie says, "not for drinking."

"No matter."

The customs official chucks the cologne into a nearby trash can.

Perfect, Charlie thinks.

He hopes that now the official's had a small victory that the rest of the inspection will be more cursory. That hope is soon dashed. Each and every cassette box is opened to ensure they actually contain cassettes, and then each of the books is flipped through, with the text heavy contingent of Hemingway, Orwell and Steinbeck, given shorter shrift than the books with pictures and photos in them.

Charlie waits. His shirt has stuck to the film of sweat that now sheathes his back. He wonders if there are people behind him looking for just such a sign. He dares not look around to check.

The customs official comes to his radiology textbook book, and Charlie holds his breath. Lying within its back cover are his passports, expertly hidden by a Brooklyn bookmaker. The official begins leafing through it, choosing every so often a random page to scrutinize more fully. Nothing seems to catch the official's eye and as he gets deeper into the book, his inspection becomes more perfunctory.

Almost there.

The official goes to close the book only for his eyes to pass over something that so offends him that his face looks like it's received an instant sunburn. He flips back through the pages until he comes to whatever caught his attention.

"This is an abomination," he screams.

Everyone looks in his direction.

"I don't understand," Charlie says.

The official grabs a fistful of Charlie's hair and pushes his face into the fold of the book. Charlie glimpses a topless woman having one of her breasts squeezed by a mammography unit.

"I'm an X-ray technician," Charlie says.

The official lets go of Charlie's hair and begins to tear one page from the book after another. Charlie realizes it won't be long before he gets to the back cover and rips it too.

"Stop," Charlie shouts.

The customs official is so shocked by Charlie's command that he does just that.

"That is not a bad book," Charlie says. "I promise. It's for my job."

The customs official draws his baton and hurdles the desk. The first blow lands square in Charlie's gut. Charlie crumples to the floor and lays there wheezing as further blows rain down.

This is insanity, he thinks.

The blows stop. He glances up and sees a couple of the official's colleagues dragging the official away. A couple of others grab a hold of Charlie and drag him across the hall and into a windowless interrogation room. They drop him on the floor and leave, the door slamming shut behind them.

Charlie lies there. The back of his thighs throb in pain. He tries to regain a semblance of composure but fails. He can't believe that his minutely thought out plan has come undone so quickly.

How could you be such a fucking idiot?

The door opens, and a grey haired customs official wanders in holding Charlie's tattered textbook. He looks down at Charlie and frowns.

"What are you doing there?" he says.

Charlie could state the obvious but he decides it's probably best not to.

"I'm not sure," he says.

"Well, please, take a chair," the official says.

Charlie claws his way off the floor. His bruised buttocks make contact with the room's sole plastic chair, and he winces.

"Nothing broken, I hope?" the official says

"I don't think so," Charlie says.

"Good, good. That would have been most unfortunate."

Charlie chooses to remain silent.

Isn't that what all lawyers instruct their clients to do?

"You must understand, Mr. Stapinski, that my colleague is a very upright and moral individual, and that photo and the certain illustrations accompanying it are quite despicable. So despicable that can you really blame him for the way he acted?"

The official smiles at Charlie. Charlie realizes the question wasn't rhetorical.

"No, I totally get it," Charlie says.

"That's good to know since if I had seen such photos, unwarned, I dare say it would have caused a similar reaction in me. Now that said, I have since taken the time to examine this book of yours and it does, as you mentioned, match with the area of expertise on your work visa."

To Charlie's astonishment the official places the torn textbook in his shaking hands.

"I have removed all the offending pages," the official says.

The official opens the door and leads Charlie through the customs hall. On the far side another official waits with Charlie's two repacked bags.

"Welcome to Saudi Arabia," the older official says. "I hope you have a pleasant stay."

FIFTEEN

NOOR KNEELS ON her prayer rug, her evening prayers complete. They provided her with little comfort.

I am pregnant, she says to herself. *My God, I'm pregnant.*

Two days earlier when Asra had said the phrase, Noor had instinctively known she was right. Yet that evening she'd still had Malaya bring her a pregnancy kit in the desperate hope that she was mistaken. She wasn't. Noor had burst into tears. The very thought of carrying this monster's child was overwhelming. Malaya had stayed with her and held her tight until her tears had subsided. Afterwards Noor had sworn Malaya to secrecy.

Can I abort it? she wonders.

Technically she isn't sure how she would go about doing it, but she realizes she doesn't need to. So long as she sticks with her plan to kill the Prince, her execution will take care of the rest. Together, she and the child will be freed from this hellish existence.

But why do you think your child will live a hellish existence? a voice inside her says.

Have you seen how the women are treated in this compound? she replies.

But what if it's a boy. He'll lead one of the most privileged existences known to man.

And become a monster no different than his father.

Not necessarily. After all Tariq was the product of two saints and look how he turned out.

Noor convinces herself that if it's a boy she has a chance to form his character, to create an individual who might help change this society from within. Who's to say he can't embody the same qualities of Baba or Charlie? Why would she deny him the chance?

And if it is a girl? the voice asks.

Then, dear God, I promise we'll escape.

Energized, Noor stands and heads to her closet. She retrieves her bounty of pills from the back of the scarf drawer and flushes them down the toilet. From now on her destiny is to protect and nurture this child.

She retreats to her bed and turns off the light. For the first time in two days she falls swiftly to sleep.

***

THE LIGHTS BURST on.

Noor attempts to focus. A blurred, thobed figure strides towards her.

"So I'm a coward, am I?" he yells in Arabic.

There is no voice that could induce more terror in Noor. It's the Prince.

Noor attempts to scramble from the bed but before she can, he grabs a hold of Noor's hair. He hauls her off, and she lands on her shoulder. Noor cries out in pain. Oblivious, the Prince drags her across the floor like a butcher might a lamb whose throat he intends to slit.

"Please stop," she screams.

The Prince tosses her down. Noor spins around to see his foot poised to slam into her belly.

"I'm pregnant," she screams.

The Prince pauses. The vein in the middle of his forehead engorged, his jaw clenched, his gaze so venomous that he seems possessed.

"I promise," Noor says. "I'm nine weeks pregnant."

The Prince lowers his foot.

"Take off your clothes," he says.

Noor staggers to her feet.

Hurry, she tells herself. *Better to be raped than for my child to be harmed.*

She tears off her silk nightgown and pulls her panties down. Noor hears rustling. She assumes the Prince is undressing but when she looks back she sees he's unwrapping his agal, the black cord that holds his headdress in place. He doubles it up to create a whip.

"No," she says.

The Prince grabs her by the hair and frogmarches her over to the bed. He shoves her face first into the mattress. Noor grips a hold of her sheets.

Swoosh. The agal strikes her buttocks. Noor screams. It feels as if someone has lit her backside on fire.

"Stop, I beg you," she says.

Swoosh. The full length of the agal connects again. And then again and again.

Noor loses count of how many times the Prince strikes her. The pain is so intense she forgets how to breathe.

Finally he stops. Noor lies there gasping, unable to move. For a moment she thinks the Prince must have left. But then she experiences another form of tortuous pain as he forces his way inside her. She would scream but the violence of the moment has rendered her mute. The Prince grunts his way to a swift conclusion and withdraws. She hears him walk away, and as his footsteps fade so does her own consciousness.

***

TARIQ WAITS IN the vast reception room. He can't help but shiver. Even in here, at its furthest end, he could hear Noor's screams. They were so bloodcurdling he can only assume, now they've stopped, that Noor is dead.

And to think it was all going so well, he thinks.

In fact up until an hour ago it had been a dream. At Ri-yadh Airport they had been met not only by an honor guard but the Crown Prince himself. Inside the dazzling royal terminal the Prince had introduced the returning Saudi mujahids to the Crown Prince. When it had been Tariq's turn, the Prince had called him 'the bravest and most loyal mujahid I've ever had the honor of fighting beside'. To Tariq's astonishment, the Crown Prince had bestowed Saudi citizen-ship upon him right there and then.

Finally I have arrived, he had thought.

They had travelled into town in a fleet of Rolls Royces. Despite the punishing heat, crowds of men had lined the route waving paper Saudi flags. The Crown Prince had honored them with a sumptuous feast in a gilded hall the size of a soccer field. Everyone seemed to be there to meet them; there must have been over five hundred Princes alone. After all they were Saudi Arabia's conquering heroes, men whose exploits in Afghanistan had expunged the shame of having had Crusader armies in this the most holy of lands.

Afterwards they had travelled to the Prince's compound. The Prince had insisted on seeing his mother, and when Tariq had enquired as to Badia's whereabouts, he was told that she was living in Princess Fadilah's palace also. It was the first time he had felt perturbed. This wasn't what he'd told Badia to do. She was meant to be staying close to Noor. Yet as he had stridden down the palace's long, gleaming corri-dors, his worries had subsided. He couldn't have been more excited. There had not been a night since he'd last seen her when he hadn't dreamed of Badia's naked body. Yet when he had entered her bedroom, instead of running towards him, Badia had stood there not with a smile but with a look of untold distress.

"I have something terrible to tell you," she had said, and she had proceeded to tell him about the incident between Noor and Princess Fadilah. Tariq had been so shocked that for a minute he had remained rooted to the spot. And then, he had turned and run back to the Palace entrance. By the time he had gotten there the Prince had already left. A servant had told him that the Prince was on his way to see his fourth wife. Tariq had requisitioned a car and sped over himself. A male servant had led him to the reception room, and it was in here that he had heard Noor's screams.

God damn you, Noor, he thinks. *How could you do this to me?*

At the other end of the room, the mahogany double doors swing open. The Prince lumbers in, his shoulders drooped, his headdress askew. Tariq scrambles to his feet and waits for the Prince to reach him. When he does, he bows.

"I apologize profusely for my sister's behavior," Tariq says.

"I'll be divorcing her the first moment I'm able," the Prince says.

Tariq does his best to hide his surprise. He hadn't expected her to still be alive. The Prince collapses in his chair and indicates that Tariq should sit. A servant comes over and hands the Prince a warm hand towel, as another pours each of them a cup of tea. The Prince unfolds the towel and places it over his face. He breathes in deeply, the towel creating the impression of a death mask.

"It's my fault," Tariq says. "She's angry over my father's death and is spouting lies as a consequence."

"My mother attributes it to her peasant stock," the Prince says. "Says I should have never married such a woman."

Tariq stays silent. He is no fool. There is nothing to be gained by contradicting the Prince's beloved mother.

The Prince takes the cloth off and drops it on the floor. A servant rushes over to take it away.

"Yet if she provides me with a son," the Prince says, "she'll have accomplished something none of my high born wives have achieved."

"She's pregnant?" Tariq says.

"Nine weeks. I just spoke with my doctor. He says we should know the child's sex within a few more. If it is a girl I'll divorce your sister immediately."

But if it's a boy, she'll remain your wife, her child taking pride of place as your first born son.

An electric thrill runs through Tariq. The Prince stands, and Tariq jumps to his feet.

"Don't worry, Tariq, I don't blame you. In fact you're the most curious of talisman. The most awful things befall me when you're around, yet right afterwards so do the most wonderful."

The Prince chuckles as if Tariq is a scientific mystery and walks out of the room. Tariq stands there marveling at how he's escaped disaster once more. He thinks about going to his sister but then he remembers Badia. He walks as calmly as he can towards the exit. If it weren't for the servants he'd be running.

SIXTEEN

RALPH, THE RADIOLOGY department's chief administrator, smoothes down the few remaining strands of hair on the crown of his head.

"You want to do what?" he says.

"I'd like to work seven days a week," Charlie says.

"Any specific reason?"

"I want to make as much money as possible."

And have the best possible chance of hunting down Noor's hospital records.

"But everyone needs to rest at some point," Ralph says.

"I don't. I was in the ..."

Charlie catches himself just before he says 'army'.

"What I'm trying to say is in the States they work you like a dog. I'm used to it."

Ralph shakes his head. The strands of hair flop out of position.

"I'm sorry, Joe, I can't do it. Hospital policy dictates that everyone takes at least one day off a week."

"All I'll do is sit around my apartment."

"That's your choice."

Ralph extends a hand. It's clear Charlie's introductory interview is over.

"When would you like me to start?" Charlie says.

"Since you're so eager, why not today. Ask for Mike Cooper. He'll show you around."

Charlie exits the administrative offices and heads for the radiology department through a set of gleaming corridors and lobbies. The hospital is spotless with arrangements of fresh flowers everywhere, check-in staff in suits and ties, crystal chandeliers, and elevators with gold plated doors. Beside a copse of trees a pianist plays soothing music on a baby grand, and the air is filled with a scented freshness reminiscent of a mountain hillside. He enters the radiology department and asks for Mike Cooper at reception. Soon after a bear of man with curly red hair and a matching beard bounds out.

"Joe?" the man grins.

"That's me."

"Mike Cooper. God it's good to see you."

Mike hugs Charlie like they're long lost fraternity brothers.

"Come on," he says, "let's find you some scrubs."

Mike takes Charlie through a set of double doors and into a locker room. He opens a drawer filled with medical scrubs and tosses Charlie a set. Charlie starts putting them on.

"So what you think so far?" Mike says.

"Hospital seems cool," Charlie says.

"No, I meant the country. It your first time in a Muslim country?"

"Yeah."

"Fucking whack-a-do, right?"

"Certainly isn't Manhattan."

Mike lets out a barrel of a laugh.

"No it fucking ain't. So Manhattan, that where you from?"

"Born and raised."

"Long Island myself. Great Neck, ever hear of the place?"

"Wasn't Gatsby from there?"

"Town's claim to fame. Awesome place to grow up. Safe, good schools, close to the city. Full of Persian Jews now."

"That a bad thing?"

"You kidding, some of those guys are my best friends. Over here though, fuck, they'd line them up and crucify the lot of em. Well maybe not crucify em, I mean that's a Christian thing, ain't it? More likely they'd chop their heads off."

Mike assumes the pose and swings an imaginary sword.

"Watch out! Head coming through."

He bellows with laughter. Charlie does his best to grin. Charlie finishes putting on his scrubs.

"So what now?" Charlie says.

"Let the tour commence."

Mike takes Charlie on a whirlwind tour of the radiology department and introduces him to every member of staff they come across. The doctors are all European, American or Arab, while the technicians are a mix of Europeans, Filipinos, Malaysians and Indians. They come to a room taken up by a CT scanner so modern and monstrous it looks like it belongs in space. Mike admires it while Charlie does his best to remain calm. He hasn't got a clue how to work the thing or, for that matter, half the equipment Mike's shown him.

What was I thinking? he thinks. *I'm going to be exposed in a day.*

"Just got it," Mike says. "First one off the production line."

"Might take me a little time to get up to speed," Charlie says.

"You and me both. Fact is most of our equipment's the very latest. Hospital only wants the best. Problem is no one but the Indians knows how to use it."

"Why?"

"They're smart that way. Anyway by the time you do finally get up to speed they go and fucking replace it again. You got to start all over."

"So what do you do?"

"I get one of the Indians to help me."

"Then what's the point of having us around?"

"When a Saudi enters a diagnostic room and sees he only has an Indian technician or a Filipino, for that matter, he freaks the fuck out. Saudis think they're a bunch of dumb and dirty retards."

Charlie frowns. Mike holds a hand up.

"Their words not mine. Now a European, on the other hand, they'll trust, while Americans, like you and me, well we're the gold standard, dude. It's why we're paid more than anyone else. Most of the time, I just stand in the room and banter with the patients, while the Indian and Filipino technicians man the machine and do the real work. The Saudis haven't a clue."

Mike stares at the CT scanner.

"Still it's a beauty, don't you think?"

"Sure is," Charlie says, his hopes rising.

Maybe I can get away with this after all, he thinks.

Mike leads him out of the room.

"So where are the female patients examined?" Charlie says.

"Why do you care?" Mike says.

"I've seen no mammography equipment, that's all."

"Looking to get an eyeful of Arab titties, are you?"

Charlie is so thrown by the accusation he's unable to answer. Mike explodes with laughter and slaps Charlie on the back.

"Dude, I'm pulling your leg."

He taps on the corridor wall.

"They're through there. It's strictly a female-only facility."

"That the same throughout the hospital?"

"For technicians yeah. They'll let male doctors see em, but only the parts that are affected, everything else has to remain covered and even that's not good enough for some of em."

"What happens then?"

"You mean if there isn't a female doctor around?"

"Yeah."

"Well many of em just prefer their women to die."

They arrive at the technicians' station. Charlie leans against the counter trying to be as nonchalant as possible.

"So are all the female records over there too?" Charlie says.

"Guess so."

"Nothing's on computer?"

"Not yet. They've been promising us this hospital wide system for a couple of years now, but like so much round here it's become a total rat fuck. Look, I got a patient waiting, but why don't you come by my apartment later and we'll have a beer. I'll fill you in on all the real shit that goes down around here."

"I thought you couldn't drink in Saudi Arabia."

Mike bellows with laughter.

"Dude, more drinking goes on around here than at an Irish bar back home."

"Where you get it?"

"Brew my own. Shit's fucking exquisite."

So exquisite, Charlie suspects, that he decides to keep Mike at arm's length from here on out. The last thing he wants is to be deported for drinking.

"Do you mind if I take a rain check," he says. "I'm pretty exhausted from the flight."

"Course not. Hell, why don't you get out of here. I'll cover for you."

"Really?"

"Dude, you and me, we're in the trenches together. Nothing we won't do for each other, right?"

"Right."

Mike slaps Charlie on the back and propels him on his way. Charlie stares at the wall to his right. The women's section is mere inches away but it might as well be on another continent.

What am I going to do? he thinks.

His whole plan had been predicated on having access to

Noor's records. That way he could work out when her next appointment was scheduled at the hospital.

Think, think, think, he tells himself.

He wanders down a series of immaculate corridors and enters the sun-drenched lobby. Amidst the forest of trees and babbling fountains the pianist plays a Chopin piano concerto. It offers him no inspiration. He's at a loss.

SEVENTEEN

NOOR LIES FACE first on her bed, the pain so intense she daren't turn over. From what Malaya told her this morning she had been out for most of the day.

Why couldn't it have been longer? she thinks.

After the Prince had left, Malaya and another maid had rushed in. The wounds on Noor's buttocks were so severe that the other maid had wanted to call a doctor. However Malaya knew that was pointless - without the Prince's permission no doctor would be allowed onto the compound - and so together they had washed Noor's lacerations and bandaged them with gauze.

"It's all right," Noor had said when she finally awoke. "I survived."

"Yes you did, your Highness," Malaya had said. "As did your child."

The relief had been such that it had anesthetized the pain.

Noor places a hand on her belly.

"You're still there," she whispers.

She closes her eyes hoping to sense her baby move. It doesn't.

"That's all right, my love. It's early days."

The door opens. Noor assumes it's Malaya.

"Congratulations. I hear you're pregnant."

Noor freezes.

Tariq.

Tariq comes around the side of the bed. She sees he's wearing a thobe and a ghutra headdress.

He might as well be a Saudi, she thinks.

They stare at each other. Noor refuses to show him a hint of emotion. He returns the compliment.

"What did you hope to achieve, Noor?" he says. "My downfall?"

"There's nothing you can do to me," she says. "Not anymore."

"Oh, I wouldn't be so sure, there must be something. I could give you advice, for instance."

Tariq climbs onto the bed. The mattress shifts and with it her position. To her chagrin she can't help but wince. He lies down beside her, his face mere inches from her own.

"What would you have me do?" she says. "Act like a good Muslim wife?"

"It'd be a lot less painful if you did."

"I can endure pain."

"Physical pain, yes, emotional pain, now that I'm not so sure."

His hand works his way onto her belly. He strokes it with his fingers.

"I mean, could you really bear to lose someone else you loved?"

"You wouldn't," Noor says. "He'd kill you if you did anything to his child."

"Come on, do you take me for a fool? This child of yours is the most blessed gift you could've given me."

"Not if it's a girl."

"I won't lie, I'd prefer it to be a boy, but if it's a girl it will speak to your incredible fertility. After all the Prince only implanted his seed in you once and look at the result. My

suspicion is he'll forget about divorcing you, especially if you
grovel to his mother and beg her forgiveness."

"Never."

"You will if you wish to have any involvement in your
child's life."

Noor's heart beats faster. Her wounds only throb more.

"You see if you keep up this act, dear sister, the Prince will
take your child away from you the minute it's born. He'd be
an idiot not to. I mean, really, do you think he wants the
mother of his child, especially if it's his first born son, to
whisper in his ear that his father is a coward and a monster,
that everything the Prince holds most is a fraud?"

Tariq places his hand on Noor's cheek.

"You're stubborn, Noor. You always have been. It's your
greatest failing. To think if you hadn't been, if you had only
taken my advice and accepted this marriage from the very
beginning, you would have spared not only our father's life
but that of your lover's. Well now, I implore you to finally
listen to me. Apologize to the Princess Fadilah, apologize to
her like you've never apologized to another human being
before, and then once that's done, devote yourself to being a
righteous wife who thinks not of her own needs but those of
her husband and her future children. You do that, dear sister,
and I assure you, with Allah as my witness, the Prince's
temper will subside, and this child growing in your stomach
will stay in your care."

Tears flow down Noor's cheeks.

"Do you understand?" he says.

"I do," she whispers.

"Good."

***

NOOR ENTERS PRINCESS Fadilah's sitting room and all conversation stops. This time the women don't look at Noor with hostile curiosity but rather with morbid fascination. It's as if Noor were a defendant at an inquisitional court. Princess Fadilah, the grand inquisitor, sits ensconced in her love seat and peers at her from beneath her baggy eyelids. Noor walks over to her. She attempts as best she can not to limp. She bows her head.

"Salaam alaikum," Noor says. "I want to fervently apologize for the words I said the other day. They were falsehoods, the enraged rantings of an embittered woman."

"Then why say them?" Princess Fadilah says.

"Satan had a hold of my soul. He hid from me all that was good here and poisoned me toward not only you but your son. I have since prayed fervently to Allah and He has released me from Satan's grip. He has shown me the right course. I know now that your intentions and those of the Prince are and always will be noble."

"And this talk of my son being a coward."

"Nothing but lies, no more true than if I'd said the earth was flat. I'm aware of the truth now. I know how bravely the Prince fought to free our people from the grip of the unbelievers. As you said, the Prince will be remembered as one of Islam's greatest leaders."

Princess Fadilah doesn't say anything but rather kicks off her shoes and extends her distended feet. Noor knows what she must do. She gets down on her knees and kisses both of them before working her way up and kissing both of Princess Fadilah's outstretched hands. She returns to her standing position.

"I accept your apology," Princess Fadilah says. "Now please, join us."

Noor looks up, certain that Princess Fadilah is playing a game. But all Princess Fadilah does is smile. She points to an empty chair.

"Please," she says.

Noor sits down. The conversation starts up again like a gathering breeze. It is a schizophrenic mix. Princess Fadilah and her daughters babble gaily away while the wives speak in a more subdued fashion. Noor presumes the Prince has made his rounds by now and meted out his own peculiar form of greeting to each of the wives. After a while Noor needs to go to the bathroom. She excuses herself. Once there she has to crouch over the toilet. She dare not place her buttocks on the seat. She hears a knock and pulls up her underwear. Asra enters. She gives Noor a sympathetic smile.

"How you feeling?" Asra says.

"I've had better days," Noor says.

"You did good in there. I've never seen the Princess be so forgiving."

Asra goes over to the mirror and fixes her lipstick.

"How are you doing?" Noor says.

"I'm not as beat up as you."

"But he beat you?"

"He said I disgusted him, that I need to lose weight immediately."

"And what was your response?"

"I told him I'm trying but nothing seems to work. That I fear I'm genetically made this way."

Of course you did, you clever girl.

"You know he didn't even want to have sex with me. He had something on his mind. I think it was you."

Noor shivers.

"Why do you think that?"

"In the morning he brought you up. How you should be my role model. The way you look, the way you speak, the way you carry yourself."

"He beat me within an inch of my life."

"How's that expression go? 'You're always hardest on the ones you love.'"

Noor puts a hand on a dresser to steady herself.

That's why the Princess was so conciliatory, she thinks. *The Prince asked her to be. And the moment the Prince tires of me, she'll pounce.*

Asra smacks her lips and twirls around.

"We should go back in," she says.

Back in the sitting room, Noor sits down next to Princess Hadiya. They make small talk with Hadiya giving Noor all sorts of advice about her pregnancy.

"We all hope it's a son," she says.

Hadiya's comment seems genuine, but Noor can't be sure. On the one hand if Noor has a son it will relieve the pressure on the other wives, yet on the other hand it will exalt Noor above all of them.

"I pray whatever it is, it's healthy," Noor says.

A flicker of pain etches itself across Hadiya's brow.

"I'm sorry," Noor says. "I didn't ..."

"No, there's no need to be. After all everything in this life has been pre-ordained by God. It was Allah's will."

Noor looks away. For the briefest moment she catches Princess Fadilah staring at her with undisguised scorn. Princess Fadilah quickly replaces her expression with a beneficent smile. Noor does her best to return the smile and turns back to Princess Hadiya.

"When we go to the mall tomorrow, we must look at baby clothes," Princess Hadiya says.

"That would be nice," Noor says.

Noor's mind, however, is elsewhere.

You're an idiot if you wait for Princess Fadilah to pounce, she thinks. *No, somehow you must escape before she's able.*

EIGHTEEN

"HOLD YOUR BREATH, please," Charlie says.

Standing in nothing but his underwear, the elderly Bedouin gives Charlie a blank stare. Charlie mimics the action. The Bedouin finally gets it and does as requested. Charlie takes an exposure and comes out from behind the protective shield. He replaces the film in the x-ray machine and without even bothering to ask, turns the Bedouin sideways and raises his scrawny arms above his head.

"Okay, hold that pose."

Charlie pops behind the shield.

"Now one more breath."

He takes a deep breath, and the Bedouin copies him. Charlie takes a second exposure.

"Okay, you're done," he says.

The Bedouin descends into a fierce coughing fit. It goes on for so long that Charlie fears he's going to topple down dead right there. The Bedouin finally gets it under control and spits a large globule of yellow mucus onto the floor. Without complaint Manuel, the Filipino technician, sets about cleaning it up.

Charlie pulls out the first film and examines it. A large white mass covers most of the Bedouin's right lung. Despite his limited experience Charlie knows the man's screwed. He pulls out the second film. Same result. The Bedouin lights a cigarette.

"The doctor will be right in," Charlie says.

Charlie heads out to the technician's station. Doctor Angerman is standing there chatting up Jenny, a leggy Aussie nurse. While Saudi women might not be allowed in this part of the radiology wing there's no rule against Western women being here. In fact, as Charlie's quickly discovered, there's nothing the Saudi patients like more than to gawk at the Western nurses' breasts, especially Jenny's, whose are by far and away the department's most impressive.

"What have you got?" Doctor Angerman says.

"Looks like lung cancer. Pretty advanced I'm afraid."

Doctor Angerman throws the film up on the x-ray board.

"Yep, he's fucked."

Doctor Angerman swipes the x-rays and hails a Jordanian nurse to help translate.

"I'll see you later," he says to Jenny.

He heads for the examination room. Jenny rolls her eyes. Charlie scans the empty corridors.

"Where's everyone else?" he says.

"It's Thursday afternoon," Jenny says.

Charlie gives her a blank stare.

"Department pretty much shuts down for the weekend."

"Course. I forgot Friday's the start of the weekend."

"So what are you going to do?"

"Probably just take it easy."

"You should come by the compound's main pool tonight. There's going to be a rager. Bunch of cool people."

"Like Doctor Angerman?"

Jenny laughs.

"Way cooler."

Charlie shakes his head.

"I don't know."

"What you got other plans?"

"I'm just not that social, that's all."

Jenny screws her eyes up.

"You're a mysterious one, aren't you Joe Stapinski?"

"Don't mean to be."

"Then come, I want to find out what you're all about."

Jenny winks at him and waltzes off down the corridor. Charlie waits until she's turned the corner. He looks around and sees no one. He heads to the records room and closes the glass door behind him. He pulls back the sliding cabinets and searches for a folder with the Prince's last name on it. He doesn't find one. He pulls out a random folder and reads it. He realizes everything is filed under first names. He resumes his search and sees two folders with the Prince's first name. He opens the first. It's for a boy born in 1984. He replaces it and opens the second. The patient shares the Prince's last name and was born in 1957.

It's him, he thinks. *It has to be.*

Charlie hears voices down the corridor and edges further into the room. He scans the folder's contents. There's an x-ray of the Prince's right hand from five years earlier. The pinky finger is clearly broken.

'Patient says injury occurred when striking his wife,' the accompanying doctor's note reads.

He didn't even feel the need to lie, he thinks.

The voices get louder. He flips through the folder.

Come on. Where's the address?

On the very last page he finds a print out. The only problem is the address is written in Arabic. He rips the page out and shoves it in his pocket. The door swings open and he twists around to find Ralph and a middle-aged Saudi standing there.

"Ah, there you are, Joe," Ralph says.

"Just putting away a patient file," Charlie says.

"May I introduce you to Abdul Jameel, the executive in charge of our department."

"Salaam alaikum."

Abdul Jameel smiles, clearly pleased by Charlie's use of the Muslim greeting.

"Wa alaikum asalaam," Abdul Jameel says.

"So how's everything going?" Ralph says.

"Good. Actually I was going to come and see you. I was hoping to change my schedule back to five days a week."

"I thought you wanted to work every hour God gave you."

"Yeah, might have bitten off more than I can chew."

"Well, I suppose, that can be arranged."

"If it's okay I'd prefer to work nights. Mike told me you always need a tech on hand."

"I don't know, Joe, it's not so—"

"Oh come on," Abdul Jameel says. "Surely it can't be that difficult to accommodate the man."

Ralph forces a smile.

"Of course not. I'll rearrange your schedule right away."

"It was a pleasure meeting you Joe," Abdul Jameel says.

"You too, sir," Charlie says.

The two of them carry on down the corridor. Charlie puts the folder back. Now he needs to find someone to translate the address for him.

NINETEEN

THEY COME FOR her at two-thirty in the afternoon. Any earlier would be inconceivable since most of the princesses don't rise from their beds until one.

They travel in a five vehicle convoy, Princess Fadilah and the uglier of her two daughters, Princess Mysha, sit squashed in the back of a Mercedes saloon, while Princess Ismah, the second daughter, the four wives and Badia ride in three separate Toyota S.U.V.s. Besides their drivers, they're accompanied by three young, male relatives who sit up front. Noor presumes they're their chaperones.

Noor sits in the back of the last S.U.V. next to Asra. Asra makes constant eye contact with Noor through the slit of her niqab, and is on the verge of saying something only to pull back when she spies Prince Salman, their acned, sixteen year old brother-in-law staring at them in the mirror. Noor turns away and gazes out the window. It's her first real look at Riyadh and it's not made easy by the black gauze curtains that hang over the passenger windows. Designed to obscure the S.U.V.'s interior from passers-by, they afford the vehicle's passengers nothing but a hazy vision of the bright outdoors.

Apart from the spaceship looking Ministry of Interior and the tall, imposing Ministry of Petroleum there are few sights to see. Riyadh is a flat city dotted with bland, characterless buildings baking under a relentless sun. The sidewalks are deserted but for an occasional Bangladeshi sweeper.

There's no color, no vibrancy, no life to this place, Noor thinks.

It sums up the life she's been condemned to.

They arrive at the mall and descend into its subterranean garage. They pull up outside a marble lobby where a platoon of top-hatted valets in tails wait to greet them. No one inside their car moves. Noor looks over at Asra.

"Princess Fadilah has to get out first," Asra says.

Noor watches as Princess Fadilah's two daughters haul her out of her Mercedes. Only when she is safely on her feet and waddling towards the glass doors does everyone else get out. Princess Fadilah heads toward an elevator marked 'Ladies Only.' The ten women squeeze into it, and despite their combined tonnage, it whisks them effortlessly to the first floor. They step out. One of the women turns in a circle as she takes in the three story central atrium with its domed roof and cascading waterfall. Noor guesses it must be Badia and is proven correct when Badia comes over and squeezes her arm.

"Isn't this exciting?" Badia says.

"Wonderfully," Noor says.

Noor casts her eye over the other women in the mall. Every one of them, and there are many, is shrouded in a black abaya.

This is what a convention of witches must look like, she thinks.

Behind them their male chaperones step off a separate elevator, and Princess Fadilah makes a beeline for a perfume store. Everyone follows in a pack. They pass a Starbucks where a group of bored teenage boys are slouching. One catches Noor's eye and she can't help but stare back at him. With his smooth skin and blackened eyebrows, there's something weirdly androgynous about him.

Inside the perfume store, under the glass counters, is an array of different flower oils, herbs and spices; jasmine, rose, bergamot, citrus, jojoba, vanilla, amber, musk, oud. The list of ingredients is endless. Noor hangs back and watches as the women select different ingredients, and the army of clerks race away to create their concoctions. While they wait, the women set about choosing a bottle in which to put their personalized perfumes. There are almost as many choices here as there are ingredients, the bottles intricate affairs made from gold, jade, crystal and ivory. Princess Fadilah presents Badia with a diamond encrusted bottle, and Badia shrieks with delight. Noor turns to Asra.

"How much does that bottle cost?" she asks.

Asra shrugs and asks a clerk.

"Ten thousand dollars," Asra says.

To think we lived off fourteen dollars a week, Noor thinks.

Princess Fadilah tires of the store and with a click of her tongue announces their departure. She lumbers across the open expanse of the atrium like a matriarchal elephant leading her herd across the plain. They return to the elevator bank and the women head to the third floor. When they step off they are met by a large sign blazing the words 'Warning: Ladies Only Floor'. Just beyond the sign a long bearded man stands in a thobe so short that Noor can see his ankles. His red and white checkered ghutra is draped over his head like a discarded dishcloth. Asra grips Noor's arm.

"Mutaween," she whispers.

Noor gives her a blank look.

"Religious police."

The man scrutinizes the women making sure the hems of their abayas drape all the way to the ground, the arms of their abayas hang well over their wrists and their niqabs cover the whole of their heads.

"We will meet in exactly one hour in front of the first floor elevators," Princess Fadilah says.

The women scatter in different directions like a pack of dogs let loose on a beach. Noor notices Princess Hadiya looking for her, no doubt so they can search for baby clothes together. She shivers.

She already treats my child as if it's her own.

Noor looks for help and finds it in the form of Asra.

"Come on," Asra says.

She grabs Noor's arm and drags her toward a Chanel store. As soon as they pass through the doors, Asra rips off her outer garments and leaves them in her wake for a sales assistant to pick up. Noor stands there thinking Asra's lost her mind.

"It's okay," Asra says, "once you're inside the store you can be naked for all they care. Well maybe not naked but you get my drift."

Noor looks around. The other Saudi women are similarly uncovered as are the female Caucasian sales assistants. Noor follows suit and hands her outer garments to one of them.

"We have an account here," Asra says, "so get anything you want."

"I don't need anything," Noor says.

"Oh come on, stop being such a wet blanket."

"Well I suppose I could get some trousers."

Asra turns to one of the sales assistants.

"Find her some cool pants," she says.

Noor blushes as the assistant scurries away to fulfill her request. Asra swaggers around the store, picking out dress after dress until the two assistants traveling in her wake can't carry anymore.

"Let's go," she says and they head to the fitting rooms.

Noor can't help but observe the one, she and Asra are sharing, is bigger than her old mud hut back in Kacha Gari. Asra, as usual, has no scruples about taking off her clothes in front of Noor. Noor shudders on seeing the black and purple patches that mark Asra's body. Asra notices Noor staring.

"Don't worry," she says, "this is just his version of a leaving present."

"He's divorcing you?"

Asra breaks into a broad grin.

"Can you believe it, Noor. I'm going to be back with my parents in a week. Paris, inshallah, in a month."

"And your daughters?"

Asra's smile fades.

"Fadilah's going to bring them up," she says.

"And you're okay with that?"

"There's nothing I can do. So why cry about it?"

Asra pulls on a sleeveless white dress that's so short it barely covers her crotch. Noor's eyes water over.

"You think I'm awful, don't you?" Asra says.

"No, I was just admiring your dress. It will look amazing on the Champs Élysées."

"I didn't think you'd been?"

'I haven't, but I might as well have. Victor Hugo, Émile Zola, Hemingway. I can see it now, you strolling down it drawing admiring glances from passers-by."

"With a gorgeous Frenchman on my arm," Asra giggles.

"Someone who treats you right."

"Oh, don't worry, he will."

Asra tosses Noor's items at her.

"Now come on, jump into those."

Noor undresses, no longer ashamed to be naked in front of her sister wife. She puts on a pair of severe black pants and a white collared shirt. Noor tucks the shirt in and Asra giggles.

"What?" Noor says.

"You look like a man," Asra says.

Noor stands there stunned. She can't believe she hadn't thought of that idea earlier.

"I'm sorry," Asra says, "I didn't mean to offend you."

"No, no," Noor says, "I had a thought. I'd like to buy the Prince a gift, a new thobe in fact."

"He has hundreds of them."

"I know, but maybe he'll take it as a sign that I've come around."

Asra shrugs.

"Fuck it."

Without bothering to change, Asra grabs her pile of dresses and exits the fitting room. Noor hurries after her. Asra tosses the dresses at the waiting sales assistant.

"I'll take them all," she says.

She grabs her abaya, niqab and gloves from another assistant and puts them on.

"Well come on," she says to Noor.

"Don't I need to change?"

"Don't worry, they got it."

Noor struggles into her outer garments and the two of them make for the elevator. They get off at the first floor. Asra strides over to Prince Salman who's lounging with the other chaperones at the Starbucks.

"I need you," she says.

"Really?" he says.

"Yes, really."

Like the spoilt teenager he is, Prince Salman pouts and struggles to his feet. They head to a men's store festooned with dazzling white thobes.

"Okay. Let me show you what he likes," Asra says.

"If it's all right I'd prefer to choose it myself," Noor says. "If you want to go to another shop, I'll wait for you here."

"It's not allowed," Asra says.

"We could go to the electronics store," Prince Salman says. "It's across the way."

"Fine, just don't go anywhere" Asra says.

Asra and Prince Salman saunter out, and Noor finds herself alone. It's a surreal feeling. She could walk out the door and keep going.

Yet how long would it be before they found you?

Not long, she suspects. A woman walking around Riyadh on her own would attract the attention of the Mutaween more swiftly than an unaccompanied toddler.

An elderly sales clerk approaches.

"Can I help you, Ma'am?"

"I'm looking for a thobe and a ghutra for my husband."

"Do you have his measurements?"

Noor glances across the way. Prince Salman is occupied with a Nintendo game console while Asra looks at a selection of Walkmans.

"He's my size," Noor says.

The sales clerk frowns.

"Do you have an issue with that?" Noor says.

"No, ma'am, it's just that—"

"It's 'Your Royal Highness.'"

The clerk pales.

"I'm sorry," he says. "It's just that I can hardly take your measurements, your Highness."

"Then guess," she says. "And give me the best you have."

Noor glances out the store. Prince Salman and Asra are wandering back empty handed.

"Hurry," Noor snaps.

The harried clerk grabs a thobe from a hanger and a ghutra and an agal from a drawer. He shows them to Noor.

"Do these seem—"

"Please wrap them."

Asra and Prince Salman enter the store. The clerk enfolds Noor's items in brown paper.

"You already got it?" Asra says.

"I don't want to be late for Princess Fadilah."

Asra glances at her Cartier watch.

"Shit."

Asra nods at Prince Salman who produces an American Express card. By the time they return to the elevator bank, Princess Fadilah and the other women are indeed waiting.

"Sorry," Asra says, "we had a couple of errands to run."

Princess Fadilah fixes the three of them with a piercing glare and turns for the elevators. When they arrive at the parking lobby their cars are waiting for them, their purchases already loaded. On the return trip, Noor finds herself in the same S.U.V. as Badia. Badia can't stop reminiscing about all the incredible clothes she bought.

"This truly is a dream," she says.

At the compound the convoy splits up as each vehicle delivers its occupants to their respective palaces. As they approach Noor's, a van passes them carrying a group of veiled women.

"Who's that?" Noor says to the driver.

"The dayshift, your Highness," he says.

"You mean the maids don't live at the palace?"

"No, your Highness, most of them don't at least."

"Where do they live?"

"Across town at a servants' compound."

The S.U.V. pulls up and an attendant rushes over to open the door. Noor climbs out and looks back at the van.

I've found my way to escape.

TWENTY

CHARLIE LIES ON his bed in the encroaching gloom and listens to the mournful wails of the evening muezzins. They entrap him from every direction, reminding him in their own strident way that this endeavor is futile and doomed to fail.

The doorbell rings. Charlie waits. He hopes whoever it is goes away. It rings again and again.

Shit.

Charlie rolls off the bed and heads down the hallway. He opens his front door to find Mike standing there in a New York Jets football jersey.

"It's the weekend," Mike grins, "and you, Joe Stapinski, are coming out with me."

"I don't know, I kind of–"

Mike barges past Charlie and surveys the barely furnished townhouse.

"Like what you've done with the place," he says.

"Mike, I'm really not up for it tonight."

"Well you should be, this party's gonna be off the charts."

All the more reason, Charlie thinks.

"Hell if you don't go people will start talking. Who's that weirdo that stays holed up in his apartment? Maybe he's a CIA agent or something."

"If I were a CIA agent it wouldn't make much sense for me to stay in my home the whole time."

"Won't stop the rumors spreading. Saudi's not the most logical of places."

Charlie rubs his forehead. Mike is like a bothersome fly he's unable to swat.

"You think there'll be anyone at the party who can read Arabic?" Charlie says.

"What kind of fucked up question's that?" Mike says.

"Will there?"

"Sure, there will be all sorts of people."

"Okay, then give me a minute."

Charlie heads for his room and changes into a fresh shirt. He hears Mike prowling around his living room.

"So how you finding the job, so far?" Mike shouts.

"Good, not too stressful."

"Our hospital's the bomb. The others, National Guard especially, they're a totally different story, some seriously screwed up shit comes through those doors. I have a buddy who's an ER nurse over there. Every day, hell every hour they wheel in a car wreck victim, it's like brains and mangled body parts everywhere. You know why? None of these fuckers wear seatbelts, not a single one, not even the infants. And you know where the kids like to stand?"

Charlie waits.

"Do you?" Mike shouts out.

Charlie sighs.

"In the trunk?"

"No, right between the two front seats. When there's a head on collision, boom the little shit goes flying through the windshield like a heat seeking missile. At the hospital all the parents say is 'It was Allah's will', and all my buddy wants to scream is, 'Then why did Allah allow seat belts to be invented in the first place, you stupid fucks.'"

Mike goes silent.

Finally.

Charlie lifts up his mattress and retrieves the piece of paper with the Prince's address on it. He enters the living room to find Mike sifting through his collection of books.

"Some pretty heavy shit here, dude."

"I like to read."

"Figured that out."

Mike comes upon the tattered radiology textbook.

"Shit what happened here? The dog eat it?"

"Customs. They didn't like some of the photos."

Mike grins.

"I'm sure they didn't."

He tosses it on the floor.

"Right, let's get the fuck out of here."

By now, the sun is well below the horizon yet outside a fierce heat still percolates in the air. Mike's Cadillac Deville waits with its engine running. Charlie frowns.

"Who's going to fucking steal it?" Mike grins. "You lose a hand round here for that kind of shit."

Charlie climbs into its icy interior, and Mike takes off blatantly ignoring the numerous speed limit signs. The compound reminds Charlie of his grandfather's retirement community back in Florida with its one story bungalows and two story townhouses straight out of the sixties, and its vast gas guzzlers parked out front. The only difference is there's less humidity and fewer lawns. Charlie hears the sound of bottles clinking and twists around in his seat. In the back is a cardboard box filled with twenty mason jars.

"What's in those jars?" Charlie says.

"Oh, that's just siddiqi, my friend."

Mike cracks up.

"You get it," he says. "Siddiqi means 'my friend' in Arabic so when I said em together–"

"What is it, Mike?"

"Chill buddy, it's homemade liquor okay. It's for the party tonight. I'm going to make a killing."

Charlie grabs a hold of the door handle.

"Stop the car," he says.

"Are you tripping?"

Mike keeps driving. Charlie leans over and grabs the wheel.

"I said stop the fucking car."

"Shit, chill dude."

Mike pulls over to the side of the road. Charlie reaches for the door handle only to hear the whoop of a police siren. Mike glances in the rear view mirror.

"Oh shit," he says. "Now look what you've done."

Charlie glances in the side mirror and sees two uniformed police officers in berets and tan uniforms step out of a police cruiser.

"What do we do now?" Charlie says.

Mike bangs his head on the steering wheel.

"We're fucked, buddy, totally fucked."

Charlie swallows. His heart pounds frantically. He thinks of making a run for it but fears one of the cops might shoot him in the back.

"Oh sweet Jesus," Mike says, "that's a lot of fucking booze back there. It's gonna be 'eighty and out' for us."

"Eighty and out?"

Mike brings his head up. He has the look of a condemned man.

"Eighty lashes then out on the first flight home."

There is a rap on Mike's window. A mustached, Rayban wearing officer peers down at them. Mike rolls down the window.

"You got me officer," Mike says. "My friend too."

Charlie spins towards the officer.

"I promise you, I had—"

"Shut up," the officer says.

He turns his attention back to Mike.

"Now what have you got for me?"

Mike reaches down and pulls the trunk lever.

"Ten bottles of the finest sid in the whole of Riyadh," he says.

"The finest, you say."

"You find better, Officer Ahmed, and I'll give you your money back."

"I never pay you money."

"That's the point."

Officer Ahmed bursts out laughing.

"You're a funny one, Mike Cooper. Very funny indeed."

Officer Ahmed strolls to the back of the car and lifts out another cardboard box. The other officer slams the trunk shut and together they saunter back to their cruiser. Charlie grips the armrest in an attempt to control his trembling. Mike grins.

"You really thought you were fucked, didn't you? Classic ... wait till I tell the boys."

Mike puts the car in gear and drives towards the center of the compound. He chuckles the whole way. He pulls up outside a collection of stores; a McDonalds, a couple of hairdressers, a dry cleaners, and a supermarket. He jumps out and grabs the siddiqi.

"Hurry up," he says.

Like a chastened lamb, Charlie follows him down a paved walkway. They come upon a large, lit up pool in the shape of a palm. Two hundred ex-pats are gathered around it, dressed like they're out for a night in Jamaica. Another thirty or so frolic in the water. *Jump* by Kriss Kross blasts from a set of speakers and whenever it gets to the chorus half the crowd do exactly that. Mike joins in, unconcerned that his sloshing siddiqi might go crashing to the ground. The song transitions into a slower Vanessa Williams number.

"I'll go get you a drink," Mike says. "You sure as shit look like you need one."

Mike carts the box over to a makeshift bar. Charlie closes his eyes and takes a deep breath. He decides to slip away.

"So you came after all," a woman says.

Charlie turns to find Jenny in a one piece bathing suit with a multi-colored wrap tied around her waist. Her long blonde hair is wet and slinks to one side.

"It feels more like Club Med than Saudi Arabia," Charlie says.

"That's the dirty secret," she smiles.

"Not to the Saudis, I assume."

"No."

"Then why—"

"Because if they didn't let stuff like this happen, half the ex-pats would be on the next plane home."

"What happens on compound, stays on compound."

"You're learning."

Charlie and Jenny watch as two women perched on their respective mates' shoulders grapple in the pool. Finally one topples over, taking her opponent's bikini top with her. The crowd lets out a roar as the topless women raises her arms in victory.

"Don't worry," Jenny says, "everyone's shocked when they first arrive. You come thinking you're going to live like a monk and instead every night feels like Friday night back home."

"Not the Friday nights I remember."

"There was one company back in England who had a supply manager who was a total alkie, so they came up with the genius idea of posting him to their Riyadh office. Three months later they had to fly him home in an air ambulance. Poor blighter had cirrhosis of the liver."

Charlie laughs. Mike sidles up with a couple of red plastic cups. He hands one to Charlie.

"Shove that down your hatch."

Mike downs his in one go. Charlie follows suit and immediately regrets it. It feels as if the liquid is dissolving his insides. He bends over gasping for air.

"Mike, you're such an asshole," Jenny says.

"Oh fuck off, Joe knows how to take a joke. Don't you, Joe?"

Charlie does his best to straighten up. He puts a hand up.

"It's okay," he says.

"No, it's not," Jenny says. "This little prick always goes too far."

"You'd know how far my little prick can go," Mike says.

"Sorry when I said 'little' I was trying to be kind. I should have said totally, fucking miniscule."

Mike reddens.

"Watch out, Joe," he says, "this one's got a thing for fresh meat. It's that convict blood in her, can't keep her hands off anything shiny and new."

"Why don't you go back to the hole you crawled out of," Jenny says.

"Really, I didn't know your vagina was still available."

Jenny launches herself at Mike. He stumbles backwards and ends up in the pool. A cheer goes up. Mike rises sputtering obscenities. Jenny turns her back on him.

"So you feel like dancing?" she says.

"I'm not much a dancer," Charlie says.

"What are you much of?"

"Actually I was hoping to find someone who reads Arabic."

Jenny shakes her head.

"You really are a strange one, aren't you?"

Over her shoulder, Charlie watches Mike clamber out of the pool. Mike rushes at Jenny.

"Excuse me?" he says.

Charlie intercepts Mike and, with his shoulder lowered, drives Mike back into the pool. An even greater cheer erupts. Charlie turns back. Jenny smiles at him.

"Strange but utterly fascinating," she says.

She holds out her hand.

"Come on, Frank's over there. He's a whiz at Arabic."

Charlie takes her hand, and Jenny leads him towards a cabana.

TWENTY-ONE

"AH THERE IT is, your Highness," the doctor says.

The Arab-American doctor moves her wand over Noor's belly and taps a couple of keys on the ultrasound machine.

"It has the cutest nose, tiny, little feet ... and oh, there it goes rubbing its eyes."

Tears form in Noor's own.

"I wish I could see it," she says.

"And I wish I could show you, your Highness, but the Prince was very explicit. He wants to be the first to learn the child's gender."

"So you can tell?"

"It's still very early, nothing's certain."

The doctor hits another key. The machine spits out a couple of pictures.

"But in this case I think it's pretty obvious. If it's a boy, what you see is a turtle, the tip of his penis peeking out from behind the testicles, while if it's a girl, and I don't mean to be crude, the genitalia look more like a hamburger inside a bun."

Noor can't help but blush.

So stupid, she thinks, *over something so natural.*

"Anyway, I'll leave you to get dressed. Take your time. Like I said turtle for a boy, hamburger for a girl."

The doctor takes the pictures and leaves. Noor lies there wondering why she thought it so important to repeat that information.

Of course.

Noor scrambles off the table and over to the ultrasound machine. There on the monitor is a frozen image of her fetus. Noor stares at it in wonder.

You're a turtle.

The ride from the hospital can't be over quick enough, and once home, Noor summons Malaya to her sitting room.

"I want to become more involved in the running of the palace," Noor says.

"But that's my job, your Highness, there's no need for you to worry."

"I want to. I need to feel useful, Malaya, surely you can understand that."

"Of course, it's just ..."

Malaya takes a moment to choose her words carefully.

"If the Prince thought I was somehow failing in my duties ..."

"He won't. He'll never know."

Noor detects an overwhelming weariness in her house-keeper.

"How long have you lived in Saudi Arabia, Malaya?" she says.

"I arrived on April Third, Nineteen Seventy-Four."

"My Lord, you must have saved a lot of money."

"I send most of it home."

"But still? You'd be a wealthy woman in the Philippines if you were ever to go back."

"I dare say I would, but you need your passport to leave Saudi Arabia, your Highness."

"Have you ever asked for yours back?"

"Once. Ten years ago."

Malaya fights back tears. Noor understands full well the pain she must have endured for being so presumptuous.

"I can get it for you," Noor says.

"That's most kind of you, your Highness, but it's a fruitless task. There's a policy, you see, for all the maids."

"But you don't understand. I'm having a boy. The Prince is going to be so overjoyed he'll grant me anything."

"You really think so?"

"Absolutely."

Malaya rushes over to Noor. She takes Noor's hand and kisses it.

"Oh thank you, your Highness. You don't understand, I have two sons, a daughter. At most I thought I would be leaving them with my mother for two years, and now they're all grown with children of their own."

"Then you can make up for being away so long by being an amazing grandmother."

"Yes," Malaya says. "That I will."

Noor stands.

"So why don't we start with a tour of the maid's quarters," she says.

"Give me one moment."

Malaya retreats into the sitting room and Noor hears her speaking to someone over the internal phone system. Malaya returns.

"I'm sorry but I had to tell the chefs to depart."

Of course, Noor thinks. *God forbid they see me.*

Malaya leads Noor towards a part of the palace that Noor suspects no royal has ever set foot in. They walk along the ornate corridor that leads from her quarters, and halfway down Malaya pushes on a mirrored door that's so well concealed Noor's never noticed it. They head down a metal staircase into a basement that is bathed in harsh, artificial light, and through a large kitchen filled with both gleaming top of the line appliances and an ancient open oven. Pots are bubbling on the stove, and pita bread is baking in the oven. It's clear the cooks were here not long ago. Beyond the kitchen is another corridor off which are vast store rooms stocked with every conceivable food a Saudi royal might desire. Every so often they come upon a maid. At first they do a double take on seeing Noor and then they avert their gaze and cower as if Noor's there to conduct a witch hunt. Finally, they reach the maids' quarters. They seem to consist merely of a locker room and a small dimly lit room with six plastic chairs arranged in a circle.

"Is this the break room?" Noor says.

"I suppose you could call it that, your Highness, though technically we're not allowed a break while on duty."

"Not even to eat?"

"We are given five minutes to eat at the start and end of our shifts."

Noor wanders back into the locker room and opens one of the lockers. Inside she discovers an abaya and a niqab. Noor rubs the rough fabric in her hand.

If you're going to disguise yourself, she tells herself, *you'll need one that's similar.*

Noor turns to find Malaya standing behind her.

"I hear most of the maids don't live here," Noor says.

"Yes, there are two shifts. One arrives at five in the morning and the other at five at night."

Hence why I saw the van leaving the palace at five thirty.

"How many maids live at the palace?" Noor asks.

"Just three of us," Malaya says.

"May I see your room?"

Malaya blushes.

"There is really nothing to see," she says.

"Still I would like to see it if that's all right."

Malaya nods and leads Noor down a whitewashed corridor. She opens a door on her left and flicks on a light. Noor steps inside. Malaya's bedroom is smaller than a prison cell and has barely enough room for a narrow bed and a bedside table.

"I'd love to see a photo of your children," Noor says.

"I have none," Malaya says.

Noor frowns.

"Surely you're aware the Prince forbids any photos of people."

Of course, aniconism, Noor thinks. *Another antiquated practice that Baba used to rail against.*

Noor realizes something.

"You have no idea what your children look like now, do you?"

Tears form in Malaya's eyes.

"To be honest, your Highness, I have lost all memory of what they looked like when I left them."

Noor shivers.

Will I forget what Charlie and Baba looked like too? she wonders.

A maid comes running up to the door and speaks in a strange language to Malaya. The color drains from Malaya's face.

"The Prince is looking for you," Malaya says.

"Where is he?" Noor says.

"In your bedroom."

They head through the basement at a hurried clip and up the stairs. When they reach the door, Noor puts a hand on Malaya's arm.

"You should take a look first."

Malaya nods. She opens the door and disappears. Moments later she returns.

"It's safe," Malaya says.

"You're an angel," Noor says.

Noor kisses her stunned maid on the cheek and steps into the corridor. She walks back to her quarters, doing everything she can to keep her breathing measured. She finds the Prince in her bedroom, rummaging through her dressing table drawers.

"Where were you?" he says.

"I got waylaid in one of the bathrooms," Noor says. "I've been feeling really nauseous of late."

The Prince nods. Her excuse clearly suffices.

"Take off your dress," he says.

Noor reaches around and unzips it. The dress drops to the floor. She stands there in her underwear. The Prince walks over and places his hand on her hardened belly. His touch is cold and clammy.

"The chief doctor says he's almost certain it's a boy," he says.

"That's wonderful news."

"You don't seem surprised."

"I'm just glad he's healthy."

The Prince chuckles.

"A Saudi woman would be dancing around the room in joy," he says.

"I don't think of girls as a curse," Noor says.

"And nor do I. After all one must accept whatever Allah, in his infinite wisdom, decides. But still a boy, especially in this household, is a gift from Allah, one that I'll always cherish."

The Prince gets down on his knees and lays his bearded cheek on her stomach.

"From the moment I laid eyes on you, Noor, I knew you were special."

"I feel as if I have been nothing but a disappointment."

"Oh no, for what you're going to give me I would have put up with a hundred times more insolence."

"I never wish to be insolent again."

"I believe that. Truly I do."

The Prince traces his fingers across the front of her underwear. To Noor's shame, her nipples harden. Noor bites her lip, readying herself for what is sure to come.

"There's nothing I want more than to possess you, my dear," he says. "But I won't. Not until he's born."

The Prince stands and looks into her eyes.

"Nothing, I repeat nothing, can be allowed to risk my son."

"I understand," she says.

"Good."

The Prince smiles.

"I have one favor," Noor says. "It's Malaya."

The Prince's face darkens.

"What has she done?" he says.

"Nothing. She's too old for her job. For all her attentiveness and devotion, the burden is too onerous for someone her age."

"So what would you have me do?"

"Find someone new. Send Malaya back to the Philippines to live out her days."

The Prince nods.

"I will give it my full consideration."

"Thank you."

Noor kisses the Prince gently on the lips.

"I am so glad you've been patient with me," she says. "I finally feel like I belong here."

"You do. Forever."

"Yes, forever," she says.

TWENTY-TWO

TARIQ SITS IN the reception room and waits for his sister's anguished wails to permeate the walls. They don't come. It strangely perturbs him.

For Tariq the last week has been both glorious and unsettling. Glorious for he'd been able to delight in the caresses and company of his beautiful wife. Unsettling for he'd felt utterly isolated, holed up in a luxurious villa on the compound with not a word from the Prince. He'd become increasingly paranoid, wondering if he had somehow fallen out of favor. And then two hours ago, the Prince had requested he come see him. He has no clue why.

The door opens and the Prince sweeps in. Tariq scrambles to his feet, relieved to see the Prince is smiling. In fact the Prince's grin is so wide it seems to occupy the whole of his face.

"It's a boy," the Prince shouts.

Tariq finds himself rendered speechless.

"Come," the Prince says, "you have no words of congratulation?"

"Of course, congratulations, your Highness."

"I tell you, Tariq, this child will be an historic figure. I'm convinced of it."

The Prince flops into his chair, and Tariq follows his example. Six servants emerge carrying silver pots of tea and gold trays laden with hors d'oeuvres. There's everything a Saudi could possibly desire including warm pita bread, fresh herbs, dishes of olives and dates, hummus, fattoush, lamb kibbeh and grilled eggplant. The Prince tears into it as if he hasn't eaten in days.

"Please," the Prince says indicating the food.

Tariq takes a sambousak. The pastry, mince meat, cheese and pine kernels melt in his mouth. He can't help but groan with pleasure. The Prince smiles.

"Are the doctors certain?" Tariq says.

"Ninety percent, that's what the chief gynecologist told me. Besides I saw the pictures. The child is hung like a stallion."

The Prince stuffs a couple of falafel in his mouth and looks out across his expansive reception room as if he were a sailor fixing his eye on the horizon.

"This sister of yours," he says. "She is a most unusual creature; unique you could say."

She is that, Tariq thinks.

"That's why I'm so convinced this child will be a unique individual."

"Two unique parents must by their very natures produce a unique child."

"One day, inshallah, he'll be the ruler not only of this Kingdom but of a caliphate stretching from India to Spain."

"Like Saladin."

The Prince stuffs a grilled eggplant in his mouth.

"Anyway I must apologize for not having seen you lately," the Prince says. "I've been on an endless cycle of lunches and dinners, reacquainting myself, you could say, with my extended family. I promise you, you've not seen such a collection of indolent blasphemers in your life. They may say the right things, but none of them truly believe the words that come out of their mouths; if they did they'd never have allowed those heathens to station their troops in our land in the first place. No, all they care about is the price of oil and how that affects their ability to buy the useless baubles they desire. Allah blessed this land with oil, Tariq, so we might use its wealth to spread the true faith to every corner of the planet. He certainly didn't want us to languish in a swamp overflowing with the idolaters' toys."

Tariq cannot help but glance at the Italian furniture, the French crystal chandeliers, the fine English Wedgwood china, and the million dollar Swiss watch on the Prince's wrist, and think that is precisely what they're doing right now.

"I wish I could be of use to you at this time," Tariq says.

"You're going to be of great use," the Prince says. "You're going to be my go between with bin Laden."

Tariq sits up.

"I have to be careful right now," the Prince says. "One thing I've learned from these dinners is that bin Laden preoccupies the members of my family almost as much as the oil price. They see him around every corner, fear he'll launch an insurrection any moment."

"Will he?" Tariq says.

The Prince shakes his head.

"Yet you'd think he was about to, the way he spouts off to any dignitary that makes the trek to Sudan. You need to go there next week and tell him to stop talking in this manner - at least about the royal family."

"Why would he listen to me?"

"Because you're my personal envoy. Make crystal clear to him that, for our plan to work, we need to lull everyone into a false sense of security ."

"I don't understand."

"The war against the Soviets was an overt one and took eight years. This one will be covert. It will be waged in the shadows and it will take at least as long just to infiltrate our people into the right positions in the Kingdom. When we strike, I want the actual fighting to be over in a day."

"Strike who? The Americans?"

"No, as I've told bin Laden on countless occasions, striking them is no more effective than hitting a beehive with a stick. Our goal needs to be grander than that and much closer to home."

Of course, Tariq thinks, *you want to topple your own family and rule Saudi Arabia yourself.*

"That's all you want me to tell him," Tariq says.

"I may have a few more particulars by the time you leave, but the most important thing is that your mission be secret. I could never go myself. I've led my family to believe that bin Laden and I have had a falling out."

"I hope by now you can trust my discretion."

"I wouldn't be sending you if I didn't."

The Prince takes a slug of tea to wash down his food.

"Now there's one other matter I wish to discuss. I have two unmarried sisters. I won't lie to you, neither of them is a great beauty, but you'd do me a great honor if you were to marry Princess Mysha, the elder one. I think it would be the perfect way to cement our relationship."

Tariq stares slack jawed at the Prince. For a moment he believes he heard him wrong. It's too incredible otherwise.

"I promise her *mahr* will be a generous one," the Prince says.

Oh God, it is true.

"Of course. Of course I will," Tariq blurts out. "It would be an honor."

"Good. I'm glad you're disposed to the union. There's one thing. My mother, while thinking highly of your present wife, would prefer that Mysha be your first and primary wife.

Tariq feels a twinge of regret.

How I will miss Badia, he thinks.

But it is no more than a twinge. By marrying Princess Mysha, he will become a part of the Saudi royal family. And besides, if all goes to plan, he'll be able to remarry her as his second wife once he's gotten Mysha pregnant.

"I totally understand," Tariq says.

"Good, then I will tell my mother she can begin preparing the wedding celebration once you return from Sudan."

The Prince sits back with his fingers entwined across his pudgy belly. Tariq stands. He learned a while back that this is the signal for him to leave.

"Ma'salaam," he says.

"Yes you too, Tariq."

Tariq heads for the doors, his mind a daze. He can quite honestly say he's never been happier.

TWENTY-THREE

CHARLIE GLANCES DOWN at his marked up map and then back up at the high wall beyond the intersection. In the midday glare it gleams like it's made of gold.

No doubt about it, he tells himself. *Noor's somewhere inside there.*

The light turns green, and Charlie drives on past the walls of the palace compound. He spies a massive teak gate up ahead and slows. In front of it two Rayban wearing guards keep watch from inside a small, air conditioned guard house. As Charlie drives by, he feels their gaze fall upon him. He presses down on the accelerator and carries on till he reaches another intersection at the end of the compound.

What now? he thinks. *There's no way I can do another circuit around the walls.*

On the opposite corner he spies a restaurant built to look like the Taj Mahal. He turns into its vacant parking lot and heads for the entrance. The place is empty but for a Bangla-deshi waiter folding napkins.

"Salaam alaikum," Charlie says.

"Wa-alaikum asalaam," the waiter says.

"Are you open?"

"But of course. Please sit anywhere."

Charlie heads for the corner table and positions himself in such a way that he can look back up the road. A hundred yards away he can make out the palace gates. The waiter approaches.

"I'll have a glass of water, thanks, and whatever your signature dish is," Charlie says.

"Signature, I do not understand this word," the waiter says.

"The dish you like most."

"Oh, then without a doubt that would be al Kabsa. You can have it with beef, chicken or lamb, your choice?"

"Chicken be great."

The waiter retreats and shouts out the order to the kitchen. Charlie stares out the window at the gate. He detects movement and leans forward. A white S.U.V. swings out and heads his direction. The light at the intersection changes to yellow. The S.U.V. accelerates and powers through the intersection a good couple of seconds after it has turned red. A delivery truck has to swerve in order to avoid colliding with it. The S.U.V. flies past the restaurant, and Charlie has just enough time to detect the blurred faces of two bearded men in red and white ghutras. He realizes his vigil is useless.

Even if Noor does leave the palace how will I know it's her? She'll be covered head to toe.

The waiter approaches. Charlie stands.

"I'm sorry," Charlie says. "I have to be somewhere."

"But your food is almost ready."

"I promise, I'll come back another time."

Charlie hands the man a twenty dollar bill and hastily exits the restaurant. He drives back to his compound and feels a hot sweat envelop him. He bangs his head against the steering wheel.

"What was I thinking?" he screams. "This was stupid. Stupid, stupid, stupid. I'm never going to rescue her."

He looks up and sees the traffic in front of him has come to a stop. He drills his foot against the brake. His tires squeal wildly. His car halts inches from the bumper of the car in front. Charlie pants, tears of frustration now flowing down his cheeks. He looks out his side window and sees a young boy staring at him from the backseat of an S.U.V. The boy puts his fingers in his mouth and sticks his tongue out. Charlie can't help but chuckle. The traffic starts up again, and he follows, his mind now calm and clear.

You gotta go home, he thinks. *There's no point sticking around here hoping for a miracle. Of all people, you know they don't exist.*

He enters the compound's gates. As ever there is a heavy police presence out front. It includes an armored police truck with a machine gun turret. He wonders what they are doing there; protecting the ex-pats or stopping their citizens from seeing the freedoms they allow within those walls.

He enters his townhouse and finds a message on his answering machine. He plays it. It's from Jenny, from an hour ago. She wants him to come to Deira souk with her. She needs to buy a birthday present for her father. He erases the message and goes and lies down on his bed. He wonders how long Ralph will take to approve his exit visa. He prays not more than a week.

And then something occurs to him.

He jumps off the bed and races to the kitchen. He empties his trash can and searches for the paper napkin that Jenny had scrawled her home phone number on at the party. He finds it. It's soaked with coffee granules. The number is barely visible. He picks up the phone and dials it. Jenny picks up on the fourth ring.

"It's Joe," he says.

"Hey, I was about to jump in a cab," Jenny says.

"You don't have a car?"

Jenny laughs.

"God, Joe, you really are new to town. Women can't drive around here."

"Then I'll drive you, that is if the invitation's still open."

"Of course it is. I'll tell the cab driver to bugger off."

"Great. See you in five."

Charlie is true to his word and five minutes later, he is outside the door of a townhouse identical to his own. He rings the doorbell. Jenny answers it in an abaya and black headscarf.

"Your call was an unexpected surprise," she says. "The way you disappeared the other night I was afraid that was the last I was ever going to see of you."

"I'm not a late night kind of guy."

"Let's go, the shops shutter once Friday prayers start."

Jenny fills the drive to the souk with mindless gossip. From her telling, it seems Mike not only provides booze to all the ex-pats on the compound but also to a healthy portion of the doctors who work at the hospital. Charlie lets her prattle away. He decides this is not the time to be asking his favor.

They park off a large, crowded square and make their way across its wide, rectangular paving stones. On one corner is a light brown castle with circular towers; it reminds Charlie of the sandcastles he and his mother used to make in the Hamptons when he was a kid. On the other corner is a large, bricked mosque with such straight lines that it seems as if it's been constructed from Lego. Beyond the square is the souk. To Charlie, it has a similar feel to Qissa Khawani bazaar. The alleys are tight and winding and, like in Peshawar, the souk is divided into different sections. In one carpets are piled high at the shop's entrances, their owners calling out as they spy a couple of gullible Westerners stroll by. There is the gold bazaar, the walls of each store heaving with gold necklaces and breast plates so pure they dazzle even under the garish fluorescent light. There are the spice stores whose wares sit in ceramic pots and exude a panoply of scents, and produce stores with bulging baskets of dates and figs. Despite wearing an abaya and headdress, Jenny can't help but receive lascivious stares from the shop owners and male shoppers. They pass one store, and Charlie sees a couple of teenage boys pucker their lips at her. He steps towards them. Jenny grabs his arm.

"Ignore them," she says.

"Thought they were meant to respect women around here?"

"Saudi women sure, but Western women, hell it doesn't matter how you dress, they think you're a whore. The other day, I had to take this guy's blood pressure and I walk into the examination room and his cock is out, standing rigid to attention."

"Did you call security?"

"You crazy, I'd be on the first plane home."

"So what did you do?"

"I told him I liked men with bigger cocks and carried on with the exam. His erection wilted before my eyes."

Charlie laughs. They continue past a series of stores where thobes hang like sets of curtains, and then finally come to the part of the souk that Jenny's been so intent on tracking down. On the walls of the stalls hang an assortment of *jambiyas*, curved daggers sheathed in ornamental holsters. Jenny and Charlie stop in front of one store. The gnarled Berber owner seems more intent on chewing the twig in his hand than being of any assistance to them.

"I'm not sure if this one speaks English?" Charlie says.

"That's okay," Jenny says, "I've picked up a little Arabic."

Charlie looks in Jenny's direction.

"What?" she says. "You thought I was a dumb blonde?"

"Not for one second."

"Good."

She points to a dagger and asks the Berber if she can look at it. He reaches up and places it on the glass counter. Jenny twirls it in her hand. The sheath is silver with little other ornamentation. She pulls out the blade and points its tip at Charlie.

"I think this is something every warm blooded man should have, don't you?" she says.

"More like every warm blooded woman."

Jenny laughs.

"What will your dad use it for?" Charlie says.

"Who the hell knows. He'll probably put it on his office desk, and show it off to all his co-workers."

"Not use it on them, hopefully."

"Nah, he's a cuddly bear."

Jenny asks the Berber the price. He gives it to her. Jenny snorts and gives him an offer of her own. The Berber waves his hand at them as if to tell them to piss off.

"Fine," Jenny says, "let's go."

She grabs Charlie's hand and leads him away.

"I once bought a bike using just this technique," Charlie says.

"Any second now," Jenny says.

Sure enough, Charlie feels a hand on his arm. He turns to see the Berber gesticulating at them to return. The Berber mentions a price and Jenny counters. Three rounds later they have a deal. Jenny returns to take possession of her prize. From the direction of the square, a muezzin starts calling the faithful to afternoon prayers. Soon after other muezzins begin their own recitations. There are so many it's disorientating.

"Fuck," Jenny says. "Hurry."

Jenny searches in her bag for her purse. Out the corner of his eye, Charlie sees two bearded men in hitched up thobes and loose ghutras heading their way. They each carry a cane and are barking at the chastened store owners to slide down the metal fronts of their stores.

Jenny finds her purse and pulls out a wad of cash. She hands the correct amount to the Berber. The Berber puts the dagger in a brown paper bag. Angry shouts erupt behind them, and Charlie feels a stinging whack to the back of his thigh. He swings around to see the two bearded men glaring at him.

"What the hell?" he says.

The men scream at them like a pair of staff sergeants.

"It's okay," Jenny says, "we're finishing up."

Behind them the Berber locks up his store.

"No wait," Jenny shouts, "what about my dagger?"

The Berber races way with the other storeowners, and the two men chase after them as if they were errant sheep. In a matter of moments everyone is gone.

"What was that all about?" Charlie says.

"Mutaween, religious police," Jenny says. "Now we'll have to bloody wait."

"For how long?"

"Thirty minutes, maybe a little longer. On Fridays the imams like to deliver fiery sermons."

"About evil people like you and me?"

"Exactly," Jenny says, slipping her arm through. "We're deliciously evil."

The two of them wander through the deserted souk and come upon the open square. They find a bench in the shade and sit down, the magnified voice of the imam vibrating out through the walls of the mosque.

"So I was wondering if you wanted to make a little cash on the side?" Charlie says.

"I don't come cheap, you know," Jenny says.

Charlie blushes.

"I didn't mean it like that."

Jenny laughs.

"I'm screwing with you, what is it?" she says.

"I had this patient in the other day. He tells me his sister got married to this Prince, and well the guy supposedly has a reputation for beating his wives."

"Not uncommon around here."

"Well he's desperate to know how she's doing. When they were growing up they were really close."

"I don't think it's within my power to arrange a meet and greet."

"No, but you have access to the female records. If he knew when she was coming in for her next appointment, he could engineer some chance encounter in the lobby."

"You sure he's not some kind of unrequited lover or something."

Charlie shakes his head.

"His last name's the same as hers."

"Doesn't mean shit around here."

"I promise, he's one of the good ones."

"How much is he offering?"

"Two thousand dollars. Thought we could split it fifty fifty."

Jenny stares out across the baking square.

"I don't know. I don't want this to come back and bite me in the arse."

"It won't. He won't even know you helped me."

"Then tell him it's four thousand. These bastards can afford it."

"I'm sure he'll agree."

"You got the girl's name?"

Charlie hands Jenny a slip of paper. She reads it.

"Princess Noor," she says. "It's like something out of a fairytale."

If only it was, Charlie thinks.

Across the way, a crowd starts to flow out of the Great Mosque and flood the square.

"Ah, finally," Jenny says.

She jumps to her feet.

"Let's go get my Dad's pressie."

Charlie stands only to be drawn to the sound of blaring police sirens. A convoy of police cruisers and a yellow van enter the square. The crowd parts and the cruisers spread out to create a perimeter. A buzz permeates the air.

Charlie takes Jenny's hand.

"Come on, let's get out of here," he says.

They head for the bazaar. A young man with a trim beard approaches them.

"Welcome, my friends," he says. "Welcome indeed to Chop-Chop Square."

Charlie puts a protective arm around Jenny.

"We're just leaving," Charlie says.

"No, you must come. As honored foreign guests, you must take pride of place at our special event."

Charlie sees four other young men have surrounded them. The men grab Charlie and Jenny by the arm and frogmarch them through the crowd.

"Joe," Jenny screams.

"It's okay, I'm right here," Charlie says.

Charlie twists toward the grinning young man.

"Look we really don't need to see this."

"No you must. Saudi justice, number one in the world."

They burst through the front of the crowd and emerge no more than thirty feet from the center of the square.

"Sit, sit," the young man says.

The man's friends shove them to the ground and stand in a semi-circle behind them. There's nowhere to run. In the center of the square, a powerful African man in a dazzling white thobe paces around like a batter waiting for his turn at the plate. He holds a curved sword that twinkles in the sun. Nearby another man in white kneels on the ground. His head is covered by a tube of white cloth and his hands are tied behind his back. Charlie feels Jenny's hand intertwine with his. He looks over at her. She's gone pale white.

"Close your eyes," he says.

She tries but is unable. The young man points at a middle aged man standing not far from the accused. The man has the countenance of a vengeful Old Testament prophet.

"That man," the young man says, "he is victim's family. Only he can save the prisoner's life now."

"How?" Charlie says.

"Money. Like with all things."

Charlie watches as a couple of policemen approach the middle aged man. They engage in an intense conversation. It looks no different than a haggling session in the souk. The executioner waits with his hand on his hip. The middle aged man shakes his head and walks away. An excited murmur rises in the crowd.

The executioner approaches the condemned man. Jenny's nails dig into Charlie's palm. The executioner assumes a wide legged stance and raises the sword above his head. All around catcalls and insults are shouted at the condemned man.

Charlie feels his throat tighten.

The executioner lowers the sword and touches its razor sharp edge to the one exposed part of the man's body, his neck. The condemned man's neck instinctively straightens and in a flash the executioner brings the sword back up and then down.

A roar goes up.

The head rolls away.

Blood gushes from the man's severed neck like water from a burst water main.

Jenny leans over and vomits onto the paved stones in front of her.

For a moment the man's headless corpse kneels there, but then like a felled tree it tilts to one side and collapses to the ground. Two men in blue jumpsuits place it on a stretcher while another grabs the head and places it in a bag. From atop a police cruiser, a megaphone screeches in Arabic. The young man leans in.

"He was an adulterer. It's a warning to all to do what is right in the eyes of Allah."

The young man slaps Charlie on the back and smiles.

"Otherwise chop, chop. Saudi justice," he chuckles.

The young man slips away with his friends. Charlie wraps his arm around Jenny.

"You okay?" he says.

Jenny turns towards him. Tears stream down her cheeks.

"I want to get out of this country so badly," she says.

"Me too," Charlie says.

Charlie pulls Jenny to her feet and guides her towards their car, her father's dagger long forgotten.

TWENTY-FOUR

"I'VE CONSIDERED YOUR request regarding that servant," the Prince says.

Noor ends her pretense of being asleep and looks up at the Prince.

"Princess Hadiya believes her to be of vital importance to the running of this palace," he says.

"Princess Hadiya does not spend her every waking moment here," Noor says. "The woman is too old to do her job properly."

"It's settled. She stays."

"But I really think—"

"Do you doubt my judgment?"

"I'd never presume to."

"Good. Then like I said, it's settled."

The Prince rests his right cheek on Noor's belly.

"He's strong," the Prince says. "I can sense that."

"Just like his father," Noor says.

The Prince crawls up the bed and places his lips on Noor's. His tongue delves into her mouth, and Noor forces herself to respond. His hand gropes her breasts and he lets out an agonized moan. To her astonishment, he flips her over.

No.

He fumbles to release himself and soon after she feels a searing yet familiar pain. Noor cries silent tears; not for herself but for Malaya.

I failed you, she thinks.

Soon after the Prince lets out a guttural groan and collapses beside her. Noor lies there motionless. He rolls off the bed and stumbles to the bathroom. As the Prince relieves himself, Noor fantasizes about the many varied ways she could kill the Prince, only to conclude that nothing will kill him more than the loss of his son after she escapes. The Prince returns to the bedroom and comes over. He kisses the top of her head.

"I must be away to work. I will see you in three days, inshallah," he says.

Not if I have anything to do with it, Noor thinks.

She watches the Prince walk out of the room. Malaya takes his place. She offers Noor a broad smile.

"Would you like me to draw you a bath, your Highness," she says.

Noor averts her gaze. She can't find the courage to look her housekeeper in the eye.

"You don't need to trouble yourself, Malaya."

"Nothing is too much trouble for you, your Highness."

Noor listens to the water cascading into the tub and recalls a Virginia Woolf saying that her father was fond of quoting.

"You cannot find peace by avoiding life".

Noor rises and walks into the bathroom. Malaya is on her knees testing the temperature of the water with her elbow.

"I'm sorry, Malaya, I tried."

"I know you did, your Highness."

Noor realizes that Malaya must have been listening in.

She always has. She'd have to in order to know when I needed assistance.

"In all my time in Saudi Arabia no one has treated me with more kindness than you," Malaya says.

"But I failed you."

Malaya shakes her head.

"No, you restored my faith in humanity, your Highness. That's the greatest gift you could have given me."

Noor takes Malaya's hand and pulls her up so she is sitting on the edge of the tub.

"You're Christian, aren't you, Malaya?"

"Jesus is my Lord and Savior."

"And in the Bible, the night before Jesus is betrayed he washes the feet of his disciples?"

"That is correct."

Noor kneels down in front of Malaya and removes Malaya's shoes and socks. Malaya sits utterly still.

"Why did he do that?" Noor says.

"To show us that no one is greater than any other," Malaya says.

Noor finds a washcloth and dips it into the warm water. She wrings it out and wipes down Malaya's worn feet.

"I think his message was even more powerful than that. I think he wanted to show us that the lowliest of servants are more exalted in the eyes of God than the highest of rulers."

Malaya looks down at Noor with tears in her eyes.

"But you are Muslim, why would you believe such a thing?"

"Because the Holy Quran says something similar. 'The true servants of God the Gracious are those who walk on earth in humility.'"

Noor takes a towel and pats down Malaya's feet.

"Malaya, your place in heaven is assured, and one day you'll be reunited there with your children and grandchildren. I know it."

"And so do I."

Noor picks up Malaya's shoes and socks. She hands them to her housekeeper.

"Now go to your room," she says. "Close the door and pray to God."

"Are you sure?"

Noor kisses Malaya on the forehead.

"Go," she says.

Malaya leaves. Noor pulls off her gown and slips into the bath.

Tonight, she decides, *tonight I will escape.*

***

NOOR FINISHES PRAYING and looks at the clock. Four-forty-seven.

It's time.

She pushes her intercom buzzer. Malaya enters the bedroom.

"I'm going to bed early tonight," Noor says.

"Are you unwell, your Highness?" Malaya says.

"A little nauseous, nothing serious. I don't want to be disturbed tonight under any circumstance. No one is to enter my quarters."

"I understand."

"And please allow me to sleep in. I'll call for you when I'm in need of assistance."

"Of course."

The two of them stand there awkwardly. Malaya's expression as inscrutable as ever.

Does she suspect something? Noor wonders. *If so, would it even matter?*

"Is there anything else, your Highness?" Malaya says.

"No, thank you."

Malaya heads for the door.

"Malaya," Noor calls out.

Malaya turns back.

"May God be with you," Noor says.

"And with you, your Highness."

Malaya closes the door behind her. Noor looks at the clock. Four-forty-nine. She hurries into the bathroom and undresses until she wears nothing more than a pair of running shorts and the sneakers on her feet. She sits in front of her vanity mirror. She has practiced what she's about to do every night for the last week.

Make-up.

She wets a cotton ball with make-up remover and wipes away the little make-up and lipstick she put on that morning.

Eyebrows.

She takes an eyebrow pencil and makes her own thicker and straighter.

Beard.

She uses the pencil to create a goatee and after that mascara to give her cheeks a subtle shadow.

Hair.

She takes a hair tie and pulls back her hair.

Breasts.

She goes into her closet and opens a drawer. She extracts a collection of Hermes scarves she's tied together. She wraps the scarves tightly around her torso. She ties the scarves off and puts on a t-shirt.

Thobe.

She extracts the thobe from in between a set of hanging ball gowns. She pulls it over her head and buttons it up. It fits well but is also loose enough that her reduced bosom now totally disappears.

Ghutra.

She extracts the ghutra from the back of another drawer. She places the red and white checkered headdress on her head and places the round agal cord on top. She glances in the mirror. She looks no different than that androgynous Saudi teen she saw at the mall.

Abaya.

She throws on an abaya and niqab that she soaked the night before so that it would appear cheap and wrinkled. She looks at herself one last time in the mirror. All that can be seen are her eyes.

I'm invisible, she says to herself.

She heads back into her bedroom and looks at the clock. Five o'clock.

Time to go.

She opens her bedroom door only to remember something. She rushes to her writing table and grabs the three solid gold bracelets and two diamond rings lying on top of it. She slips the bracelets on her wrist and the rings in a breast pocket.

She heads into the sitting room and takes a quick sweep. Malaya was good as her word. No one's in there. She walks through the dining room and into the entry hall. She places her ear to the door and listens. No one seems to be there. She pulls it open and glances out.

Go.

She hurries through the hall and down the ornate corridor. She hears voices. Someone's coming. She scurries back to the hall and stands with her back against the wall.

She waits.

The voices disappear.

She looks down the corridor. She decides it must have been a couple of maids leaving at the end of their shift.

She rushes down the corridor until she comes to the hidden servants' door. She closes it behind her and makes her way down the metal staircase. She heads through the kitchen and down another corridor past the store rooms. A maid comes her direction. She keeps her head down.

"That you, Grace?" the maid says in English.

Noor doesn't respond.

"Grace?"

Noor continues on. The maid gives up and carries on her way. Noor listens for chatter. There is none. She panics.

The bus must have left already.

She quickens her pace.

When she gets to the maids' quarters she glances into the locker room. To her relief, she sees the day shift are putting on their abayas as the night shift takes theirs off. No one talks. It's as if the women have lost the power to speak. Noor hears the beep of a horn and continues down the corridor. She comes to a door and pushes it open. The evening heat attacks her. At the top of a set of concrete steps waits an idling bus. She stares at it in disbelief. It almost feels too easy.

Behind her the door swings open. It galvanizes her into action. She continues up the steps and climbs on board. The chain-smoking driver pays her no heed. She makes her way to the very back and sits by the window. Soon after fifteen abaya clad maids clamber on board. She waits for one to sit down beside her but none of them do. For reasons unknown they prefer the seats up front.

The doors slap shut and the bus rolls down a one lane road until it comes to the tradesmen's entrance to Princess Hadiya's palace. The doors hiss open and another fifteen maids shuffle on board and take the seats at the back. Two sit down beside her. Noor waits for them to say something but they don't. They slump in their seats exhausted from their day. The bus rolls away again and continues through the back of the compound. It reaches a large gate. The gate swings open. The bus rolls forward then stops. Noor glances out the window. An armed guard comes out of the guardhouse. The doors hiss open. She thinks of ducking down but it's too late. The guard looks down the length of the bus. She sits there frozen wondering if he's doing a head count. The driver says something to the guard. The guard laughs and steps off the bus. The doors slam shut, and Noor exhales. The bus swings into traffic.

Thank you, Allah, she says over and over.

She looks out the window. The palace's floodlit walls fly past and then, like a river toppling over the side of a waterfall, they fall away.

I'm free, she thinks.

She sits back and closes her eyes. She listens to the vibrations of the engine as the bus makes its way through the Riyadh rush hour.

How long do I have?

Sixteen hours minimum. There is no way Malaya or any other maid will dare enter her room until nine the next morning. If they wait until midday she'll have twenty.

It's an eternity, she thinks.

Once they arrive at the maids' compound, she suspects it'll take her half-an-hour to get away. She'll need to find a secluded place to get rid of her abaya and niqab. From there she'll take a taxi to the souk where she'll sell the first gold bracelet. That will provide her with more than enough money to hire a taxi to take her all the way to Jeddah. Six hundred and sixty miles. That's what she'd estimated by using the map in her palace. It will be night, the highway relatively empty, her driver will go at least eighty miles an hour, probably more knowing how people drive out here. She'll arrive in Jeddah at dawn and have the driver take her to the old harbor. There she'll use the second gold bracelet to bribe a fisherman to ferry her across the Red Sea. She will have another driver take her to Cairo where she will sell the final bracelet and use the money to rent an apartment. She will hide out there until she works out where to head next. Once she does, the two diamond rings are worth enough that they'll finance not only the next part of her journey but the next ten years of her life.

And that of my son also.

The bus brakes, and she senses the women fidget in their seats.

We must be here, she thinks.

She has no idea how long she's been daydreaming.

Ten minutes? Twenty? Thirty?

She opens her eyes and presses her face to the window. The bus has come to a halt in front of a barred gate. On either side are walls as high as those of the Prince's. They are topped with rolls of barbed wire.

No, it's not possible, she thinks.

The gate creaks open and the bus carries on. An armed guard glares up at her. She twists in her seat and watches the gate close behind them. The compound consists of six cinder block towers. Nothing more. It's a post apocalyptic vision with no vegetation, cracked sidewalks, washing hanging on drooping lines, and trash swirling in the evening breeze. Traipsing around it are nothing but third world women.

It's worse than a prison, she thinks.

The bus brakes and the doors hiss open. The maids edge their way off the bus. She knows if she gets off she's trapped.

Noor drops to the floor and hides behind the seat in front of her.

In the distance the call to evening prayer goes out. The driver sighs and ambles off the bus. A few minutes later he returns. The doors slam shut again and the bus turns back around. The gate creaks open, and the bus merges into the Riyadh traffic.

It's all right, she tells herself.

She suspects the bus will head to a depot. Perhaps the driver will stop at a gas station where she can slip off.

She squats there, not daring to change her position. If the journey to the maid's quarters seemed to pass in a blink of an eye, this one never seems to end. With every minute the urge to pee becomes ever more excruciating and each time the bus brakes her bladder screams out in pain. She wonders if they are heading to the driver's home.

That's all right too, she thinks. *I can get a taxi from there.*

The bus brakes and the door hisses open. Someone climbs on board. The driver says something and another man laughs. Its owner is familiar. It's the guard from the Prince's compound. She hears his boots stomp down the aisle.

It's over, she tells herself.

He stops two seats before the back of the bus and heads back down the aisle. The doors slam shut. The bus winds its way through the compound and parks. The driver gets off and the doors close behind him. Noor sits up and looks out the window. The bus is in a walled parking lot next to a row of similar buses.

Knowing she cannot hold out any longer, Noor pulls up her abaya and thobe and pees on the floor. Her urine streams down the aisle. She lies down on the backseat and waits. Every noise, every gust of wind sends a wave of fear through her. The wails for the Isha prayer come and go. Finally she suspects it's close to midnight.

It's time to go.

She creeps down the aisle and pulls the door open. From a hut in one corner she sees the orange dots of cigarettes and hears men laughing. She sneaks behind the row of buses and over to a low slung wall. She climbs over and drops down into a flower bed. In front of her is an expansive lawn. A series of sprinklers arc back and forth bathing it in water. Beyond it is the back of her flood lit palace. At least it looks like hers. It's so tough to tell. She knows she has no other choice. She takes a deep breath and sprints across the lawn, the sprinklers splattering her abaya. By the time she reaches the other side she is drenched.

Keep going, she tells herself.

She hustles down the basement stairs and tries the door. It opens.

Thank God.

She barrels inside and scampers down the corridor, her wet sneakers squeaking on the cement floor. She passes the maid's locker room.

"Who's there?" someone says.

It's Malaya.

She thinks of running but decides against it. The lights burst on, and Malaya approaches in her nightgown.

"Who are you?" Malaya says.

"Go to bed, Malaya," Noor says.

Malaya pales.

"Your Highness?"

"I said go to bed."

Malaya heads back the way she came. Noor hurries through the kitchen and up the staircase. She slips through the secret door into the upstairs corridor and runs back to her quarters. She collapses on top of her bed and finally the enormity of her failure hits her. She begins to sob and doesn't stop until sleep finally overwhelms her.

***

THE CURTAINS OPEN and light floods into the bedroom. Noor wakes with a start.

Malaya?

Someone approaches the bed.

"Good morning, sister."

Noor lies there utterly still.

"Noor?" Tariq says.

"What are you doing here?" Noor says. "I told Malaya that no one was to disturb me."

"So she said, but fortunately the Prince's commands carry more weight than yours around here."

Noor brings a hand up to her face. Her niqab is still in

place. She swings her feet off the bed and bundles past Tariq.

"Excuse me?" she says.

She stumbles into the bathroom and locks the door behind her. She starts ripping off her clothes; the niqab, the ghutra, the abaya, the thobe, the t-shirt.

"If only our father could see you now," Tariq says, "so comfortable in a burqa that you even wear one to bed."

Noor freezes. Tariq has entered the walk-in closet and is heading for the other door. It's unlocked. Noor struggles to undo the knot of Hermes' scarves.

"Though even I find this practice somewhat peculiar. To wear an abaya to bed is one thing, but a niqab?"

The scarves pull loose and Noor lets them drop to the floor. She picks up the thobe and ghutra and sprints for the shower. Tariq enters the bathroom as she squeezes through the shower's glass door. She turns on the water and throws the thobe and ghutra in one corner. She pulls her shorts off and uses them to wipe away the black make up on her face.

"What are you doing in here?" she shouts.

"There's no shame in a brother seeing his sister in her full glory, especially if she's going to be the co-founder of a mighty dynasty."

Noor turns to see Tariq staring at her through the glass door. She twists away, hoping the door will soon steam up. She forces a derisive laugh.

"Dynasty?" she says. "You've always had an abnormally elevated view of yourself, haven't you?"

"I'd prefer to say prescient."

She lathers her face with a bar of soap and scrubs it with the shorts. The side of it comes away black.

"Have you ever heard of Mohammad bin Laden?" Tariq says.

"Is he related to that mujahid back in Peshawar?"

"Very astute. He was his father actually. Once he was a poor, uneducated Yemeni and when he first arrived in Jeddah he worked as a porter. What he made, he saved and in time he had enough to start a small construction company."

Noor looks at the shorts. No more make-up seems to be coming off. She throws them on the ground only to spy her sneakers. She takes off the first.

"He was brilliant, with an eye for detail and a head for numbers and soon he managed to forge such a close relationship with the royal family that King Faisal awarded all future construction contracts to his company. Do you know how much that company is worth today?"

Noor pulls off the second of her sneakers.

"Enlighten me?" she says.

Tariq swings the door open. Noor twists off the shower and pushes past her brother. Tariq turns in her direction. Noor faces her brother naked and unashamed. Behind him the thobe and ghutra lie in full view.

"Five billion dollars," Tariq says.

"You expect to make five billion dollars," she says.

"No but I expect our family to be just as prestigious. You are married to a man who one day, God willing, will be King; your son his chosen successor. While I, his closest friend and brother-in-law, will enrich myself by helping to carry out his wishes."

"I didn't know you were married to his sister?"

"I will be when I return from Sudan."

"To be married again so soon. You seem to be making a habit of this."

"Each has been more advantageous than the last."

"And who will it be to this time?"

"Princess Mysha."

"Asra told me she was born with a penis as well as a vagina."

Tariq doesn't flinch. He casts his eyes down Noor's body in a way that makes her wonder if he's taken lessons from the Prince.

"You are too cruel," he says. "Not everyone can be as delectable as you."

Noor grabs a towel and wraps it around herself. She heads for her closet. To her relief Tariq follows her.

"And this is why you came to see me today?" she says, "To tell me all this?"

"Oh no, I came because I told the Prince I'd chaperone you and the women to the mall."

"Have fun, I'm not going."

"Oh but you must, Princess Fadilah and Princess Hadiya are desperate to buy baby clothes for your son."

"Then they should buy him some."

"They want you there with them."

Noor yanks open a drawer and extracts some underwear and a bra. Tariq stands there with his arms crossed and watches her slip them on.

"One can only imagine how upset the Prince will be if you decline," he says.

Noor straightens.

"I assume there's something in it for you?" she says.

"The Prince did mention that I should buy myself a watch while I'm there. I could buy you one too if you wish."

Noor nods towards a shelf where twenty jeweled watches lie.

"I have plenty," she says.

"Then you must understand how appropriate it is that I have more than one."

"When do we leave?"

Tariq smiles.

"I will come by at one-thirty."

"Don't be late," Noor says.

"Don't worry, I won't."

Tariq leaves, and Noor collapses into a nearby chair, all her false bravado gone. Malaya enters.

"Can I be of assistance, your Highness?" she says.

"The thobe and ghutra in the shower, could you get rid of them, please," Noor says.

"Of course."

Malaya heads for the bathroom. She pauses at the door.

"I'm sorry that whatever you were attempting didn't work out, your Highness."

"I guess it's not meant to be for me either, is it?" Noor says.

Malaya gives Noor one of her soft smiles.

"Perhaps not in this life."

No, Noor thinks, *in this life I'm forever condemned.*

TWENTY-FIVE

"HI YA."

Charlie turns and discovers Jenny standing in the doorway of the examination room.

"Hey, how you doing?" he says.

"Nightmares are mostly gone. Hope you don't think I was a total wuss."

"You kidding? Most brutal thing I've ever seen."

Not quite, he thinks. *Wali was worse. Way worse.*

"You'd think being a nurse, I'd be used to blood and people dying on me," Jenny says.

"I think the way you reacted says a lot about you. Shows you have humanity."

"Unlike these fucking Muslims."

Charlie frowns.

"Come on," he says. "That's a little harsh."

Jenny shakes her head.

"You haven't been around them as long as I have, Joe. They're all bastards."

Charlie would argue the point but he knows he can't. What can he say? That some of the finest, bravest and most genuine men he's had the honor of knowing - Aamir Khan, Wali, Shamsurahman - were Muslim. That the woman he loves with all his soul prays towards Mecca five times a day.

"Maybe there'll be a day when one surprises you," he says.

"I doubt it."

Jenny looks down the corridor and closes the door.

"I got what you wanted."

She extracts a piece of paper from her pocket and hands it to Charlie.

"Good and bad news," she says.

Charlie unfolds it. It's a record of Noor's last appointment.

"Seem like your patient's sister is pregnant, but, as of now, there's no follow up set."

Pregnant.

Charlie doesn't respond.

"Joe?"

He looks up.

"I guess we can check back in a week," he says.

"Screw that, it was enough of a risk just snatching this. Tell your guy it was the best we could do."

Jenny holds out her hand, and Charlie hands the piece of paper back.

"You okay?" she says.

"I'm a little off. Sore throat. Sinus headache. Patient sneezed in my face a couple of days back."

"What did I tell you? Bastards, the lot of them."

Charlie forces a smile.

"I think I'm going to take the day off," he says.

Jenny takes his hand.

"Promise you'll call me when you're better," she says. "I'll cook you dinner."

"Promise."

Jenny kisses him on the cheek and leaves. Charlie collapses against the examination table. Up until now he's managed to block out any thoughts of the Prince having sex with Noor, but he can't any longer. He shivers as he imagines Noor lying there screaming as the Prince brutally rapes her.

You can't give up, he tells himself. *Not now.*

He gathers himself and heads out of the room. Down the way, he spies Mike leaning against the nurse's station chatting with a couple of the Indian technicians. Charlie walks over.

"Hey, Mike, would you mind covering for me? I'm not feeling well."

"Told you you'd get VD if you fucked that bitch," Mike says.

"Well will you?"

"My schedule's kinda full."

Charlie pulls out his wallet and holds out three hundred riyals. Mike snatches the bills.

"But I guess I can make it work," Mike says.

Charlie takes the service elevator to the hospital's subterranean garage and gets in the Toyota Corolla he'd bought for a pittance off a departing Danish paramedic a couple of days earlier. He races up the garage's parking levels as if he were doing laps on a race track and hurtles through the midday traffic. Even the crazy drivers of Riyadh find his driving perturbing. Twenty minutes later, he pulls into the restaurant's parking lot. He runs inside. The kitchen door swings open and the Bangladeshi waiter bounds out smiling.

"You kept your promise," the waiter says.

Charlie makes for the table by the window.

"Chicken al Kabsa and a glass of water, correct?" the waiter says.

"Perfect," Charlie says.

The waiter heads for the kitchen. Charlie's gaze never diverts from the palace entrance.

I'll wait here for a week if need be, he says to himself.

A few minutes later the waiter returns with a glass of iced water. Charlie drains it.

"From your accent I sense you American?" the waiter says.

"New York," Charlie says.

Down the way an armed guard ambles out onto the road and stops an approaching bus.

"Oh, I have dreamed many times of one day paying a visit to that glorious city."

A black Mercedes sedan accelerates out of the compound followed by three white S.U.Vs. Charlie leans forward.

"Of course obtaining visa is of considerable difficulty, especially for Bangladeshis such as myself."

The five car convoy approaches.

"I wonder, perhaps you know of someone who could assist myself in this regard?" the waiter says.

The Mercedes flies past the restaurant. Charlie can only make out the driver since the back passenger windows are obscured by curtains. It is the same for each of the SUVs.

He slumps back in his chair, once more thwarted.

"Do you?" the waiter says.

And then it comes to Charlie. The curtains mean women and four cars means lots of them.

Noor.

Charlie jumps out of his chair and races for the door.

"Sir," the waiter shouts after him. "Why do you keep doing this?"

Charlie bursts into the parking lot and sprints to his car. He fumbles for his key and it falls onto the baking asphalt. He snatches it back up and unlocks his car.

Come on, come on.

He jumps in and inserts the key into the ignition. The car engine thrums to life and he screeches out of the parking lot barely missing a loading van coming the other direction.

He scans the road ahead. He can't see the convoy. He pushes down on the accelerator.

Sixty, seventy, eighty, ninety ...

Up ahead the light turns red. He floors it and closes his eyes. Horns blare, brakes screech, but there's no impact.

Thank you God.

He catches sight of the bus a hundred yards ahead. There's still no sign of the convoy. He wonders if they turned at the last intersection.

They must have.

He spots a road up ahead. He prepares to brake and do a u-turn, only to pass the bus and find the S.U.V.s and the black Mercedes right in front of it. The bus had been obscuring them.

Calm down, he tells himself. *Calm the fuck down.*

He allows the convoy to pull four car lengths ahead and follows it through downtown Riyadh. He wonders where they're going. Eventually the convoy turns off the main thoroughfare and heads towards a building that looks like a massive ice cube. They descend down a ramp. The ramp splits in two directions. The convoy goes left and comes upon a barrier manned by a guard. Charlie follows. The barrier rises and lets them through. Before Charlie can make it past, the barrier comes down again. The guard comes over to the window, and Charlie rolls it down.

"Go back," the guard says. "VIP entrance."

"I am a VIP," Charlie says.

The guard casts his eyes up and down Charlie's dinked up Corolla.

Up ahead the convoy has stopped in front of an extravagant marble lobby. Top hatted Indian bellboys rush to open the doors, and a group of nine fully covered women disembark along with three thobed men. Charlie tries to work out which woman is Noor. Three are so gargantuan that he discards them immediately, but out of the other six, it's impossible to tell.

The guard smacks his hand down on the hood of the car.

"Back now," the guard says.

Charlie throws the car into reverse. He reaches the split and screeches down into the mall's lower parking level. He sprints for the elevators. There another set of bellboys guide waiting customers into a set of elevators.

A couple of families are ferried upstairs, one after the other, and then one of the bellboys gestures at Charlie. He enters an elevator with two Saudi men. A twangy form of Arabic muzak is playing. He glances at the control panel and sees there are three shopping levels. In bold letters a sign proclaims that 'The third floor is for women only. No males whatsoever.'

He steps off at the first floor and scans his surroundings. The mall is an incongruous sight; luxury stores like Cartier and Gucci sharing real estate with fast food joints like KFC and McDonalds. There are plenty of women, and every single one of them wears an abaya and niqab. For the most part, a male relative accompanies them. Charlie searches for a large group but fails to find one.

Shit, he thinks. *They're on the third floor.*

He hears the elevator ping and looks to see whom it might be. He notices a good proportion of the men at Starbucks do the same. A couple of women get off. A man stands and walks over to them.

Of course, Charlie thinks. *This must be where the men and women rendezvous.*

Charlie makes his way down the concourse and pretends to window shop. Tag Hauer, Benetton, Lacoste. Every minute or so an elevator door dings, and he and the men swing their heads in its direction. More often than not a couple of women get off and one of the men gets up to greet them. How they can tell so quickly whose women are whose is beyond Charlie.

Charlie comes to a Rolex store and edges inside while keeping a line on the elevators.

"May I help you, sir?" a man asks in an impeccable British accent.

Charlie turns to see a sales clerk with a pencil thin mustache in a Saville Row suit and a knotted tie.

"Just browsing," Charlie says.

The elevator dings, and Charlie glances out the door. It's only a solitary woman.

"You seem to me like an outdoors type," the clerk says. "So may I be so bold as to suggest our Cosmograph Daytona. It's waterproof, can you believe, to three hundred and thirty feet."

The clerk opens a glass cabinet and hands Charlie a chunky gold wristwatch.

"Now this watch, and to call it a mere watch is to do it a grave disservice, has some features I think you'll admit are quite extraordinary."

The elevator dings again. Charlie looks towards the elevator bank. He never sees who gets off because all his attention is drawn to the one armed man entering the Rolex store.

Tariq.

Charlie spins away.

"Would you like to try it on, sir?" the store clerk asks him.

Without thinking, Charlie sticks his right arm out. The manager places the watch around Charlie wrist. Charlie hears Tariq's uneven stride approach. It gets ever closer until Tariq is standing right behind Charlie.

"I'd like to buy a watch," Tariq says.

"If you'd allow me to finish up with my present customer, sir, I'll be right with you."

The clerk turns back to Charlie.

"What do you think?"

Charlie shakes his head and unstraps the watch. He goes to hand it back to the clerk only for Tariq to swipe it.

"Let me take a look," Tariq says.

Charlie edges further into the store. His heart beats furiously.

If Tariq's here, he thinks, *Noor's got to be.*

"How much?" he hears Tariq say.

"Just over eight thousand dollars, sir."

Tariq snorts.

"It's too cheap," Tariq says.

"Then may I suggest the Daytona Diamond. The example I am going to show you is a little over fifty thousand dollars."

With the help of a reflecting glass display case, Charlie watches the clerk bring out another watch. The clerk hands it to Tariq who slaps it on his wrist.

"I'll take it," Tariq says.

"Wonderful," the clerk says cheerfully.

He is clearly used to such snap decisions.

An elevator dings. Charlie has to force himself not to look.

"Hurry up, I've got to go," Tariq says.

Noor.

The clerk runs Tariq's credit card, and Tariq signs it with a flourish. Tariq heads for the door.

"Sir, the box," the clerk shouts after him.

"Keep it," Tariq says.

Charlie waits a moment then follows after Tariq.

"Are you sure I cannot be of any assistance?" the clerk says.

"Not today," Charlie says.

He bursts out of the store. Twenty yards ahead he sees Tariq with two other men and a group of female Saudis. A whale of a woman leads the way. The group pass by the waterfall at the center of the mall and come to a children's boutique. The women trundle inside. Tariq shows off the watch to his two male cohorts. Neither seem overly impressed. They slink off into a nearby Mont Blanc store. Charlie waits for Tariq to follow them. He never does, preferring to gaze in adoration at his watch. Charlie realizes he is unlikely to get a moment alone with Noor.

You need a note, he thinks.

He rushes inside a nearby Body Shop and approaches the sales clerk.

"Excuse me," he says. "Do you have a pen and paper?"

"A moment, please," the clerk says.

Charlie waits as the clerk rings up a middle-aged ex-pat. Halfway through the transaction the man decides to lose a couple of items. The clerk voids the sale and starts all over. Charlie runs back to the entrance.

Thank God.

Tariq is still there. He returns to the sales register. The customer is counting out what he owes.

"Oh for fuck's sake," Charlie says, "it's just a pen and paper."

Both the clerk and customer stare at him in shock.

"Hurry up," Charlie snaps.

The clerk fumbles in a drawer and produces a pad and pen. Charlie scrawls down his home phone number and rips off the top sheet. He darts back out. Tariq's gone. He looks the other way and sees the group heading for the elevators.

Fuck.

He sprints after them.

The group pass an electronics store, and one of the young men says something to the women. The whale argues with him, but he pays her no heed and saunters into the store. The whale snaps at Tariq. Tariq reddens and hustles after the young man.

Now or never, Charlie says to himself.

Charlie heads towards the women. The closer they get the more his throat constricts. He passes next to them and glances into the electronics store. Tariq is remonstrating with the young man to hurry up. The young man grabs a high end camera, and they head for the cash register.

Charlie continues on another ten yards and turns around. Two of the women are chatting to each other, two are staring at the ground, the whale, along with the third man, are looking impatiently at the electronics store and three are gazing off into the distance.

You've got to get Noor's attention.

Charlie spies a trash can next to him. He backs into it and sends it clattering to the ground. The women look in his direction.

He freezes. There she is, standing next to a column. He's sure of it. Noor's iridescent green eyes are unmistakable.

Noor stares blankly back at Charlie, and Charlie wonders if she recognizes him. Then her legs wobble, and she has to strike out a hand to steady herself. The desire to run over to her is overwhelming. Tariq and the young man exit the electronics store. Charlie spins away.

Do it.

Charlie drops the piece of paper on the floor and starts walking. He knows he can't look back or God forbid wait by the elevators so he slips inside the Starbucks. He stares out the window and watches the group pass by. Noor never looks his way. A bellboy ushers the group into a waiting elevator, and the doors close behind them.

Charlie runs out of the coffee shop and makes for the trash can. A Bengali janitor is already upon it, getting ready to sweep up its upturned contents.

"Wait," he shouts.

The Bengali janitor stops what he's doing. Charlie scans the ground. The piece of paper is gone.

TWENTY-SIX

IT'S IMPOSSIBLE, NOOR thinks. *You're dead.*

As the S.U.V. whisks Noor and Princess Hadiya back to the Prince's compound, Noor becomes increasingly convinced what she saw at the mall was an illusion no more real than the time she thought Charlie was sitting beside her at the pool.

Dear God, I'm going mad.

Noor begins to cry. She looks out the window in an attempt to keep her tears hidden from Hadiya.

I'm finally going mad.

The piece of paper lies in the sleeve of her abaya, but she dare not take it out.

What would be the point anyway? You imagined it all. It's nothing but a piece of rubbish.

The S.U.V. sweeps through the palace gates. The guards salute as they pass.

Allah, what have I done to incur such wrath? Why toy with me in this way?

Princess Hadiya taps Noor's shoulder. Noor startles. She wipes her eyes with her sleeve.

"I'm sorry. I was daydreaming," Noor says.

"I was saying Princess Fadilah thinks Salah would be a good name for your son," Hadiya says.

"What does the Prince think?"

"He is very much in favor."

"Then it's settled."

"If you have an opinion, Noor, you should express it."

"You don't really believe that, do you?"

Princess Hadiya turns Noor's face towards her, her amber eyes staring deep into Noor's.

"You may not believe me but, of all his wives, the Prince admires you the most. He appreciates your forthrightness."

"He has a peculiar way of showing it."

The sadness in Hadiya's eyes is profound.

"What I'm trying to say is that you mustn't lose that particular quality that endears you to him. The last thing you want is to fall out of favor."

"I think Asra would disagree."

"Asra has been condemned to a small house on the outskirts of Riyadh. She's allowed no friends, no television, no access to her daughters, and apart from a maid, whose language she doesn't understand, no human contact."

Noor feels a chill slice through her stomach. Perhaps Asra's tale about Princess Fadilah's rebellious daughter was true after all.

"Surely her family will intervene," Noor says.

"Never. In her family's eyes, Asra has forever disgraced them."

The S.U.V. pulls up outside Noor's palace. Malaya and a couple of maids wait to greet her.

"Promise me you'll think on what I've said," Princess Hadiya says.

"I will," Noor says.

Malaya opens the door, and Noor climbs out, her mind a mess. First those apparitions of Charlie, now this news of Asra. She feels as if she's no longer able to discern what is fact and what is fiction.

Perhaps I'm not even pregnant.

In her room, Malaya undoes Noor's niqab and lifts her abaya over her head. The piece of paper floats to the floor. Malaya picks it up.

"Is this yours, your Highness?" she says.

Noor stares at it.

"No," she says, "it's just rubbish. You can throw it away."

Malaya retreats from the room. Noor lies down on her bed. A single rose is laid on one of the pillows. Noor shudders. It's Malaya's way of reminding her the Prince will be visiting her tonight. Noor replays the moment the trash can had clattered to the floor. She'd looked up and there he was; more gaunt than she remembered, his hair longer, his face scruffier, but it was Charlie, there was no doubt about that. He had stared at her so intently it was as if he was able to see through her niqab and gaze upon her face. She had been so overwhelmed she'd had to steady herself against a pillar or she'd surely have collapsed. And then the paper had dropped from his hand and he'd turned away. She remembers Tariq saying something to her, what exactly she has no clue. She had turned in her brother's direction and when she'd looked back Charlie was gone. Princess Fadilah had snapped at them to get going and Noor had hung near the back of the pack. As she passed the upturned trash can, she had bent down to pick up the piece of paper. She had looked back up to see Tariq staring at her and for once she was relieved she was wearing a niqab for he couldn't see her blushing. Tariq had told her to hurry and she had picked up her pace.

Perhaps it was an angel who took your form, she thinks.

It seems far-fetched but why not? Didn't Jibreel appear to both Mary and the Holy Prophet?

Yet if that is so, a voice inside her says, *then surely the piece of paper is a message.*

Noor sits up and rolls off the bed.

"Malaya," she shouts.

Noor sprints out of the room and through her quarters.

"Malaya."

She reaches the corridor and sees the secret door swing shut.

"Malaya. Wait."

Noor flies down the corridor and throws the door open. She hurtles down the metal staircase and sprints along the dim corridor into the kitchen. A couple of male Bengali cooks stare at her in shock then cover their eyes as one might if playing peek-a-boo with a child. Noor glances at the open oven; wood and paper are burning within.

No.

"Your Highness."

Noor turns to see Malaya standing there.

"The piece of paper," Noor says. "Where is it?"

"I have it here."

Noor places a hand on the counter to steady herself.

"Did you read it?" Noor says.

"I took the liberty. It's a receipt from a store called The Body Shop ..."

Of course, why would it be anything else?

"... on which someone scrawled a phone number."

Noor feels the room spin. She sticks out her hand and Malaya places the piece of paper in her hand. Noor immediately recognizes the ragged, chicken scratch handwriting she first encountered on a hundred rupee bill back in Kacha Gari refugee camp. She gasps.

Dear God, you're alive, she says to herself.

A moment later she faints. The piece of paper wafts from her hand.

PART II

escape

TWENTY-SEVEN

NOOR WAKES TO find a niqab over her face and a male doctor taking her vital signs. Through the slit in her niqab she spots the Prince pacing back and forth in her bedroom. Tariq sits on a futon in the far corner, gazing at his watch like a child might a new toy. Noor remembers why she is lying there. The number.

Charlie's alive, she says to herself. *Oh Allah be praised, he's alive.*

She can't help but gasp in delight. The doctor's gaze meets hers.

"She's awake," he says.

The Prince rushes over.

"How do you feel?" he says.

"Fine," Noor says.

The Prince turns towards the doctor.

"Her vital signs are normal," the doctor says.

"Then why would she faint?" the Prince says.

"Low blood sugar perhaps, it's common in pregnant women."

"And my son?"

"As far as I can tell he's in great shape, your Highness, but it would be prudent for her obstetrician to do an ultrasound."

"Then get her to the hospital immediately."

"Is that really necessary?" Noor says.

The two men ignore her.

"May I ask where there's a phone?" the doctor says.

"In the sitting room," the Prince says. "My operator will connect you."

The doctor strides from the room as if determined to show the Prince how earnest he is in serving him. The Prince brings his gaze back to Noor. Noor recognizes the unconscious twitching of his eyes; if she weren't unwell and carrying his son, she's certain he'd give her a beating to remember. Instead he runs his prayer beads through his right hand like an agitated gambler might a stack of chips.

"What were you doing in the basement?" the Prince says.

"I was hungry," Noor says.

"Then why not ask a servant to get you some food?"

"I didn't want to put anyone out."

"You have twenty maids whose only job is to serve your needs."

"Exactly. I'm not used to it. I wanted to make something for myself."

"Well never again. Do you hear me?

Noor holds the Prince's venomous gaze.

You lied to me, she says to herself. *You told me he was dead.*

The doctor marches back into the room and announces the imminent arrival of an ambulance.

"I will come by and see you tomorrow," the Prince says.

He turns to Tariq.

"Go with her."

The ride to the hospital is a shrouded one. If it wasn't proper for the doctor to see her face then it certainly isn't for the two Western paramedics to see it either. Tariq sits bent over beside them. Every time Noor looks up she finds him staring back down at her.

He suspects something, she thinks. *But what? Surely he can't suppose that Charlie's in Saudi Arabia.*

'Charlie, Charlie,' every time she says his name her body tingles with joy. Yet her soul is a mess of emotions. On the one hand she's exhilarated that Charlie is alive but on the other she's terrified that he's put himself in mortal danger. There's no way they'll be able to escape together. Her last attempt has convinced her of that.

I need to call him and persuade him to leave, she thinks.

But to do that she knows she needs his telephone number. She prays that Malaya retrieved it from the kitchen.

When they arrive at the hospital, the paramedics place Noor in a wheelchair and wheel her through a lobby that rivals the elegance and splendor of her own. By the gold plated elevator doors waits an obsequious man in a dazzling white thobe. He introduces himself as the chief administrator of the hospital and he takes it upon himself to guide them up to the eighth floor that's reserved for the exclusive use of the royal family. He is quick to point out that Noor's sumptuous suite consists of a sitting room, two bathrooms, a guest bedroom and a main bedroom with a framed Picasso pencil drawing on one wall and a colorful Mondrian on the other. Both appropriately contain no human representations. Not a piece of medical equipment is anywhere to be seen. Noor soon discovers that it's all hidden behind mahogany compartments. It's as if the last thing anyone wants to admit is that the patient may be ill. Noor is placed in bed, and soon after a team of doctors and nurses come in and work on her. The nurses are exclusively female as is her obstetrician, but the rest of the doctors are male, Saudi and middle-aged. The administrator eagerly points out to Tariq that each is the head of his department.

Throughout the poking and prodding, Noor wears her niqab and abaya. When they need to view her fetus, a nurse cuts a small flap in the niqab and the ultrasound wand is slid underneath. Tariq leans against the wall and stares at her. Noor stares right back at him. Until now she never thought she could hate him any more.

But I do, and if I could kill you, I would.

"We're done," the senior doctor says.

He gestures for Tariq and the other doctors to follow him out. They confer in hushed voices in the sitting room.

You must put aside your hatred, a voice tells her. *Think of Charlie. Think of the danger he's in.*

Noor realizes she must do everything she can to ensure that Tariq never stumbles upon the real reason she went to the basement.

You need to discombobulate him, she tells herself. *Put him on the back foot.*

The doctors' voices fade away. A female nurse returns. She takes off Noor's niqab and abaya, and helps her out of her clothes. Tariq ambles back in at the exact moment Noor is fully naked. The nurse looks in Tariq's direction. She freezes.

"It's okay," he says. "I'm her brother."

The nurse takes his word for it and scampers over to the closet where an array of pristine and embroidered hospital gowns hang. Noor holds Tariq's gaze.

"Well?" she says.

"There's nothing wrong with you," he says.

"That's good to hear."

"Isn't it?"

The nurse returns with one of the gowns and helps Noor into it. Noor notices it has a Chanel label. Tariq goes to say something, but Noor jumps in before he can.

"I want you and Badia to move into my palace," she says.

Tariq frowns.

"I'm bored," Noor says. "Climbing up the walls almost as much as I suspect Asra is."

"So you heard about her?" Tariq says.

"Women tend to gossip."

"It would be up to the Prince."

"Oh, he'll agree."

"How can you be so sure?"

"Because he does pretty much anything I ask. At least of late."

The nurse finishes tying up Noor's gown, and makes her excuses and leaves. Tariq sits down on the side of the bed.

"Like what?" Tariq says.

"The name of our son."

"I was told that was Princess Fadilah's suggestion."

"Of course you were. The old woman needs to maintain some shred of dignity."

"What else?"

Noor notices the diamonds glinting on his wrist.

"Your watch," she says. "Do you think someone as self-centered as the Prince came up with an idea like that?"

Noor studies her brother. He tugs on his beard. For the first time in months he seems uncomfortable around her.

Just like old times.

"Why would you suggest such a thing?" he says. "You despise me."

"I'm testing the extent of my powers. I'm coming to learn they're quite considerable."

"You're fooling yourself."

"He hasn't beat me in weeks."

"You're pregnant."

"You can beat a woman without endangering her child."

"He will beat you again, mark my words."

"I'd be a fool not to think so. But times have changed. The Prince admires me now, certainly more than he does you."

"Liar."

"I share his bed every fourth night."

"Which you despise."

"You don't understand, Tariq, a few weeks back I had a realization that I'd do anything, endure anything, in fact go to the very ends of the earth if it'd ensure your downfall."

The color drains from Tariq's face.

"Then why tell me?"

"Because the one thing I learnt all those times the Prince beat and raped me, was that the anticipation was the worst part. The event, itself, wasn't, for at least at that point I knew it'd soon be over."

Tariq's eyes flicker toward the door as if he is wondering who might be out there.

"Go on," she says. "Strangle me in my bed. Your head will be off before morning prayers."

"You won't succeed," he says.

"Watch me."

Tariq's face turns deep red.

"Fuck you," he says.

He stalks from the room. Moments later Malaya enters. Malaya goes to say something but Noor puts a finger to her lips. She hears Tariq talking in the sitting room.

To whom? she wonders.

She glances at her bedside table. There's a phone on it. One of its lights shines as red as Tariq's face.

An outside line, she thinks.

"Do you have that piece of paper?" she whispers to Malaya.

Malaya retrieves it from her pocket and slips it into Noor's hand. The light goes off. Soon after Noor hears a door slam.

"Would you mind staying in the sitting room and coughing loudly if anyone comes in?" Noor says.

"Of course not, your Highness," Malaya says.

Malaya leaves. Noor picks up the phone. Her hands tremble. She presses the keys and puts the receiver to her ear. The phone on the other end barely has a chance to ring.

"Noor," she hears Charlie say.

Tears flow down her cheeks before she even realizes they're there.

"Noor, is that you?"

Noor nods as if Charlie were in the room with her.

"Noor, please say something," Charlie says.

"I thought you were dead," she says.

There's silence on the other end of the line.

"I thought you were dead, Charlie, I had to do things—"

"You're pregnant, I know. It doesn't matter. Not to me."

"But it does. I'm carrying the Prince's son. Even if we could escape, which we can't, do you think he would rest until he found us?"

"And do you think I'll rest until I've gotten you out of here?"

Noor bites her lip until she tastes blood.

"Please, Charlie, please. Forget about me. Start your life afresh."

"Never."

"They'll kill you."

"That's a risk I'm willing to take."

Noor's tears turn to sobs

"Do you love me, Noor?" he says.

Deny it, she tells herself.

"Noor?"

"Of course I do. With my whole being."

"Then all I ask is that you believe in us. The possibility of us."

"But how?"

"I have a plan. You need to fake an illness and get yourself admitted to the King's hospital."

"I'm already here."

This time there is silence on Charlie's end.

"Charlie?" Noor says.

"What room?" he says.

Noor pulls the phone away. The room number is emblazoned on it.

"Eight twenty-nine," she says.

"Are you ill?"

"No. I suspect they'll send me home tomorrow."

"They can't. You've got to complain of a pain in your abdomen. The lower right hand side. They'll suspect appendicitis and order a whole battery of new tests."

"They'll find nothing."

"That's okay. As long as it persists they'll want to continue monitoring you."

"And then?"

"Not tomorrow morning but the one after, I'll come for you."

Noor hears Malaya cough.

"I must go," she says.

"Two days," he says.

"Yes, two days."

Noor replaces the receiver. The door swings open. It's the nurse.

"How do you feel, your Highness?" the nurse says.

"A little queasy," Noor says.

"Any pain?"

"My stomach's tender, but I'm sure it's just a little upset."

The nurse notes it on her chart.

"Well please tell me if it gets any worse."

Oh I will, Noor thinks.

"Can I be of any further assistance?' the nurse says.

"No, thank you. I have my maid."

"Then good night, your Highness."

"Good night," Noor says.

For the first time in months Noor means it.

TWENTY-EIGHT

ANOTHER SUPPLICANT IS brought before the Prince, and once more Tariq has to wait. This one reads a painfully long poem proclaiming the Prince's greatness and then gets down to complaining about the low oil price.

Who isn't around here, Tariq thinks.

Government subsidies have been so reduced, the supplicant tells the Prince, that some days there isn't enough food for his four wives and eighteen children. The Prince listens with practiced concern while playing with his prayer beads.

If the oil price continues to stay this low, Tariq thinks, *this place will soon be ripe for a coup.*

One of the Saudi Arabia's greatest ironies Tariq is swiftly learning is that in a country so rich, tremendous poverty still exists. It's just tougher for visitors to notice since the poorer districts are kept well out of view and everyone dresses in the same clothes. It's why rich Saudis spend so much money on sunglasses, pens, watches and shoes. It's the only way for them to separate themselves and proclaim their wealth.

Tariq gazes at the snaking line of two hundred men in their white thobes and checkered ghutras. It's already two in the morning, yet the Prince will stay until he's met with every single one of them. According to the Prince, this weekly *majli* is his duty, a way to bring him closer to the people. The Prince commiserates with the supplicant and tells him he'll take care of his troubles. The man showers the Prince with further ludicrous praise. The Prince cuts him off by standing and kissing him on both cheeks.

Another follower for when the time is ripe.

An aide leads the supplicant away to a table where the Prince's accountant hands him wad of crisp riyal bank notes. The Prince leans over towards Tariq, and Tariq can't help but feel a visceral thrill. Everyone's eyes are on them.

Perhaps I'll do majlis of my own one day, he thinks.

"I have no interest in you delaying your trip," the Prince says. "My uncle's getting increasingly irritated with Osama. He even suggested assassinating him yesterday."

"Was he serious?" Tariq says.

"I doubt it, but it's all the more reason for you to deliver my message as forcefully as possible."

"Without offending him."

"That goes without saying."

The Prince nods at a servant who brings over a cup of tea on a silver tray.

"It's a relief to know Noor is well," the Prince says.

Tariq forces a smile.

"I hope I don't offend you by saying this," he says, "but you seem pleased with her."

"I am," the Prince says. "Very."

Tariq feels a damp coldness envelop his body.

Noor wasn't lying. The balance has shifted.

"One of her doctors told me that once a woman has a son the probability that she'll have another goes up exponentially," the Prince says. "Who knows? Maybe Noor will provide me with four or five sons."

The Prince gestures for the next supplicant to approach. The supplicant launches into a poetic rendition of his own. Tariq's smile becomes ever more strained. If he's learnt one thing about this culture, it's that the more sons a wife has the more influence she wields. It's no coincidence that Princess Fadilah gave her husband six.

You cannot allow Noor to become as powerful as her, he tells himself. *She'll destroy you.*

He knows what he must do. He and Badia will move into Noor's palace, and he'll wait for Noor to have her child.

And then I'll kill her.

How, and whom he'll pin it on, he's not certain of yet, but it's got to happen if he is to survive and prosper.

Who knows? Perhaps once she's gone the Prince will entrust me with their son's upbringing.

For the first time that night Tariq exhibits a genuine smile, for in his mind Noor's as good as dead.

TWENTY-NINE

CHARLIE STANDS BEFORE his barren kitchen table. First he lays on top of it their fake Turkish passports under the names of Rustu and Zerrin Dervis. He flicks to the back of Noor's passport and gazes at her smiling photo. In light of all that's happened, he can't help but consider her optimism back in Peshawar incredibly naive.

As was mine, he admonishes himself.

The two tickets he bought earlier in the day come next. They're for tomorrow's British Airways flight to London. It leaves at midday. As a precaution, he won't buy their tickets to the United States until they arrive in London.

Their American passports come after that. He picks up Noor's fake American passport and compares it to his own genuine one. They seem identical. There is no reason to believe Noor won't make it through US immigration.

And where to then? he says to himself. *Belize? Why not?*

The irony. His dream of opening a dive shop might come true after all.

Finally he places a shopping bag filled with women's clothing and necessities on the table. It had taken a couple of hours to corral these items at the mall, but he figured it would look odd if Zerrin Dervis left Saudi Arabia with nothing but the clothes on her back. He had even run the clothes through the washing machine a couple of times so they didn't look brand new.

You can't leave anything to chance, he thinks. *Anything.*

He stares at the items on the table. He's satisfied he has everything they need.

The doorbell rings, and he freezes. He waits. It rings again. A stab of fear runs through him. He wonders if the authorities could have traced last night's call. He edges over to the window and pulls back the edge of a blind. Jenny stands there in a pair of jean shorts and a pink t-shirt. She holds a covered dish in her hands. She rings the doorbell a third time.

"Come on, Joe," she shouts, "it's bloody boiling out here."

Charlie sweeps the passports and tickets into the shopping bag and shoves it under the table. He heads into the hallway and opens the door. Jenny pushes past him faster than the suffocating summer heat.

"Thank God," she says, "I thought I was going to keel over out there."

She makes for the kitchen. Charlie rushes after her. He positions himself in front of the kitchen table in order to shield the shopping bag as best he can. Jenny turns to face him. Her damp t-shirt clings to her braless breasts. She holds out the dish.

"Shepherd's pie," she says.

"You didn't need to," he says.

"It's the Catholic school girl in me. Nothing I like more than helping the sick and needy."

She opens the fridge and places the dish on its top shelf. She stands there and lets its escaping vapors cool her off.

"You know what I think?" she says. "I think you called in a sickie."

"Why's that?" he says.

"Call it a nurse's intuition."

"You won't tell anyone, will you?"

Jenny spins around and grins. The cold air has had sufficient time to harden her nipples.

"Well, Mr. Stapinski, that depends on what you're prepared to offer for my silence."

Charlie opens a kitchen cabinet and grabs a tumbler.

"How about a glass of water?" he says.

"I was hoping for something more substantial."

"I'm sorry, but I don't have any booze."

"Oh come on, Joe, get real! Do I really need to spell out what I want?"

Jenny's gaze drifts towards Charlie's crotch. Charlie freezes.

"I'm gay," he says.

Jenny's eyes flick upwards.

"Remember when we first met," Charlie says, "and you said I was mysterious, strange, something like that at least. You were right. I was hiding something."

Jenny cocks her head as if she's attempting to look at Charlie from a whole new angle.

"You don't seem it," she says.

"That's what everyone said about Rock Hudson."

"Don't tell me you got—"

"Course not. I'm just attracted to men that's all."

"Not even women with a set like these."

Jenny jiggles her breasts as if to accentuate the point.

"Afraid not. I'm sorry, I should have told you earlier. I just didn't think it was something I should go around advertising in a country like this."

"You're probably right about that."

Charlie can't help but notice that Jenny's nipples have wilted. If he could sigh with relief he would.

"We can still be friends, right?" he says.

"What you take me for?" Jenny says. "A complete tosser?"

Charlie smiles.

"If you don't mind," Jenny says, "could you point me in the direction of the little girl's room. Or is it more appropriate to call it the little boy's room around here?"

"It's down the hall, second door on the right."

"Be right back."

Jenny gives Charlie an impish wink and slips out of the room. Charlie leans back against the counter and takes several deep breaths.

Another hurdle overcome.

Charlie looks around the bare kitchen for a project to occupy himself with but fails to find one. He wonders how long Jenny will stay around. Not long, he hopes. He wants to go over his plan. He picks up the tumbler and fills it with water. He downs it in one go and places it in the sink. He drums his fingers on the counter.

What the hell is she up to? he wonders.

He listens out. He hears no toilet flush or returning footsteps. He edges out of the kitchen and down the hallway. The restroom door is wide open, its light off.

Fuck, where is she?

He hears a metallic creak and recognizes the noise immediately. It's the sound his closet door makes when opened. He hurries down the hallway and into his bedroom. Jenny stands in front of his closet. There's not a single item of clothing in it. His open and packed suitcase lies on the bed. Jenny turns and stares right at him, her earlier bonhomie no longer in evidence.

"What are you doing in here?" he says.

"I don't know, when I was peeing, I couldn't buy the idea you were gay."

"This is getting boring, Jenny."

"My brother's gay, you see, has loads of gay friends, and you're not like any of them. Not in the slightest. It got me thinking. You're hiding something. Just like that bag you were doing a poor show of standing in front of back in the kitchen.

So you tell me, Charlie, what is it?"

"Nothing."

"Your closet's bare."

"I'm going on a trip."

"That's obvious. But why take everything with you?"

"Jenny, this is not the time—"

"Are you flying the coop?"

Charlie nods.

"Saudi Arabia's not for me," he says. "I hate it."

"And that abaya and niqab, what do you call those? Souvenirs?"

Charlie looks over at his suitcase. The black garments he bought earlier stand out against the rest of his clothes like a bloody knife at a murder scene. Jenny strides out of the room.

"Jenny!"

Charlie sprints after her. Jenny quickens her pace and darts into the kitchen. By the time Charlie reaches it, Jenny has upended the shopping bag, and Noor's Turkish passport is in her hands. Jenny flicks to its last page.

"Oh my God," she says.

The passport falls from her hands and lands amidst the pile of female clothes and toiletries on the floor.

"That princess ... the one whose records you had me steal ... you're going to try and escape with her. Aren't you?"

Charlie is too shaken to deny it.

"You're off your rocker," Jenny says.

Jenny pushes past Charlie. Charlie grabs her by the arm and Jenny swings back around.

"Get your hands off me," she says.

"Please, you can't tell anyone."

"Or what? You going to kill me?"

"No, of course not."

Charlie lets go of Jenny's arm.

"No one knows anything about what you did," he says. "They never will."

"Why should I believe you? Everything you say is a lie. Is Joe Stapinski even your real name?"

Charlie doesn't respond. Jenny shakes her head in disgust.

"To think I thought you were one of the good ones," she says.

Jenny opens the door. Without looking back, she slams it shut behind her.

THIRTY

ONE AFTER ANOTHER Riyadh's muezzins warble like members of an orchestra tuning up before a recital. They urge the faithful to dawn prayers yet in Noor's case they needn't have bothered. She's been up for hours and finished her prayers long ago. She'd like to believe they had given her a certain peace, but she knows that would be a lie. Her palms sweat, her heart beats furiously and she hasn't sat in one place for more than a minute. She wonders if Charlie will really come today. She recalls reading a book once about how in Imperial Japan they never told the condemned what day they would die. The only thing the condemned knew was that executions occurred at dawn so if the guards hadn't come for you by the time the sun rose then you knew you'd have at least one more day on this planet.

My situation is similar, she thinks. *It's just the reverse.*

She wanders over to the tinted windows and touches the glass. It's already hot to the touch. To the east the crown of the fierce sun peeks over the horizon while below the still darkened city prepares for the onslaught of another scorching day. She peers down at the palm trees swaying out front. The wind is up. The Bangladeshi sweepers will have their work cut out today.

She hears a knock and turns expecting it to be Malaya. Instead it's a nurse; a new one with red hair and a pinkish, freckled complexion.

"I'm sorry, I didn't realize you were up already, your Highness.".

Your Highness, Noor says to herself. *May today be the last time anyone calls me by that accursed title.*

"I was praying," Noor says.

"You must be eager to get home. I see you're scheduled to leave this morning."

"Actually my stomach is worse, much worse. I have sharp pains down here."

Noor rubs her lower right side and winces.

"I'm sure it's nothing," Noor says.

The nurse smiles.

"I'm sure it is, but the doctors will want to check you out all the same."

The nurse helps Noor back to her bed and tucks her in. After she leaves, Malaya appears with Noor's abaya and niqab.

"The doctors will be here shortly, your Highness."

"Then I guess I better get dressed."

With tender care, Malaya helps Noor put on the abaya and niqab. Noor feels tears rise in her eyes. She takes Malaya's hand in hers.

"I want you to know, Malaya, how grateful I am for all you've done for me."

"It's going to be fine, your Highness. Nothing's going to happen to you."

"I know. It's just so often in life people leave things unsaid until it's too late. I don't want to take that risk. Without you I'd never have survived."

Malaya pats Noor on the hand.

"You coming into my life, your Highness, believe me it was *the* true godsend."

"I couldn't do anything for you."

"You did more than you can imagine. You reminded me that this life is but a temporary stopover in what is sure to be a glorious and eternal existence."

There is a sharp rap on the door.

"We best not keep the doctors waiting," Malaya says.

"No, it's best we don't."

Malaya opens the door and is practically trampled under foot by five doctors. Once more they prod and examine Noor, their brows more furrowed than ever. Another ultrasound is done, more blood is drawn, and then they hustle away to confer.

"Wait," Noor says.

The doctors turn back.

"What do you think I have?" she says.

"There's no need to worry, your Highness," the senior doctor says. "You're in good hands."

"I don't doubt it, but I want to know."

The senior doctor smiles at her as if she were a seven-year-old child.

"Your Highness, it's best if you rest."

"Then before I do, I'd appreciate you getting my husband on the phone so I can complain to him about the way I have been treated."

The senior doctor pales. He looks at the other doctors. None of them offer any support.

"We suspect appendicitis, your Highness," he says.

"Are you going to operate?" Noor says.

"Given that you're pregnant, we feel it's prudent if we observe you at this stage."

"Well don't disturb me unless it's absolutely necessary. Your night nurse woke me up countless times last night and I'm exhausted."

"We understand, your Highness."

"Good. Now go."

The doctors scuttle out of the room. Noor collapses against her pillow.

Come on, Charlie, she says to herself. *Where are you?*

***

CHARLIE STANDS AT the technicians' station and eyeballs the clock. The second hand ticks past twelve. Eight fifty-five.

Five more minutes, he tells himself.

He looks around. Mike is entering an examination room and Doctor Angerman is chatting with a nurse down the hall. There is no sign of Jenny though that's not necessarily unusual. She works in the female wing and only comes over this side for social calls. He's beyond castigating himself for what occurred yesterday. He had spent all night doing that. Now the question he keeps pondering is whether Jenny has told anyone anything. He comforts himself with the thought that if she had he'd never have gotten into the building this morning.

He looks back up at the clock. Eight fifty-six.

Four minutes.

He sees the door from reception open and instinctively steps behind a pillar.

"Is Joe Stapinski around?" he hears Ralph say.

"He was over by the tech station," Manuel says.

Charlie drops to the ground. He crawls along the floor using the counter for cover and slithers inside the storage room. Ever so gently he shuts the door behind him and turns off the light. Through the door he hears the administrator's muffled voice asking for him again. He knows Jenny must have told Ralph something.

Why else would he be here?

The question is what. Charlie can't believe Jenny mentioned Noor. Not if she wants to cover her own ass.

Maybe she told him I'm here under a false identity, he thinks.

Ralph's footsteps come to a halt outside the door. He questions a third technician. Charlie wonders why Ralph didn't bring security guards with him.

Because right now it's her word against mine.

Charlie realizes it's two a.m. in New York.

Ralph has no way of corroborating Jenny's suspicions.

"If you see him, tell him to come by my office," Ralph says.

"Can I say what it's about?" the technician says.

"His schedule."

Charlie knows bullshit when he hears it. He hears Ralph's footsteps recede and wills himself to count to a hundred. Only then does he open the door and make for the locker room. He glances up at the clock. Nine oh three.

"Hey, Joe."

Charlie turns. It's Manuel.

"Ralph was looking for you," he says.

"On my way to see him," Charlie says.

Charlie enters the locker room and finds Mike standing there.

"Ralph wants to see you," Mike says.

"So everyone keeps telling me."

"You been bad?"

"Innocent as a choir boy."

"Well something's up. Amanda said Jenny was a mess this morning. Blurting all sorts of shit about you not being who you say you are."

"Maybe that's because I turned her down last night."

Mike frowns.

"You a queer, Joe?"

"I'm not attracted to her, that's all."

Charlie looks up at the clock. Nine oh four.

"You're fucking weird, you know that," Mike says.

"So you keep telling me."

Mike shakes his head.

"I gotta take a dump."

Mike pushes past Charlie and heads for the restrooms. Charlie goes to the storage cabinet and grabs a pair of 'small' scrubs and a scrub cap. He stuffs them down his front and heads out the door.

"Joe," a technician calls out.

Charlie raises a hand.

"On my way to see him," he says.

He opens the door to reception and looks around. In one corner a group of Bedouin men and women sit in a circle on the floor as if they were out in the desert.

"Joe."

Charlie turns towards the male receptionist.

"Your nine o'clock's here?" the receptionist says.

"I'm off home. Can't seem to shake this bug."

"So who—"

"Mike. He's taking all my patients today."

Charlie hurries down the long corridor scanning the way ahead for any sign of Ralph. He makes it to the main lobby. The pianist is playing a Mozart concerto. Charlie heads over to the elevators. He shows the guard his ID badge, and the guard beckons him toward an open elevator only to put out a hand. Charlie looks over his shoulder. A couple of Saudi men are striding toward him. Charlie knows he'll have to wait. The help are never allowed to travel in the same elevators as the patrons they serve.

The gold plated elevator doors close behind the men. Charlie hears voices behind him. He recognizes them as Ralph's and Abdul Jameel's, the radiology department's executive. He spies their blurred reflections in the gleaming doors. They are on their way to the radiology department. Clearly things have escalated.

Charlie lowers his head. The elevator dings and its doors open. A couple of doctors step out. The guard nods. Charlie scuttles inside and pushes the button for the eighth floor.

Come on. Come on.

The doors close. He breathes a little easier. He looks up and watches the floor numbers pass by. He steps off at the eighth floor and enters a lobby that puts the ground floor one to shame. At its far end on either side of a set of double doors are a couple of brightly colored Matisse flower paintings and a couple of burly African guards. The suited receptionist gives Charlie a quizzical look.

"I'm here for Prince Najeeb's ultrasound," Charlie says.

"That's not scheduled until eleven," the receptionist says.

"I was told it could be done earlier."

The receptionist nods toward the door behind him.

"Wait in there."

Charlie does as he's told and enters a plain room with plastic chairs. Five technicians wait there, consigned to a similar fate. Behind them is another door guarded by yet another guard. Charlie takes a seat and looks up at the clock. Nine ten. He bites his nails and waits. Every cough echoes, every turn of a magazine page resonates, every screech of a chair seems to go on longer than is humanly possible. By nine twenty-five, he fully expects a battalion of guards to burst in and drag him away. Instead the door behind him opens.

"Joe Stapinski," a woman with a British accent says.

Charlie turns to find a middle-aged nurse standing there with her arms crossed. She is almost as burly as the guard.

"I'm Brenda, one of Prince Najeeb's nurses. You boys aren't due for a couple more hours."

"I'm sorry. I was meant to be out of here already, but then they asked me to stay on and do this job. I was hoping we could do it now."

Charlie gives her a plaintive smile. Brenda ponders his request.

Who knew it would all come down to this? Charlie thinks.

"Okay," Brenda says, "but only because I sympathize with your predicament. I was supposed to be relieved an hour ago."

"What happened?"

"My bloody replacement got in a car crash."

"She okay?"

"A broken collar bone."

"Sorry to hear that."

"Not half as much as I was. Come on, I can squeeze it in. Someone's meant to be replacing me in thirty minutes."

The guard opens the door, and Brenda leads Charlie down a series of corridors. They could be in Versailles they're so elegant. Charlie reads off the room numbers as they pass by.

801, 803, 805, 807, 809 ...

His heart beats relentlessly as he realizes they're coming ever closer to Noor's room.

817, 819, 821, 823 ...

It is now only three doors down.

825, 827 ...

And there it is. 829. It takes all his self control to keep going.

They carry on past another five rooms until they come to 841.

"Wait here," Brenda says. "Need to make sure the missus is covered up."

Brenda slips inside the room. Charlie looks back down the corridor. He figures he could sprint to Noor's room before Brenda ever comes out.

Be patient, he tells himself.

Moments later the door opens.

"All righty," Brenda says.

Brenda leads Charlie through the sitting room. One of the Prince's wives, fully clothed in an abaya and niqab, sits upright on an embroidered silk couch while a couple of five

year olds lie on the floor staring up at a Tom and Jerry
cartoon. None of them pay him any heed. They enter the
bedroom. A skeleton of a man wearing an oxygen mask lies
propped up on a bed of pillows. His eyes track Charlie as he
crosses the room.

"Your Highness, this is Joe," Brenda says. "He'll be doing
your ultrasound today."

Charlie looks for the ultrasound machine. There doesn't
seem to be one. He looks helplessly at Brenda.

"I'm sorry," he says, "but I don't come up here often."

Brenda goes over to a mahogany cabinet and opens it. The
machine is tucked away inside.

"All yours," she says.

Charlie rolls it out and plugs it in. It beeps to life.

"Your Highness," he says, "I'm going to have to undo
your pants in order to perform this procedure. Is that okay?"

The Prince glares at him.

"The old bat doesn't speak a lick of English," Brenda says.

"But he's okay having this procedure done?"

"He gave the doctor his permission last night. He's all
yours."

Charlie pulls down the Prince's pants and with Brenda's
help he turns the Prince on his side so his wrinkled butt faces
him. Charlie snaps on a pair of latex gloves and places a sheaf
over the transducer. He lubes the transducer up, his mind
working overtime on how to get rid of Brenda.

"Bend his knees please," Charlie says.

Brenda does as requested, and Charlie pushes the transducer into the Prince's rectum. The Prince moans as the
device slithers in.

"He okay?" Charlie says.

"He's got a shit eating grin on his face."

Charlie looks across at Brenda.

"Just kidding," she says. "He's staring at me like he's going
to have my bleedin head chopped off."

Charlie moves the transducer around and peers at the monitor. The Prince groans.

"Funny thing life," Brenda says. "All the money in the world can't save you from the indignity of having one of those shoved up your bum."

On the monitor, Charlie detects what he believes is the prostate. It's a lot bigger than he thought it would be. Brenda comes around and looks at the monitor. She whistles.

"Look at that thing, it's the size of a tennis ball. The poor devil's buggered."

"The doctor's going to want a lot of images," Charlie says. "It's probably going to take me another fifteen minutes, perhaps twenty."

"You're joking."

Charlie moves the transducer and clicks off an image.

"Why don't you get out of here?" he says.

"I'm not meant to leave you alone with him."

"We're not meant to drink out here either. Go on, he sure as hell isn't going anywhere."

Charlie pretends to focus on the task at hand. Outside, the wind rattles the windows.

"Screw it," Brenda says. "But once you're done, make sure you get the hell out of here."

"Scout's honor."

Brenda smiles.

"My son was a scout. Biggest fibber you ever met."

Brenda leaves. Charlie looks at the bedside clock.

Nine thirty-six.

Give it two more minutes, he tells himself.

***

MALAYA ENTERS NOOR'S room.

"An ultrasound technician is here to examine you, your Highness," she says.

Noor sees the abaya and niqab in Malaya's hands. Her heart pounds. It can only mean one thing. The technician is a man.

Charlie.

She attempts to speak but nothing comes out.

"Your Highness?"

"Have him come in," Noor says.

Malaya holds out Noor's overgarments.

"Shouldn't you put these on first?" Malaya says.

"Yes. Of course."

Malaya brings them over. Noor struggles into them as quickly as she can.

"I need you to go to the hospital shop," Noor says. "There is a scent I need. Chanel Number Five."

"I'm sure they can have someone bring it up."

"But I want you to go get it. Do you understand?"

The two of them hold each other's gaze. Eventually Malaya nods.

"As you wish, your Highness," she says.

Malaya disappears. Noor grips the side of the bed in an attempt to control her tremors. The door opens. Noor gasps. There he is in a set of blue scrubs. Tears spring in her eyes. Charlie has tears in his own. Charlie approaches the bed. She flings her arms around him and nestles her face in his neck. She clings to him and her whole body shakes as if caught up in the paroxysms of an epileptic fit. Charlie shushes her and ever so gently undoes her niqab. It falls to the floor. He stares at her, his eyes wide, his skin flushed.

"I promised I'd find you," he says.

"You have," she says.

He kisses her on the lips. Noor wishes time would stand still. The wind rattles the panes of her window, and he pulls away.

"We've got to get going," he says.

Charlie pulls out a set of scrubs tucked underneath his own.

"Quick," he says. "Put these on."

Noor springs out of bed. She rips off her abaya and hospital gown and stands naked before him. Charlie doesn't move a muscle. Noor realizes it's the first time he has ever seen her this way.

"Your make-up has run down your cheeks," he says. "I'll find you a washcloth."

He turns and heads for the bathroom. She hears a tap running. By the time he returns she has put the scrubs on. He comes over and wipes her cheeks.

"There," he smiles. "Much better."

She forces herself not to cry again. He smoothes her hair up and pulls the scrub cap over her head. He ties it at the back.

"You ready?" he says.

"Shoes," she says.

Charlie's face drops. He quickly shakes it off.

"It's okay," he says. "I have some in the car."

"But what if–"

"It's going to be fine. I promise. Now let's go."

Charlie opens the door. They slip into the living room. Malaya stands there. Noor gasps.

"It's all right, your Highness," Malaya says. "I knew the moment I laid eyes on this young man that he was the one."

"How?" Noor says.

Malaya smiles.

"Call it a grandmother's intuition. Now go. I'll delay everyone as long as I can."

"But they'll–"

"I don't want to spend the next twenty years in this country. Please, your Highness, you of all people must know that."

Noor forces back yet more tears. Malaya notices Noor's bare feet and takes off her sneakers. She gets down on her knees and slides them onto Noor's feet. She stands.

"There," she says. "You're ready to go."

Noor puts her arms around her.

"I love you, Malaya."

"And I love you, Noor. Promise me you'll never look back."

"I promise."

"Then go."

Noor and Charlie hurry into the entrance hall. Charlie opens the door and looks out. Noor can't help but be reminded of the moment her mother did the same thing many years ago in Kabul. He looks back and nods. They head down one corridor after another. Noor sees one of her doctors approaching.

He's bound to recognize me, she thinks.

The doctor looks Noor right in the eye. Noor feels as if she's going to faint. He passes by. Noor feels a surge of exhilaration.

He's never seen my face, she tells herself. *None of them have. They don't know what I look like.*

Charlie opens a door on his right and guides Noor through the technicians' waiting room to the eighth floor lobby. The suited receptionist looks up. Noor twists her head away. They come to the elevators. Charlie presses the down button. Noor feels the receptionist's eyes on the back of her neck.

"You need to sign out," the receptionist says.

The doors open. The elevator's empty.

"Excuse me," the receptionist says.

With his palm on her back, Charlie guides Noor into the elevator. Charlie presses the button for the parking garage. The doors slide closed. Charlie turns to face Noor. He does his best to smile.

"How scared are you?" she says.

"Terrified," he says.

Noor leans in and kisses him.

"What's that for?" Charlie says.

"In case we don't get the chance ever again."

"We will. I promise."

The elevator doors open. They step into a chilly subterranean garage. Charlie leads Noor to his Toyota Corolla. He opens the back door, and she slips inside. She sees an abaya and niqab lying on the seat. She doesn't need to be told what to do. She puts them on. Charlie jumps in the driver's seat and reverses out of his parking space. At any moment Noor expects a platoon of guards to burst out of the elevators and block their path. None do. Instead the car winds its way around the parking levels until it arrives at the exit ramp.

"Get down," Charlie says.

Noor drops to the floor.

Who is it? she wonders.

The car brakes, and she hears Charlie's window glide down. Moments later the car accelerates forward.

"Sorry. Parking attendant," he says.

Noor scrambles back up. She spies the top of the ramp.

"Where are we going?" she says.

"The airport," Charlie says.

She stares at him in disbelief.

"I promise, it's going to work," he says.

"I believe you," she says.

God is on our side, she tells herself. *How could we have gotten so far otherwise?*

The car emerges into the bright outdoor glare. Noor squints and stares out the window. The hospital's palm trees sway in the wind, and the spray from its many fountains blows across its deep green and manicured lawn.

It doesn't feel real, she thinks. *Not this land nor this escape.*

The car heads down the hospital driveway. Noor twists in her seat and looks up at the eighth floor. She wonders what excuses Malaya will make to stop the doctors from entering her room. Charlie brakes at the intersection and pulls off his blue scrub top. He grabs a white shirt off the passenger seat and throws it on. An S.U.V. beeps behind them. He turns right.

"We are flying as Turks under the names Rustu and Zerrin Dervis," Charlie says.

Noor nods. That makes sense. Charlie could pass as a Turk.

"I doubt they'll question you, but if they do just stick to English. None of the officials will speak Turkish."

Charlie exits onto an onramp and merges onto a six lane freeway. Charlie pushes down on the accelerator and the car surges forward.

"Where are we flying to?" Noor says.

"London. At midday," he says.

"And from there?"

"The States. Don't worry, it's all planned. Once we're through Saudi immigration it's plain sailing."

Noor prays he's right.

They come upon an interchange and Charlie slings the car around it. Soon they're heading along another freeway, this one only wider. Crammed on either side are a motley collection of skyscrapers, tall office buildings and tan colored apartment buildings. For a while neither of them says anything. It's as if they won't permit themselves the luxury until they're free. The buildings start to thin out as they approach the desert. The traffic slows, red brake lights going on one after another. Charlie brakes.

"What the hell?" he says.

Noor peers out the front windshield. In the distance a massive brown cliff has materialized out of nowhere. It stretches from one edge of the horizon to the other.

"What is that?" Noor says.

Charlie leans forward.

"A dust cloud," he says.

The cloud rolls towards them like a vast tsunami wave. The two of them stare at it in disbelief. Up ahead vehicles stop and put their hazard lights on. Charlie does likewise. He reaches his hand back and takes Noor's in his. The wind picks up as the cloud creeps ever closer. The car rocks from side to side. One after another the cars in front disappear. Charlie undoes his seatbelt and climbs into the back.

"What are we going to do?" Noor says.

Charlie puts his arms around her and draws her in. At first they are enveloped by a brownish haze, but it's not long before they're plunged into pitch darkness, the beam of their headlights the only thing still visible. The wind roars like a train passing through a tunnel. The car rattles. Sand smacks against the S.U.V. as if they're being fired upon by millions of tiny darts. Slowly but surely the sand infiltrates the air ducts. It clogs Noor's nose and stings her eyes.

Noor closes her eyes and prays to Allah. For forgiveness, for their deliverance from not only this infernal storm but also this country. Most of all she prays for Charlie.

Whatever happens to me, oh Allah, I beg you keep Charlie safe.

As if to confirm Allah's heard her prayer, the roar of the wind lessens. Charlie scrambles into the front seat and turns on the windscreen wipers. Noor opens her eyes. She's amazed to see that blue skies have already returned. Noor stares at Charlie. He's covered head to toe in a film of brown dust.

"We survived," she says.

Up ahead the cars inch forward. Charlie looks at the clock.

"We can make it," he says.

He blasts his horn at the cars ahead. Soon the traffic is miraculously back to its old madcap pace. The road is covered by so much sand that it's almost impossible to tell it apart from the desert yet no one seems to care. They drive like maniacs.

How Saudi, Noor thinks.

For once she means it as a compliment.

Twenty minutes later the airport comes into view. Charlie takes the exit for short-term parking and squeals into a spot. All around it looks as if someone has glazed every car in brown frosting. They jump out, and Charlie grabs their two suitcases from the back. Charlie rips off his scrubs to reveal a pair of jeans underneath.

"Let's go," he says.

He strides towards the terminal. Noor does her best to keep up. They pass through a set of sliding doors and enter the still spotless check-in area. Every counter has a long line winding its way towards it. Charlie ignores the hundred or so waiting passengers at British Airways and goes up to the counter.

"Rustu and Zerrin Dervis. We're here for the twelve o'clock flight," he says.

"As is everyone behind you, Mr. Dervis," the British check-in agent says. "We're rebooking you all on a flight for tomorrow."

"You can't be serious?"

"The runway is a complete mess."

"How about other airlines?"

"I'm sorry but no one's getting out of here today. Be here at the same time tomorrow and you'll be fine."

Charlie turns towards Noor. She sees the horror in his eyes. She knows as well as he does that they surely won't.

THIRTY-ONE

TARIQ STARES OUT the grimy window at the languid, turquoise waters of the Blue Nile. He could go out onto the balcony to get a better look, but he'd have to endure a hundred and twenty degree temperatures and tortuous humidity.

No, he decides, *it's better I stay in here even if the temperature's kept only marginally lower by that wheezing air conditioner.*

Tariq shakes his head. He can't believe this is the best hotel in Khartoum.

When he'd arrived, he couldn't have been more excited. He and a couple of guards had flown on a chartered Gulfstream. Sitting there in those vast leather seats he'd felt like an exalted foreign dignitary. The plane had landed, and he had expected a red carpet welcome; perhaps not an honor guard but a couple of bin Laden's highest aides and a limousine at a minimum. Instead there'd been nothing more than an ancient Land Rover driven by a one-eyed Egyptian veteran who had informed Tariq that bin Laden was at his farm in Al Damazin and wasn't expected back until the following night. On first approaching the hotel, Tariq's hopes had risen. Its facade was white, columned and colonial, its lobby filled with antique furniture and framed nineteenth century art. However, since then everything had disappointed. The bedroom had a musty smell and stains on the walls. Water dribbled from the bathroom tap and cockroaches wandered aimlessly around the bathtub. On his tour he'd been shown the pool but from its murky green color he'd surmised that he would most likely get toxic shock if he were foolish enough to swim in it.

Tariq collapses on the bed and hears something squish. He shudders to think what it is. He stares up at the listless and useless ceiling fan.

I pray I never have to return here again, he thinks.

There's a knock on the door.

Finally.

He'd ordered the bottle of water an hour ago.

"Come in," he yells.

The door creaks open.

"Put it on the table," he says.

"Put what exactly?"

Tariq freezes.

Ivor.

The American wanders over and stares down at Tariq. Ivor hasn't changed; not for the better at least. His hair is as greasy as ever, his shirt drenched with sweat, his stomach somewhat paunchier.

"How you doing, Tariq?" Ivor says.

"My guards?" Tariq says.

"Both taking well deserved naps."

Tariq wonders if they're C.I.A. induced. He struggles to sit up.

"This place is a hellhole," Tariq says. "I don't know how you stand it."

"Riyadh's made you soft," Ivor says.

"I mean of all places, why did bin Laden choose this one?"

"There aren't many others that'd take him. Your Crown Prince has made it clear to anyone who'll listen that he'll take it as a personal insult if they harbor him."

"And the Sudanese don't listen?"

"That's not a quality they're known for. Besides bin Laden's spending money hand over fist out here."

"Is he building a palace?"

"Fuck, Saudi really has done a number on you. No, he's spending his money on farms, a tannery, some construction projects. He, himself, lives in a modest place. No AC, no modern appliances, all so he can adhere to his ideal of humble living. If you can say one thing about the guy he walks the walk."

Ivor pulls a water bottle out of his back pocket. He takes a swig and offers it to Tariq. Tariq's throat is so parched that he doesn't refuse. The water is the temperature of fresh piss.

"So what you here to discuss?" Ivor says.

"The Prince wants bin Laden to tone down his pronouncements."

"Why?"

"He fears the Crown Prince will take drastic measures if he doesn't."

"Like assassinate him?"

"I guess."

"It won't be easy. The Takfiris tried a couple months back. If you can believe it, they didn't think he was fundamentalist enough. Now he's got trenches all around his home, machine gun emplacements everywhere."

Ivor wanders over to the window and gazes out at the river.

"Are bin Laden and the Prince planning something together?" Ivor says.

"If they are, surely you'd know," Tariq says.

"Unfortunately I don't have a man inside al Qaeda. Hardest organization I've ever tried to penetrate."

Ivor turns and eyeballs Tariq.

"They're not," Tariq says.

"I can't believe the Prince is acting purely out of concern. Your boss is hardly known for his selflessness."

"He's fond of him, you know that."

"Not fond enough to send you here on a Gulfstream."

Ivor takes a final swig off the bottle and crunches it between his fingers.

"Don't play me for a fool, Tariq. Why's the Prince so desperate to keep bin Laden alive?"

Tariq wilts under Ivor's relentless gaze. The last thing he wants to do is tell him the Prince needs bin Laden to be patient if he's going to pull off his eventual coup.

But what else can I say? he wonders.

The phone rings. Tariq praises Allah for the interruption.

"I better take that," he says.

He makes his way around the bed and picks up the receiver.

"Tariq?" a man says.

It's the Prince.

"You need to come back right away. Your sister's missing."

THIRTY-TWO

THE PAKISTANI PORTER places their suitcases on the room's luggage racks.

"Can I be of any further assistance, Mr. Dervis?" he says.

"No, thank you," Charlie says in the Turkish accent he's been affecting ever since they fled the airport.

Charlie hands the man a hundred riyal bill, and the porter leaves. Charlie makes certain to lock the door after him. He turns. Noor has already rid herself of her niqab and abaya. She stands there in her pale blue scrubs.

"I'm sorry," he says.

"What could you have done?" she says.

"I don't know, looked at the weather forecast."

"These things materialize out of nowhere. You couldn't have known."

Charlie glances out the window at the endless blue skies. They seem placed there to mock him.

"We need to lay low a while," he says.

Noor smiles.

"I can think of worse things," she says.

Charlie shakes his head.

"I should have got you out. We shouldn't be here right now."

Noor walks over and places her hand on his cheek.

"If someone had told me a week ago, I'd have the chance to touch you, hold you, kiss your lips, even if only for an hour, I'd have given my eternal soul for the opportunity."

Noor rises on her tiptoes. Their lips rub against each other. Charlie closes his eyes. Noor smells like the desert.

"I could never love anyone else," he says.

"Me neither," she says.

Noor's lips part, and she kisses Charlie with such desire he is unable to respond. She stops.

"It's all right," she says.

"Are you sure?" he says.

His eyes can't help but drift towards her stomach. Noor stiffens.

"It's an issue, isn't it?" she says. "Now that another has had me, you'll never think of me as truly yours."

"It's not that. I promise. It's just after everything he's done to you, how could any of this feel right?"

Noor leans in and touches her lips to his.

"Because your lips are not his lips ..."

She takes his hand.

"Your touch not his touch ..."

Noor leads Charlie towards the bed.

"And your body not his body."

Charlie halts.

"Are you sure?" he says.

"Stop saying that."

"I need to know."

"I've never been more sure of anything in my life."

They lie down on the bed and face each other. For a while they stare into each other's eyes and explore the depths of each other's souls. Charlie brings a hand up and traces the contours of Noor's face. She closes her eyes. He brings his face close and kisses her the way he always wished he could; unhurried, freed from expectation, devoid of guilt. Noor responds and once more they allow the moment to linger. Silent tears flow down his cheeks.

"Charlie," Noor says.

He opens his eyes.

"Thank you for never giving up on me," she says.

"I never will."

She rolls onto her back. He looks down at her.

"Come on. It's time," she says.

He no longer doubts her sincerity or desire.

"Would you like me to ..."

His voice drops away. In this moment he finds himself uncommonly shy.

"Take my clothes off?" she says.

He nods.

"That would certainly be a start," she says with a smile.

Charlie blushes like a teenager. He sits up on his knees and lifts her blue shirt up and over her head. He stares at her entranced.

"You're not finished," Noor says.

Charlie snaps out of his stupor and slips his thumbs under her waist band. He slides her scrub pants and underwear down, his thumbs tracing the sides of her legs as he goes. Noor closes her eyes and sighs. He takes it as permission for his hands to wander and he glides them over her body as if he were a master sculptor fashioning a block of stone. Noor's breathing grows heavy, her skin warmer to the touch, her hips arching whenever his hands roam between her legs. Finally he drops his hands away and goes to unbutton his shirt. Noor's eyes flash open.

"No, let me," she says.

She sits up and works her way down, one button at a time.

"I can't believe I never told you this," she says.

He frowns.

"It's not a bad story. I promise," she says.

She undoes two more buttons.

"Back in Peshawar, I was sitting up in the oak tree one night when I heard you come home. I expected you to go out onto the verandah to smoke a cigarette but instead you went to your room."

The bottom button comes undone, and Noor slips the shirt off his shoulders.

"I should have climbed down right then and there, but something compelled me to stay. I suppose I was curious as to what you got up to when you thought no one was about."

Noor undoes Charlie's belt and unbuttons the top of his jeans. Charlie holds his breath.

"You put on some music and disappeared for a while. For a second there I thought you had fallen asleep, but then, just as I was preparing to depart my perch, there you were standing on your balcony, a cigarette between your lips–"

"As naked as the day I was born."

"I guarantee you didn't look like that the day you were born."

"My mother always said I was well endowed from the earliest of ages."

Noor punches Charlie's arm. Charlie laughs.

"Don't be crude," she says.

"You're the one who seems so eager to get a second look."

Noor goes to punch him again but he catches her arm. He pushes her back down onto the bed, and she squeals. Their lips connect. He luxuriates once more in her kisses. He unbuttons the top button of his pants and pulls them down.

"Wait," she says. "I haven't finished my story."

He holds his position.

"When I saw you naked on that balcony, I was ashamed to admit you were the most beautiful thing I'd ever seen."

"And now?" he says.

"I'm not ashamed to admit it anymore."

"Good, because there's nothing to be ashamed of," he

says. "Not in your past and not now. This is pure, this is sacred."

"I know," she says.

"I love you."

"I love you too."

He lowers his hips and slides inside her. Noor gasps. She pushes upwards with her hips and kisses him with fervor. In that moment, Charlie finally understands what paradise is; a physical union of two souls forged in love.

For the next two hours they lose themselves in each other, all sense of time and place gone. Finally each has no more to give other than the warmth of their bodies.

"I love you," Noor mumbles over and over.

Charlie lies there with a joyful heart and, like a child listening to a lullaby, drifts off with Noor's back curved neatly into the contours of his chest.

THIRTY-THREE

TARIQ STARES OUT the window at the ghostly city, the flashing blue lights of his police escort flickering across the glass. Riyadh is eerily deserted in the early morning.

Noor's out there, he thinks. *But where?*

He can't believe she's gone far. Unlike in Pakistan, a woman traveling alone in this country would be questioned by the authorities immediately.

She must have taken refuge once again, he decides.

The question is with whom? He can't think of anyone foolhardy enough to risk the wrath of the Saudi royal family and the Prince in particular. He comforts himself with the fact that Noor will be found. No one can escape Saudi Arabia. When she is captured, any hold she might have had over the Prince will be long dead and buried.

The Prince is going to strap her to a bed until that child is born, he thinks. *And then she'll be mine.*

The police cars pull to the side of the road. Tariq's S.U.V. sweeps through the floodlit gates of the Prince's compound. The S.U.V. doesn't slow until it comes upon the magnificent arched entrance to the Prince's palace. A thobed functionary awaits Tariq.

"Salaam alaikum," Tariq says on stepping out.

"Wa alaikum salaam," the functionary says. "Come this way."

The functionary turns on his heel and leads Tariq into the cool, sterile embrace of the palace. They pass through a domed hall the size of a great mosque, the only sound their shoes on the marble floor. Tariq prepares himself. He presumes the Prince will scream and shout, and take out his understandable wrath on him.

The key is to be subservient but also confident and certain, he tells himself.

The confident part is something his deceased father-in-law never understood. They will find Noor, he'll tell the Prince. Soon. This is nothing but the latest act of a stubborn and willful woman.

They come upon a set of double doors guarded by two men who have a gun on one hip and a ceremonial sword on the other. He recognizes them. They are Algerians, two veterans of the Afghan jihad. Tariq nods at his former jihadi brethren. They stare stonily ahead.

The functionary pushes the doors open to reveal a circular office with three bay windows at its far end. It is rumored the Prince wanted it modeled on the Oval Office except he was determined it be double the size. At the far end of the room the Prince sits behind a large oak desk. Tariq is surprised to see him surrounded by at least a dozen men. The ones in tan uniforms he recognizes as police, the ones in green as National Guard and the ones in thobes, he assumes are from the Ministry of Interior. They all look his direction, their expressions inscrutable.

"Salaam alaikum," Tariq says.

A couple nod but no one else feels it necessary to return the greeting. The Prince stares at Tariq. Tariq waits for him to explode. To his distress, the Prince doesn't.

"This is the brother of my fourth wife," the Prince says.

Tariq can't help but note the turn of phrase. *Not brother-in-law but the brother of my fourth wife. It's a significant demotion.*

"We will find Princess Noor, your Highness," Tariq says. "I assure you this is nothing but an act of petulance on her part."

The Prince nods at one of the thobed gentlemen; a tall, slender man with a thin, neat mustache. The man wanders over to Tariq, his movements as graceful as a cat's. He stops closer than Tariq finds comfortable. His expensive cologne wafts over him.

"Your sister, Mister Khan, escaped the King's hospital at nine fifty-two this morning in the company of an American, an X-ray technician named Joe Stapinski."

An American, Tariq says to himself. *That makes no sense.*

The man hands Tariq a folded piece of paper. Tariq can't help but notice the man's perfectly manicured fingernails.

"Perhaps you recognize the gentleman in question."

Tariq unfolds the paper and stares at a screenshot of a black and white video image. Dressed in scrubs, Noor and the American are waiting for an elevator.

How? Tariq says to himself. *How is it possible?*

"Do you recognize him?" the man says.

Tariq is unable to respond.

"Answer him!" the Prince shouts.

Tariq's head jolts up.

"It's Charlie Matthews," he says.

THIRTY-FOUR

CHARLIE SLIDES ON his sunglasses and steps out of the elevator. He glances around the brightly lit lobby. To his relief, no one bothers to look his way. With as much nonchalance as he can muster he strolls over to the hotel shop and picks up a copy of the English edition of the Al Riyadh newspaper. There's no mention of Noor's disappearance on the front page, and, from a cursory glance, nothing on the interior pages either. He suspected so. Noor's escape will be of intense embarrassment to the Saudi royal family. The last thing they'd want is anything in the press. Charlie attempts to read a report on the latest Formula One race but the words soon blur.

How the fuck are we going to get out of here? he asks himself.

He has no answer. The only thing he knows, is they'll need to stay here at least a couple days. Charlie replaces the paper in the rack and heads for the front desk to extend their stay. A harried clerk is dealing with two thobed men. Charlie stands behind them. They reek of cologne. To his right a door opens and a suited manager scurries up to the desk. He holds a large sheath of photocopies. One of the two men grabs them. Charlie gets a glimpse of the sheet on top. It's a photocopy of a passport. Charlie turns toward the elevators.

"May I help you, sir," the manager says to him.

"It's okay," Charlie says in his affected accent. "I thought I'd lost my room key."

Charlie pulls out his key and holds it up high as if to prove the veracity of his story. When he reaches the elevators he steals a glimpse over his shoulder. The Saudi detectives are heading out the front door. The elevator dings and he steps on board.

"Hold the doors, please," a man says in a German accent.

He and another German businessmen step on board. Their conversation is constant and intense. The elevator doors open and Charlie gets off. He sprints down the corridor and knocks on the door of their room. Two taps. A pause. And a third tap.

Goddamn it, where are you Noor?

He knocks again.

The locks turn, and the door swings open.

"I'm sorry, I was praying," Noor says.

Charlie pushes past her and races to the luggage rack. He starts packing the few items he'd taken out of his suitcase.

"We've got to get to the airport now," he says. "There were cops downstairs collecting guest records."

"Are they still here?" Noor says.

"That's not the point."

"Then we have time—"

"Noor, didn't you hear—"

"Would you please let me finish my sentence."

Charlie takes a deep breath and turns to face her.

"I'm sorry. Go ahead," he says.

Noor walks over and takes his hands in hers.

"The only thing that makes sense is they're collecting records from every hotel in Riyadh and taking them to a single location to study them."

"But there could be tens of teams."

"Even so it gives us time."

"To do what?"

"Change your appearance to begin with."

"Noor, I told you ..."

Noor fixes Charlie with a look that renders him silent.

"I assume you intend us to take the flight we were re-booked on," she says.

"I don't think we have any other option."

"That's four hours from now. Time for you go to a chemist and buy some hair color, and a pair of spectacles."

"What about you?"

"They won't unveil every woman in line. It would cause a riot. I'll be fine."

Noor puts her arms around Charlie's neck.

"I know how scared you are, my love," she says.

"Only for you," he says.

"Don't be. Whatever happens is part of God's plan. I'm at peace with that."

"You know I don't believe in God."

Noor gets on her tiptoes and kisses him. Charlie feels his heart slow.

"Really," she says, "you don't believe that kiss was God given."

She kisses him again.

"Perhaps," he says.

"Then I'm making progress already," she says smiling. "Now go."

Reluctantly Charlie extracts himself from her arms and heads for the door.

"I'll be right back," he says.

***

TARIQ SITS IN a vacant office in the Interior Ministry. When they first dumped him here, his Rolex had read a quarter to four in the morning. Now it's ten-thirty.

Why didn't you kill Charlie Matthews when you had the chance? he asks himself for what must be close to the hundredth time.

He had intended to back in Peshawar, but then Ivor Gardener had called and told him there was nothing to be gained from killing him.

Oh how wrong you were, Ivor. There was everything to be gained.

He stares at the phone on the desk and a thought strikes him. He slips his hand into his pocket and comes back with the business card Ivor had forced on him as he was racing out of his Khartoum hotel room. He dials the number. Ivor picks up on the third ring.

"It's me," he says. "Tariq."

"Was wondering when you were going to call to apologize."

"I had to get back to Riyadh as fast as I could."

"Bad news?"

"Why? What have you heard?"

"Assumed from the look on your face that it couldn't have been good."

"My sister's escaped ... with Charlie Matthews."

There's a pause on the other end of the line.

"How the fuck did Matthews get into Saudi?" Ivor says.

"Under an assumed name. He found a job at the King's Hospital."

"Assume that Prince of yours isn't in the best of moods."

Tariq looks at the door to make sure it's closed.

"My sister's pregnant," he says. "With his son."

Ivor lets out a long, low whistle.

"Are they still in the country?" he says.

"I don't know. I'm stuck here at the Interior Ministry."

"You in trouble?"

"No," Tariq protests. "They want me close just in case."

"So what do you want me to do? Can't exactly send a squad of F.B.I. agents over there."

"Perhaps you could alert your border agents in case they're already on their way to America."

"You really think they're traveling under their real names?"

Tariq hadn't thought of that. He hears footsteps down the hallway.

"Please do anything you can," he says. "I'll make it up to you. I promise."

Tariq replaces the receiver. The door opens to reveal a young Interior Ministry agent.

"Have you found her?" Tariq asks.

"We need you," the agent says.

Tariq jumps to his feet and hustles out after him.

***

"THERE YOU GO, Mr. Dervis," the British Airways agent says handing Charlie their boarding passes. "Have a good flight."

"Thank you, we will," Charlie says.

Charlie walks away. Noor falls in step beside him.

"That has to be a good sign," she says.

Charlie looks around the cavernous departure hall. Every airline employee, worker, and passenger seems like a plain clothes agent to him. Even the abaya clad women could be agents in disguise.

Then why haven't they arrested us? he wonders.

He has no good answer. He steals himself from thinking they've made it.

We still have immigration to go.

Charlie spots a long line of passengers waiting to have their exit visas examined. He wonders whether his newly black hair, his pair of clunky glasses and the mustache Noor fashioned from his three day stubble will be enough.

Surely they'll recognize me from my passport photo, he thinks.

He castigates himself. What had possessed him to place in his Turkish passport a photo so American that Ralph Lauren would be proud?

Charlie glances at the departure board. He notices an Emirates flight leaving for Dubai at twelve-thirty.

"Wait here a moment," he says to Noor.

"Where are you going?" she says.

"It'll only take a couple of minutes, I promise."

Charlie hurries to the Emirates ticket desk. A young Indian agent with an eager smile greets him.

"I know this is last minute," Charlie says, "but we just got word my wife's mother is dying."

"I'm sorry to hear that, sir."

"If there's any way to get on a flight to London that would mean the world to us."

"Let me take a look."

The agent hits a few keys on his computer.

"The flight to Dubai is certainly no problem," the agent says, "but all our flights from Dubai to London are full. For today and tomorrow."

"Could you put us on stand-by?" Charlie says.

"I could, but there's no guarantee you'll obtain a seat."

"All I want is a chance for my wife to see her mother one last time."

The agent gives him a sympathetic smile and hits a couple more keys.

"The two tickets come to six thousand, four hundred and thirty two riyals."

Charlie winces. He has just over four thousand riyals in his wallet, and there's no way he can use his credit card. It's under Joe Stapinski's name.

"You know what," he says. "I only need a ticket for my wife right now."

"Do you have her passport?"

Charlie pulls Noor's American passport from his pocket. He looks back at Noor and gives her a reassuring smile. She gestures that she's going to join the line for immigration. He nods and turns back to the agent. The agent types in Noor's details.

Please hurry.

For once Charlie's prayers are answered. The agent hands him back Noor's passport and in return Charlie hands him the fee in riyals.

"How many bags will your wife be checking?" the agent says.

"None," Charlie says. "We rushed out here as soon as we heard the news."

The agent buys the explanation and hands Noor's boarding pass to Charlie.

"Please extend, to your wife, my deepest condolences."

"I will," Charlie says.

Charlie heads in the direction of the immigration line. He looks for Noor amongst the mass of abaya wearing women. One looks in his direction. He recognizes Noor's green eyes. He sidles up beside her. The bearded Saudi behind him grunts his disapproval.

"Sorry, she's my wife," Charlie says.

The man mutters away unmoved by Charlie's explanation. The line moves forward and the man barks in Arabic at the three women behind him. They shuffle forward as a pack. Charlie wonders if they're all his wives.

Who cares? he thinks.

He has no desire to ever visit a country again where such a question could even be asked.

"What was that all about?" Noor says.

"Buying us an insurance policy," he says.

The line moves forward again. Charlie glances warily ahead and scrutinizes the emotionless immigration officers at work.

After a while he notices a pattern. The immigration officers seem to take a lot longer inspecting the passports of couples than those of single men or groups like the one behind him. In quick succession a number of passengers are called forward and they find themselves at the front of the line. An immigration officer gestures at Charlie. Charlie turns to the bearded Saudi behind him.

"I'm sorry," he says, "it was rude of me to jump in front of you. Please go ahead."

The Saudi snorts as if that's the least he'd expect. He lumbers forward, the women following in his wake. Charlie hands Noor her Turkish passport.

"Go with them," he says.

"Why?" she says.

"Please, just do it."

Noor nods. She hurries after the women and melds herself to them. When the bearded Saudi places his four passports down on the counter she slips hers in as well. The Saudi spins around to confront her but before he can say anything the immigration officer has stamped all five passports and handed them back to him.

Another officer calls Charlie forward. Charlie walks up and hands over his Turkish passport. Out of the corner of his eye he sees the bearded Saudi chuck Noor's passport at her. She scrambles to pick it up off the floor.

No matter, Charlie thinks. *She's through.*

It's only then that he realizes he has Noor's tickets on him. If he doesn't get through, she's screwed.

"Mr. Dervis," the immigration officer says.

Charlie turns back.

"How long will you be out of the country?"

"Only three days," Charlie says in his affected accent. "I go to London for business meeting."

The officer skims to the back of his passport. He looks at the photo. Charlie senses his right hand begin to tremble and shoves it in his pocket in an attempt to steady it. The officer looks back up at Charlie.

"I wear glasses now," Charlie says. "Eyes not so good."

The officer looks down at the passport again.

He's not buying it. Say something.

"I tell you, I much prefer to stay here if I could," Charlie says.

The officer's attention wanders from the passport.

"Why?" he says. "I hear London is very pleasant at this time of year."

"The weather perhaps," Charlie says. "But it's full of tourists, the food is terrible and the women ..."

Charlie snorts.

"... let's just say they dress like whores."

"That's because they are whores," the officer says.

With a flourish the officer stamps Charlie's passport and hands it back to him.

"I wish you a swift return, Mr. Dervis."

"Me too."

Charlie can hardly believe he's through. He sees Noor standing by a nearby pillar and walks over to her.

"Everything okay?" he says.

Noor's eyes sparkle.

"We did it," she says.

***

"THERE YOU ARE, Khan. What took you so long?"

The Interior Ministry official sits behind a mahogany desk, a cigarette stuck firmly between his long elegant fingers, its smoke swirling upwards like some ghostly apparition.

If you wanted me to be closer, Tariq wants to say, *then perhaps you shouldn't have stuck me on the other side of the building.*

He takes the one available chair. The official picks up a sheath of photocopies off the desk.

"Look through these," he says.

"You think one of them might be them?" Tariq says.

"Can you believe that not a single photo of your sister exists?"

It makes sense. The Prince was adamantly opposed to possessing photos that had human beings in them.

"What about the American?" Tariq says.

"Stop asking questions," the official says. "Look at the photos."

Tariq leans forward and grabs the sheath. He skims through a whittled down stack of Riyadh hotel guests: American businessmen, German engineers, French bureaucrats, British flight attendants, and Arabic women.

Then he sees him, staring at the camera with a look of steely determination, that scar down his left cheek as perceptible as it was on the night he first met him in Peshawar.

"That's him," Tariq says. "That's Charlie Matthews."

The official snatches the photocopy.

"You're certain?"

Tariq looks down at the next sheet.

"Yes," he says, "because that's my sister."

***

NOOR DOES HER best not to fidget. She sits at the gate in a section filled solely with women and children.

Even here we're separated, she thinks. *Even when we're pretending to be husband and wife.*

She watches Charlie. He is asking the gate agent, for what must be the fifth time, when they're going to board.

"Any minute, I assure you," she hears the agent say.

Ever since they arrived at the gate, time seems to have stood still, the clock on the wall ticking by so slowly that it seems like some Sisyphean device constructed to torture her. Over the speakers, there is an announcement of final boarding for the Emirates flight to Dubai.

Why can't that be ours? she thinks.

Charlie makes his way to his seat. He glances in Noor's direction and offers her a reassuring smile.

What have I done to deserve such love? Noor wonders.

She closes her eyes and her mind wanders. That morning while she had been dyeing Charlie's hair, he had told her of Belize, of its sparkling blue waters, its soft, moist heat, its laid-back culture. She pictures them walking down one of its beaches at sunset, she in a sarong and top, he in a pair of rolled up linen pants and a cotton shirt, a band playing in the distance.

Noor imagines what she thinks to be the banging of drums. They get ever louder. Noor realizes they are the sound of feet stamping down the concourse. Her eyes fly open and she swivels in her chair. Twenty policemen are sprinting in their gate's direction. A phone rings at the counter. The gate agent answers it and reacts with shocked silence.

No, she thinks. *It can't be.*

"You've got to get out of here."

Noor looks up. Charlie is beside her. He shoves an American passport into her hands along with a boarding pass.

"It's for the Emirates flight. You can still make it," he says.

Noor feels as if the ground below her seat is about to cave in.

"I'm not leaving you," she says. "Not again."

"It won't be forever. Remember it's you they want not me."

"But ..."

Charlie grips Noor's arms so tightly it hurts and hauls her to her feet. The policemen are no more than fifty yards away.

"Please, I'm begging you," Charlie says, "if you won't do this for me, then do it for your son."

Charlie shoves Noor away from him.

"No," she says.

"Go now," he says.

Charlie turns away. Like a soldier ordered to charge at enemy lines, he runs in a haphazard fashion towards the policemen. The policemen draw their guns. Passengers scream and throw themselves on the floor. Someone barks a command and the guns are lowered. Charlie breaks through a series of desperate tackles. For a moment it seems like he'll make it past only for a couple of policeman to crash into him and send him tumbling to the ground. Soon a small scrum is on top of him. Charlie kicks and flails as the policemen try to restrain him.

Noor is about to cry out when she feels her baby kick for the very first time. She stands there stunned. The baby kicks her again and this time it galvanizes her away from the carnage, past one gate then the next until she spots a display for the Emirates flight. An agent closes the door to the gangway.

"Wait," she shouts.

The agent looks in her direction. Noor holds out her boarding pass. The agent takes a cursory glance at it and swings the door open.

"One more," he shouts.

Noor runs down the gangway and reaches the door of the plane. She shows the attendant her boarding pass. Her hand shake uncontrollably.

"It's okay, ma'am," the attendant says. "You made it."

The flight attendant guides Noor to her seat and within seconds of sitting down, the plane backs away from the gate. Noor leans over the woman beside her, desperate to get a look at what's going on in the airport. It's impossible. The glare on the glass is such that there is nothing to see. Before long the plane has turned towards the end of the runway.

Noor collapses back in her chair and for the first time she realizes the enormity of what's happened.

Oh God, she thinks, *I've lost him again.*

***

A COUPLE OF policemen haul Charlie to his feet. Charlie glances out the window and sees the Emirates jet making its way down the taxiway.

Please let Noor be on it, he prays.

There are three planes ahead of it. He knows he needs to buy Noor some time. He tries to wrestle free and another policeman punches him in the gut. He gasps. A slender man in a flowing thobe appears before him. Charlie stares up into his grey, feline eyes.

"Where is she?" the man says.

"What are you talking about?" Charlie says.

The man nods at the policeman. The policeman punches Charlie again. The man swivels around and walks away. The policemen drag Charlie along behind him. They arrive at the British Airways gate. A contingent of policemen have cordoned it off. The passengers are huddled together, the decorum of separating the sexes gone as the men stand protectively by their women.

"I ask you again," the man says. "Which one is she?"

Charlie stares at the passengers' faces. The Arabs stare back at him with contempt, the Westerners with the fear he will somehow implicate them.

"No one is getting away, Mr. Matthews, so please make this easy on yourself."

Charlie spies the obese Saudi and his three wives from the immigration line. Charlie points at them.

"Over there," he says.

"Show me," the man says.

The policemen frogmarch Charlie toward the little group. The Saudi frowns. Charlie points at his shortest wife.

"I'm so sorry, my love," he says.

The official shouts out a command in Arabic and a policeman goes to grab the woman. The Saudi lets out a roar of indignation and barrels into the policeman. The wives scream. Other policemen join the fray and jump on top of the Saudi. Unlike Charlie he doesn't go down easily. He is like a bull elephant being attacked by a pride of lions. A police captain finally manages to grab a hold of the wife and the man in the thobe rips off her niqab. A terrified acne ridden teenager stares back at him.

It suddenly occurs to Charlie that his escorts are no longer holding onto him. He turns tail and starts sprinting down the concourse. He passes first one gate and then another. He begins to wonder if in the melee they've forgotten all about him.

Then he feels something punch him with incredible force on his right shoulder. He loses his balance and tumbles. His forehead slams into the metal armrest of a nearby lounge chair and he ends up on the floor. From down the concourse he hears more screams. This time they sound more muffled. He tries to pick himself up but finds his right arm is useless and his head a daze. He wonders what the hell happened. He glances at the polished floor and sees specks of blood.

They shot me, he thinks.

From his position on the floor, he's able to stare out the windows. He sees the Emirates plane soaring into the air and smiles.

It's okay, he thinks. *I did it.*

Right after, everything goes black.

THIRTY-FIVE

NOOR STARES AT the back of the seat in front of her.

This must be a dream, she keeps telling herself. *It's too surreal not to be.*

Yet every shake of the plane reminds her it's not, and despite what Charlie had said, she knows they won't let him go.

If anything they're more likely to behead him.

Her throat constricts, and she throws up into her niqab. The vomit spills down it onto her abaya. A couple of nearby passengers groan and their assistance lights blink on. A flight attendant comes hurrying down the aisle.

"Are you feeling unwell, ma'am?" she says in Arabic.

Noor says nothing.

"Is your husband on board? A family member perhaps?"

Noor shakes her head.

Go away. Please go away.

"Then how about I help you to the bathroom?"

Noor nods. Anything to be left alone.

The attendant grips Noor's arm and lifts her up. She leads her past the aghast and the curious, and opens the bathroom door.

"I'll be outside if you need me," she says.

Noor staggers into the restroom and collapses onto the toilet. She tries to breathe. It's not easy. The vomit has worked its way up into her nostrils. She rips off her niqab and throws it to the floor.

I have to save him, she says to herself.

She thinks about giving herself up in Dubai. Perhaps that will save him. The baby kicks, not once, but three times. It startles her, as if he's rebuking the plan she's just formulated. 'Do it for your son', that's what Charlie had said. Noor knows if she returns to Riyadh she may not change Charlie's fate, but she will certainly seal her son's.

Can you really deliver him into the Prince's hands?

Noor knows she can't.

I'll never do that.

She cries once again. There is a knock on the door. It's the flight attendant.

"Are you all right in there, ma'am?" the flight attendant says.

Noor struggles to her feet. She pulls the abaya up and over her head. She splashes water on her face and swills it around her mouth. She spits out the rancid taste of her own fear and self-pity. She opens the door and holds out her niqab and abaya.

"Would you mind disposing of these?" she says.

The flight attendant can't help but wince.

"Of course not," the attendant says. "You should get back to your seat. We'll be landing soon."

Noor sits back down and opens her American passport and boarding pass. A small number of Saudi riyals fall out. Her eyes water up.

He thought of everything.

Noor forces back her tears and skims to the back page of her passport. She gazes at her smiling photo from all those months back. It feels as if it was taken of a different person in a different lifetime. She reads the name on the passport:

Sarah McDowell. She can't help but think of Sarah, the wife of Abraham, a woman who was barren all those years only to be blessed by God with a son in her old age.

It's a sign, she thinks. *My son is a blessing.*

That's what her father had called his children, his blessings', even after Tariq had so cruelly turned his back on him. She remembers Baba telling her once that when it came to children a pauper and a billionaire were the same, for each would spend every rupee they had if it meant they could save their child's life. 'You will see,' he'd said to Noor under the shade of the eucalyptus tree, 'one day when you have a child of your own you will feel the same way and have the same protective instincts as your mother did all those years ago.' Noor had scoffed at him. She was never going to get married, she had told him, let alone have a child.

But now I do.

She realizes Baba was right. She will do whatever it takes to protect her son. Noor places the riyals back in her passport and looks at her second boarding pass. The one from Dubai to New York. There is no seat number on it only the word 'standby'. She has no idea what that means but she knows one thing for sure. Sarah McDowell is going to do everything she can to get on that flight.

THIRTY-SIX

CHARLIE OPENS HIS eyes to discover an Indian doctor in heavy rimmed glasses holding a bottle of smelling salts under his nose.

"He's awake," the doctor says in English.

The doctor takes out his retinoscope and shines its light into each of Charlie's eyes. Charlie stares up at the white-washed ceiling. The events that led him here soon come back to him.

I must be in a hospital, he thinks.

The doctor puts the end of a stethoscope to Charlie's naked chest.

And Noor?

The doctor listens intently.

It's okay, Charlie tells himself. *She got away.*

Charlie becomes increasingly aware of a deep, throbbing pain in his right shoulder.

"Could you give me something for my shoulder?" Charlie says.

The doctor refuses to look him in the eye. He steps away without answering.

"He is in good shape," the doctor says.

Soon after a door clicks shut. The man who interrogated him at the airport comes into view. He peers down at Charlie in the way a cat does when it has its prey cornered. He still wears a gleaming white thobe, his red and white ghutra perched perfectly on his head.

"How are you feeling?" the man says.

"I was shot," Charlie says.

"That's what happens when you flee the scene of a crime. However you were fortunate, the bullet went straight through. It was the fall that knocked you unconscious."

"For how long?" Charlie says.

The man shakes his head to indicate that he'll be the one asking the questions.

"My name is Abdullah, and I work for Al Mukhabrat Al A'amah. The General Intelligence Department."

The man leaves the name hanging out there. Charlie has no clue as to its significance.

"I understand you're in a somewhat weakened state but my hope is this interview can be conducted in an efficient manner so that we can hand you over to your embassy by the end of the day."

"You're letting me go?" Charlie says.

"You have broken innumerable laws, Mr. Matthews, but given this case's embarrassing nature and the fact that Princess Noor has been safely reunited with her husband, we would prefer it if you just left the country."

Charlie can do nothing more than stare at Abdullah. It's as if the reason for his very existence has been ripped away.

"Oh come, Mr. Matthews, did you really think Princess Noor was going to elude us? I'll admit making us believe the two of you were on the same flight was a clever trick. But you forgot one thing. Princess Noor is a woman, and a woman's ability to act rationally in a stressful situation is almost slight to none."

"Noor has dealt with stressful situations all her life," Charlie says.

Abdullah shrugs.

"All I can tell you is she was sobbing uncontrollably when we apprehended her. If it's any consolation, it was your name she kept on repeating."

Abdullah takes out a voice recorder.

"I am going to record this interview. I hope you're comfortable with that."

Charlie says nothing. Abdullah takes his silence as permission to proceed and presses the record button.

"Now, as far as we can tell, you entered this country using the identity of one Joe Stapinski, am I correct?"

Charlie continues to stare off into space. He imagines Noor right now, her terror, the fury reigning down on her.

"Mr. Matthews, please answer the question," Abdullah says. "Did you enter Saudi Arabia using a false identity, namely that of Joe Stapinski?"

"Yes," Charlie says.

"And did you and Princess Noor attempt to leave this country using two counterfeit Turkish passports, under the names of Rustu and Zerrin Derva?"

Charlie wonders what the Prince will do to Noor. Nothing too extreme, not with his unborn child in her belly.

But once his son is born.

"Mr. Matthews?"

"Dervis not Derva. That's the name we used," Charlie says.

Tears stream down Charlie's cheeks.

Once the baby is born, Noor is as good as dead, he thinks.

Abdullah takes out a pressed handkerchief from his front pocket and dabs away Charlie's tears.

"Shhh shhh," he says. "I understand your distress, truly I do. When I was your age there was a girl I very much wanted to marry, but my father would not allow it. I cried for days, yet look at me now. You will survive this, I promise. I have only a couple more questions and we're done."

Charlie nods. All he wants to do is crawl up into a ball and die.

"You used the names of Rustu and Zerrin Dervis for your British Airways' and Holiday Inn reservations, is that correct?"

"Yes."

"But those weren't the only identities you were carrying on you, were they?"

"I had my real passport."

"Under the name Charles Matthews, yes we have ascertained that. But Princess Noor, she had a second false passport under a different name too, didn't she?"

"Yes."

"And what was that name again? I apologize but I have a tough time pronouncing it."

Charlie goes to say it when a thought crosses his mind.

What's so difficult about Sarah? he thinks. Or McDowell for that matter. This man's English is better than mine, he should have no trouble pronouncing it.

Abdullah continues to smile at Charlie.

Unless he doesn't know it.

"The first name's easy," Charlie says.

"But of course," Abdullah says.

"So what is it?"

Abdullah's expression of equanimity falters.

"Please pronounce the name Princess Noor was using when she was apprehended," Abdullah says.

Charlie turns his head to the side and glances at the Roman numerals on Abdullah's Cartier watch. Twenty five minutes past two. He does a quick calculation.

Noor's flight's about to land in Dubai.

Abdullah follows Charlie's gaze.

"You're not going to tell me, are you?"

Charlie shakes his head.

"So be it," Abdullah says.

Abdullah steps aside and for the first time, Charlie gets a view of the rest of the room. It doesn't consist of much; just two metal chairs and a couple of young, muscled toughs leaning against the wall. The men could be twins and wear a simple wardrobe of white T-shirts, cargo pants and black army boots. Abdullah nods at them. They straighten up and stroll over.

One of the men grabs Charlie by the leg and pulls him off the hospital bed. Charlie lands on his wounded right shoulder. He howls. From behind a boot connects with one of his kidneys. He gasps, the pain so intense he's rendered mute. He's struck by a whirlwind of further kicks. One lands in the small of his back, another connects with his wounded shoulder, another blasts into his thigh. He feels a rib crack and one of his knees buckle. The attack is so shocking in its brutality that Charlie only starts to feel its full effect when the men pull him up and drag him into one of the chairs. One of them grabs a hold of Charlie's hair and yanks his head back. Abdullah stands in front of him like some sixteenth century inquisitor.

"What was the other identity Princess Noor was using, Mr. Matthews?" he says.

"Fuck you," Charlie says.

Abdullah shakes his head. He steps back and the two young men approach once again. Charlie can't help but notice that one of them is holding a metal pipe in his hand. Charlie expects another beating but instead the other tough grasps his wrists and cuffs them. He pulls Charlie's cuffed wrists over his knees while his cohort inserts a long metal pipe in the gap between Charlie's knees and forearms. The two young men lift up the metal pipe and Charlie flips over. He hangs upside down like a trussed chicken with his feet and ass in the air, his nose inches from the floor. Abdullah arranges the two chairs and the two young men rest the pipe between them. They all disappear from view. Charlie tries to turn his head to see what they're doing. It's impossible.

What the fuck? he thinks.

He hears a hiss, and moments later the tip of a cane strikes the soles of his bare feet. Charlie screams. He has never experienced such pain. Instinctively his legs jerk and in so doing they pull on his cuffed wrists. His shoulders feel as if they're going to be ripped from their joints.

The cane comes down again and again, and every time it does his legs jerk and a wave of torment passes through his body. Charlie's eyes bulge, his eardrums roar and he bellows in agony.

Charlie loses count of how many strokes they give him. It's at least ten, perhaps twenty. By the time they stop, he is a moaning, babbling mess.

"Mr. Matthews."

Abdullah crouches down beside him. Charlie tries to focus but the pain is too acute.

"I don't want this to continue, believe me, but I need the second identity that Princess Noor is traveling under. And I need it now."

Don't do it, a voice deep inside him yells.

Charlie shakes his head. Abdullah sighs and disappears from view. This time the cane eviscerates his backside.

Charlie howls.

It comes down again and again, each time striking fresh flesh for maximum effect. It feels like he is being flayed alive.

"Please stop," Charlie screams. "Please."

The beating halts.

Charlie opens his eyes expecting Abdullah to be right there beside him. He isn't. Instead there's another hiss and the cane connects with his balls. Up until this moment in his life, Charlie had never wished to die, not even in those darkest moments in Pakistan. But right here, right now, if they were to give him a gun he would surely shoot himself to alleviate the agony.

"I'll tell you, I'll tell you everything," he cries out.

Abdullah crouches beside Charlie and strokes his cheek.

"I don't need everything, Charlie. Just the name."

Charlie cries. He so desperately doesn't want to give it up, but the idea of enduring another round of the cane is unbearable. And then it occurs to him.

You don't need to give him the real one.

"Mr. Matthews?" Abdullah says.

Charlie tries to think of another. Abdullah straightens.

"Wait, wait," Charlie cries out. "It's Elma Kuyt."

"Pardon me," Abdullah says.

"Elma Kuyt, it's a Dutch name."

"Spell it for me."

Charlie does so. After each letter he takes a desperate set of gasps before he relays the next.

"What flight did she get on?" Abdullah says.

"She didn't," Charlie says. "I told her to leave the airport and hole up in a hotel."

"The Holiday Inn?"

"I don't know. We didn't have time to choose one."

"But definitely a hotel?"

Charlie nods. Abdullah pats Charlie's cheek.

"I can't tell you how appreciative I am for your cooperation," he says.

Abdullah straightens, and Charlie watches the hem of his swishing robe leave the room. Moments later the young men extract the metal pipe. Charlie tumbles to the floor.

***

"THE FLIGHT IS full, ma'am," the gate agent says. "The earliest we can get you to New York is Thursday."

"I understand," Noor says, "but if there's anyway I can get on today's flight–"

"There isn't. Every passenger has checked in. I'm sorry."

The gate agent picks up her microphone. She announces the commencement of boarding for first and business class passengers. Noor stands there in the shirt and pants she bought at the airport mall to replace her soiled scrubs. She scans the passengers waiting to board. They're a mixture of harried families, cozy couples and weary businessmen. She is about to give up when she spots a straggly haired man lounging against the far wall. He is not much older than herself and is listening to a battered Walkman. She hurries past the boarding passengers and goes up to him.

"Excuse me?" she says.

The young man removes one of his headphones.

"What's up?" he says.

"I need to get to New York tonight. However, for me to do so, a passenger has to give up their seat."

"And you thought I'd be an easy mark," he says with an impish smile.

"You're my last hope."

"What's in it for me?"

Noor pulls out her passport and holds out her money.

"I have one thousand one hundred Saudi riyals here. That's almost three hundred dollars."

The young man shakes his head.

"Cost me least that much to spend a couple more days in this place."

Over the loudspeaker, the gate agent announces general boarding. The young man struggles to his feet and goes to return the headphone to his ear.

"Please," Noor says. "I'll do anything."

The young man raises an eyebrow.

"Anything?" he says.

Noor swallows.

You've endured worse, she tells herself.

She nods.

"Then I'll take that sweet ring of yours," he says.

Noor's eyes flash to her left hand and her ten-carat diamond ring. She'd totally forgotten she was even wearing it.

"It's yours," she says.

The young man stares at her in astonishment.

"You're shitting me?" he says.

"Not if you get me on that flight."

He grabs Noor's hand and yanks her towards the gate agent.

"Wait up," he shouts.

THIRTY-SEVEN

"I CAME AS soon as I received word from our station chief," Ivor says.

"How did he find out?" the Prince says.

"I hate to tell you, your Highness, but even in Riyadh secrets don't remain secret for long."

The Prince reddens.

He's thinking about all the other princes shitting themselves with laughter, Ivor thinks. *It's eating him alive.*

A thobed man enters the room.

"If you'll excuse me," the Prince says.

"Go right ahead," Ivor says.

The Prince joins the man at his desk. They confer in hushed tones. Ivor appraises the Prince; his pearl white thobe, his two thousand dollar Italian loafers, his antique Patek Phillipe watch.

For all your swagger, you're not bin Laden's type, he thinks. *You're too soft. Too caught up in your own image and not enough in the daily grind of the global jihad.*

Ivor has read the breathless accounts of the Prince's personal piety and battlefield exploits in the Arab media.

But I know better, I was there in Pakistan. I heard firsthand about your battlefield paralysis, that bitch that committed suicide.

Ivor wonders what it is about the Prince and his wives. They all go to amazing lengths to get away from him.

The Prince and the man look in his direction. Ivor smiles at them, and they return to their conversation.

What am I going to do about Al Qaeda? he thinks.

After four months in Sudan, he has no hard intelligence on the group other than the fact that its leader harbors a virulent hatred of America and the Saudi royal family. His bosses back at Langley have totally lost interest. When he had arrived in Sudan, he had hoped that Tariq would provide him with some; after all the Prince hadn't sent Tariq to Khartoum to exchange recipes with bin Laden. But Tariq had gotten so used to the good life here in Saudi Arabia he clearly felt no need to feed him anything.

After all I did for him, Ivor thinks.

Ivor wonders if finding Tariq's sister again might facilitate things, but he suspects that, even if he does, he'll be back in the same position.

I need to give Tariq an incentive to help me. I need to shake him from this cozy perch of his.

The Prince and the man embrace, and the man heads from the room. The Prince returns to his chair.

"Good news, I hope," Ivor says.

"I was informed that the American provided us with the name my wife is traveling under. She should be apprehended shortly."

"How can you be so sure he gave you the correct one?"

The Prince chuckles.

"Given the methods we employ, we don't receive incorrect information."

Ivor shrugs. The Prince is probably right.

"What do you intend on doing with Matthews after this is all over?" Ivor says.

"We have no record of such a man ever entering our country, so as far as I'm concerned he doesn't exist."

And thus there'll be no record of him dying in it either.

Ivor almost feels sorry for Charlie.

"And Tariq?" he says.

Ivor is gladdened to see the Prince's face redden a second time. Tariq clearly causes the Prince as much discomfort as the opinions of his fellow princes.

"Tariq Khan should be no concern of yours, Mr. Gardener," the Prince says.

"Now he's moved to Sudan, I'm afraid, he's gonna have to be."

"He hasn't moved to Sudan."

"Oh, I'm sorry, I got the impression he had. Made sense, you know, considering how badly he's let you down."

The Prince works over the prayer beads in his hand.

Come on, you bastard, Ivor says to himself, *take the bait.*

"He will, however, be moving there shortly," the Prince says.

You beauty.

"It had nothing to do with me," the Prince says. "He finds Riyadh claustrophobic. Too prosperous for his liking."

"Once a peasant, always a peasant," Ivor says.

"I'm afraid so."

"Well I'll keep an eye on him for you. Khartoum may not be as dangerous as Peshawar, but it's a strange place. Things can come at you when you least expect them to."

"I'd most appreciate that."

The Prince stands and sticks out a hand. Ivor shakes it.

"It's always a pleasure seeing you, Mr. Gardener. I must say I've missed our little chats."

"Me too. I hope all this ..."

Ivor searches for the right word.

"Unpleasantness comes to an end soon."

"Inshallah, it will."

Ivor strolls out of the Prince's office, the first part of his mission accomplished. As long he plays Tariq right, he should have a mole inside al Qaeda within a week.

Fuck me, he thinks, *Charlie Matthews should pop up in my life more often.*

***

TARIQ SITS IN the center of the open plan office. Everything is so shiny and modern he might as well be in the offices of a top investment bank. Outside the night lights of Riyadh gleam bright. Inside, in a glass walled conference room, the same bevy of officials from the previous night sit around a long obsidian table with the man he now knows as Abdullah, giving orders at the far end. Young officers rush in and out delivering documents. They always go to Abdullah first and only after he reads them are they disseminated to the rest of the room. Tariq wishes he could be in there with them.

It's okay, he tells himself. *The important thing is they're going to find Noor.*

Earlier a junior officer had boasted that Abdullah had broken Charlie Matthews in record time. Now they knew the name Noor was using, it was only a matter of time before they reeled her in.

And once Noor is back at the palace you can start repairing your relationship with the Prince, he tells himself.

Tariq has thought long and hard about this. He's well aware the Prince blames him, and that it will take time for the Prince's anger and bitterness to drain away.

But once his son is born, he thinks, *his mood will improve. Everything will change for the better.*

The main double doors swing open. Tariq is shocked to see Ivor Gardener walk in with another thobed official from Abdullah's dreaded Al Mukhabrat Al A'amah. Tariq shivers.

What the hell's Gardener doing tangled up with them?

Tariq tries to catch Ivor's eye, but Ivor never looks his way. The official leads him over to Abdullah's corner office. Not long after, Abdullah joins Ivor. The two men embrace like old friends, and Abdullah shuts the door. Tariq sits there paralyzed as he imagines Ivor selling him out, telling Abdullah all about his deal to spy for the C.I.A. It won't matter that Tariq never gave Ivor anything. The sense of betrayal the Prince will feel will render their relationship irreparable.

He'll throw me out of Saudi Arabia, he thinks. *Perhaps even hand me over to Al Mukhabrat.*

Tariq hyperventilates. After today, he is more than aware of what they do with people in their custody.

The door to Abdullah's office opens. Abdullah is the first out. His body coiled, his expression one of utter fury. He looks Tariq's way.

Run, Tariq thinks.

However his legs won't respond. Abdullah shouts at a couple of toughs, and together they stalk towards him. Tariq closes his eyes and waits to be dragged from his chair. The trio pass by. He opens his eyes and twists around in his seat to see them marching out of the office. Tariq turns back to find Ivor standing in front of him.

"It seems our friend, Charlie Matthews, has been telling fibs. Had everyone on a wild goose chase for Elma Kuyt, a U.N. official."

Tariq swallows.

"Do you think my sister's gotten away?" he says.

Ivor picks up a Scotch Tape dispenser and snaps off a piece of tape. He rolls it between the thumb and index finger of his left hand.

"She may have gotten further but she's not got away, not with the combined intelligence capabilities of the Saudi and U.S governments now after her."

"Thank God," Tariq says.

"I'd prefer for once, Tariq, if you just thanked me."

"I am very appreciative, I promise."

"Yet ever since you've got to Saudi you've treated me like some bum cousin, despite the fact that you'd be baking your ass off in a shithole of a refugee camp if it weren't for me."

"It's not like that. I've been very busy."

Ivor looks contemptuously at Tariq's wrist.

"What? Buying Rolexes? And to think I saved your sorry ass today. Really I don't know why I bother."

Ivor shakes his head and makes for the exit. Tariq jumps up from his chair.

"What do you mean?" Tariq says.

Ivor turns back.

"When I visited the Prince this morning, he was adamant that he was going to put you on the first flight to Pakistan."

Tariq feels a scourge of fear creep through his insides.

"He feels like someone who thought he'd bought a flaw-less diamond only to discover the man who sold it to him knew all along it was a fake."

"But you said you saved me."

"I gave him an alternative to consider. Something that'd allow him to vent his anger without severing your relationship forever."

Tariq racks his brain. He can't imagine what that might be.

"I told him to send you to Khartoum instead."

Please God, no, Tariq thinks.

"You seem displeased," Ivor says.

"It's a hellhole," Tariq says.

"In the summer, I can't say it's pleasant, but if you play your cards right, you'll only have to endure one of those."

"I can come back. He said that."

"I suggested a year would be sufficient punishment, and he didn't argue otherwise. I can get you back in the Prince's good graces, Tariq, especially once I've tracked down that sister of yours, but I need to know you'll be a real friend to me from now on."

Tears rise in Tariq's eyes. He reaches out and grabs Ivor's hand.

"I promise, I'll be the best friend you've ever had," he says.

Ivor nods.

"Then I'll see you in Khartoum."

Ivor wanders way. Tariq slumps in his chair.

Khartoum, he thinks. *How could I be so cursed?*

THIRTY-EIGHT

CHARLIE CAN ONLY guess how long he's been lying on the floor. Ever since the two young toughs left no one's come in or out, and as much as the pain has allowed he has drifted in and out of sleep. Charlie suspects it has to have been at least eight hours, perhaps even as much as twelve, for his stomach has been rumbling for some time now and his throat is so parched that every time he swallows it's like he's swallowing glass. How he's wanted to bang on the locked door and shout for water, but every time he's thought of doing so he has refrained. The last thing he wants to do is draw attention to himself and reduce Noor's chances of escaping.

He's no fool, he knows at some point they will see through his deception and come again. His back spasms as if to enunciate the point. He screws up his eyes, his whole body still screaming in pain. The soles of his feet seem to have swollen to double their size, his buttocks refuse to allow even the slightest pressure on them, while his balls moan with such intensity he doubts they will ever be the same again.

In an attempt to take his mind off the pain he has tried to calculate how long it will take Noor to get to New York. Two hours to get from Riyadh to Dubai, and then a two hour layover has her leaving Dubai at four p.m. local time. And then what? He knows from experience it takes eight hours to fly from Islamabad to London and then five hours from London to JFK. Islamabad and Dubai are on a similar longitude, he'd guessed. If so her flight should take around thirteen hours. She'll land at five a.m. He has as little as two hours and as many as five to hold out.

Up until now he's never been a religious person. Even when his mother died or when he'd lost Noor that first time, he hadn't reached out to God. Yet here, lying face first on a cement floor, bathed in fluorescent light, he finds himself begging God not only to help Noor escape, but for him to endure what is to come.

"Please God, I may not deserve anything in this life, but Noor surely does."

He hears footsteps approach. They have an urgent, menacing quality to them. The door flies open and he twists onto his back. Abdullah comes first, a cane high above his head. Charlie scuttles backwards. The cane arcs through the air and its tip catches him across the cheek. As blows of frustration and fury rain down on him, Charlie lies there with his eyes closed, blood spurting from the wound. He hardly flinches. Unlike earlier, these ones are too indiscriminate to cause serious pain. The beating ends, and Charlie waits. He can hear Abdullah breathing heavily, and then say something in Arabic. Charlie opens his eyes to see the toughs advancing on him.

They haul him to his feet and pull his arms behind his back. One of them cuffs his wrists while the other throws a metal chain through a ring in the ceiling. Charlie stares up at it in wonder. He hadn't noticed it until now.

The other end of the chain is clipped to his cuffs, and he hears the chain rattle as it is pulled through the ring. All of a sudden Charlie's arms fly backward and he is hoisted in the air until he dangles a foot off the ground. He screams in agony. It feels as if his arms are going to be torn off.

Abdullah walks up to him. Charlie can't help but notice that his ghutra is askew.

"I have to deal with all sorts of scum in this job, Mr. Matthews. Killers, drug smugglers, adulterers," Abdullah says. "And the ones I always have the most contempt for are the ones who lie to me because all they do is waste my time. Nothing else changes. Not the verdict, nor in your case the eventual apprehension of your slut girlfriend."

One of the toughs walks over and hands Abdullah a bowl and a wooden spoon. In the bowl there seems to be some form of red paste. Abdullah stirs it.

"My wife, for some time now, has had a reputation for making one of the most potent chili pastes in the Kingdom."

Abdullah scoops a dollop onto the handle of spoon and brings it so close to Charlie's eyes that they sting. Charlie's breathing quickens.

"I could ask you a second time to give me the real name that Princess Noor is traveling under, but now I know your true character I have no faith you will. Instead, you have forced me to take you to a place where giving up that name is not a choice but a necessity."

Abdullah nods, and Charlie's pants and boxers are yanked down until they're bunched around his knees. Abdullah walks behind him. Charlie's heart begins to pound so fast he's certain he's going to have a heart attack.

"Please no, I beg you," Charlie screams

"You have no one to blame but yourself, Mr. Matthews," Abdullah says.

Charlie feels Abdullah's other hand part his butt cheeks. He kicks his legs violently. His right shoulder pops out of its socket, but he hardly cares.

Not this. Please not this.

From the front, the second tough grips his legs, and Abdullah rams the chili smeared handle up Charlie's rectum. Charlie screams his contortions so wild that the tough holding the chain loses his grip. Charlie tumbles to the floor and writhes around howling. It's as if someone is incinerating his insides with an oxyacetylene torch.

"Oh God, oh God, oh God," he screams.

Soon after he shits himself.

"What name is she traveling under, Mr. Matthews?" Abdullah says.

Charlie doesn't reply. Right now Abdullah might as well be in another universe. Abdullah shouts out something in Arabic. The chain clatters through the ring and soon enough Charlie is back hanging in the air like a bloody carcass in a slaughterhouse. Abdullah reappears.

"Come, Mr. Matthews, you know this torment will only get worse."

How could it possibly? Charlie thinks.

"Tell me the name and I promise to relieve your pain immediately."

Charlie gasps for air like a recently caught fish.

"Mr. Matthews?"

Abdullah stirs the bowl with the spoon handle.

Sarah McDowell, a voice in Charlie's head rings out. *Say it.*

Charlie shakes his head.

Abdullah rips off the bandage covering Charlie's right shoulder, and drives the paste covered spoon handle through his gunshot wound.

Charlie howls, his feet kicking wildly. This time the tough holds on. Charlie feels the tendons in his left shoulder rip. His body is like a war ravaged country. No part of it is unaffected.

"Tell me the name, Charlie," Abdullah says.

Tears stream down Charlie's cheeks. He knows there's no way he can endure any more of this.

"Sarah McDowell," he says.

"Spell it for me," Abdullah says.

Charlie does, one gasped letter after the next. Abdullah turns and leaves, and the tough, holding the chain, lets go. Charlie falls to the floor. Mercifully he blacks out.

***

NOOR SITS IN the darkened cabin. All around her passengers sleep. It's the last thing she's capable of doing. She is consumed with working out a way to save Charlie without endangering her son. She thinks about informing the American authorities of Charlie's predicament when the plane lands in New York, but she soon discounts the idea. She has no way of knowing if the Americans will protect her. More likely they'll return her to Saudi Arabia.

She stares down the aisle. A man rises from his seat and helps his four year old daughter towards the restroom. Noor thinks of her own father and tears spring in her eyes.

Oh Baba, what should I do?

She listens out for his warm voice but hears nothing. She feels utterly forsaken.

The man and little girl emerge from the restroom. The man is about to sit down when a three-year-old boy pops out. The man sighs and treks down the aisle with his other child.

Of course, Noor thinks. *Charlie's father. He has contacts in high places. After all look what he did for us back in Pakistan.*

Noor convinces herself that if she can get to him, he'll be able to protect Charlie.

A weary flight attendant comes down the aisle.

"Excuse me," Noor says. "How long is it until we land?"

The attendant glances at her watch.

"A little under three hours," the attendant says.

Noor grips the arms of her chair.

Please Allah, protect Charlie until then.

***

THE PHONE RINGS and pries Ivor out of a deep and blessed sleep. He looks at the alarm clock. Ten past five.

Jesus.

He's been asleep a little over two hours. He crawls across the hotel's mammoth bed and grabs the receiver.

"Yes," he says.

"We've located her, Mr. Gardener," the Prince says. "She's on a flight bound for New York."

"Congratulations, your Highness. I assume your people are in touch with ours."

"They are making the appropriate calls as we speak."

Ivor yawns.

"Then if you don't mind me asking, why are you calling me?"

"I was hoping you could liaise with your colleagues in the United States. Help make my wife's return as uncomplicated as possible."

"Of course, it'd be my pleasure," Ivor says.

Once I've had a good night's sleep.

"Good. One of my drivers is already at your hotel waiting to take you to the airport."

The Prince hangs up. Ivor stares at the phone.

Gracious as ever.

He swings his tired legs out of bed. In the corner a pile of crumpled clothes waits to be put on.

PART III

eternity

THIRTY-NINE

NOOR SITS UPRIGHT in her seat with her eyes closed. She knows it's absurd to be so terrified.

But what if the plane crashes, she thinks, *and I never get the chance to call Charlie's father.*

Noor feels a heavy bump and then a second, slighter one. A couple of passengers break out into applause. She breathes and cranes her neck forward to get a view out the window. In the distance the glittering lights of Manhattan beckon her like some magical kingdom. She grips her passport and customs form tightly in her hand.

There must be phones at the airport, she thinks.

The journey to their gate seems to take forever, and when the plane does arrive half the passengers jump up and occupy the aisles. Noor finds herself hemmed in.

"Excuse me ... I have a connection to make."

She turns and sees a burly, bearded man pushing his way down the aisle, a carry-on cradled in his arms like a new born child. He passes Noor's seat.

"Excuse me," he says.

Noor jumps up.

"I do too," she says waving her passport in the air.

She slips into the man's wake and sticks close as he blunders down the aisle. They arrive at the end of their section. A flight attendant puts out an arm. Better dressed passengers are coming from the other direction.

"I'm sorry, sir, but business and first have priority," the attendant says.

"That's bullshit," the man says, "I'm going to miss my flight."

The man moves to the right and the attendant steps sideways to block his path. A gap opens up. Noor sees her chance and bursts through.

"Ma'am," the flight attendant shouts.

Noor scrambles out the door and runs down the gangway. She enters the terminal building and sees a sign for immigration. She sprints down what seems like an endless passageway and weaves her way through the weary business class passengers ahead of her. She finally comes to a steep escalator. She plunges down it and arrives in a cavernous immigration hall. From another entrance she sees a multitude of college kids emerge.

Hurry.

She gets to the ropes before they do. To the left is the line for citizens and green card holders, to the right the one for visitors. She heads right only to stop in her tracks.

What are you thinking?

She turns back and winds her way around the snaking rope line until she gets to the front of the line. There are only a couple of passengers ahead of her.

Noor slows her breathing.

"Next."

Noor looks up. A mustached immigration officer beckons her over. She walks up to his booth and attempts a smile.

"Passport and customs form, please."

"Of course," she says.

She hands her documents over. The immigration officer flips to the back of the passport and enters her information into his computer.

"Where have you been?" he says.

"Dubai," she says.

"For work or pleasure."

"A little of both."

He taps more keys and peers at the screen. Noor fears it's flashing a warning to have her arrested. The officer holds out the passport and customs form.

"Welcome home," he says.

Noor stares at him.

"Ma'am, you're done," he says.

Noor jolts out of her daze and grabs her documents.

"Thank you," she says.

She heads towards the chain of baggage carousels, and winds her way through the obstacle course of passengers, carts and luggage. She joins a line making its way towards a couple of customs officers. Beyond is an exit with the words 'Welcome to New York' emblazoned above it. She can hardly believe it. She looks to her right. Some forlorn passengers are having their bags searched. She sees a door fly open. A customs official rushes out. She looks back and sees a couple of immigration officers pushing their way through the crowd. She spins back around.

"I'm sorry," she says to the family ahead of her. "I have a plane to catch."

She repeats the excuse all the way down the line and hands her form over to one of the officers. He frowns.

"No bags?" he says.

"They were stolen," she says.

She looks over her shoulder. The immigration officers have reached the end of the line.

"Sorry to hear that," the customs officer says.

He turns his attention to the next passenger. Noor keeps going. The exit gets ever closer.

Noor hears a shout. An immigration officer has spotted her. She runs around a corner and finds herself in the main terminal building. A line of people, three deep, wait behind a barrier for passengers to emerge. She see two Arabic men at the front of the line. One spots Noor and points her out to his friend.

Saudis.

She sprints for the exit. She almost barrels into a cop.

"Watch where you're going," he says.

Noor pays him no heed. She hears more raised voices. She reaches a revolving door and looks back. The cop has now joined the chase, the Arab men close behind him. She bursts into the warm, sticky air. Passengers are everywhere, as are yellow cabs, buses, and limos.

She stands there paralyzed.

Ahead a cab brakes as a pair of Japanese tourists cross in front of it. Its driver lays on the horn. She sprints over to the cab and wrests its door open. She dives into the backseat only to find a blonde haired man in a cream trench coat sitting there. Noor scrambles into the seat beside him and looks out the back window. The sidewalk is overflowing with law enforcement officers.

"Miss, please get out," the Pakistani driver says. "This not your ride."

"No it's all right," the man says. "I'm happy for her to ride with me."

"It cost you more."

"Fine."

The driver mutters a curse and accelerates away. Noor turns around.

"You are wanting to go to Manhattan, aren't you?" the man says.

"Yes," Noor says.

That's exactly where she wants to go.

***

IVOR BRINGS THE crystal glass to his lips and takes a hefty swig of his Coke. Outside the engines of the Saudi Royal 747 whir as a fiery sun rises over the airport and desert beyond. He lies on a bed in his own suite, his head propped up on a pair of soft pillows, a vase of fresh flowers on the side table beside him, a television playing CNN in the corner.

Fuck me if this isn't the life, he thinks.

There is a knock on the door.

"Come in," he says.

Abdullah enters. Ivor judges from the half drunk glass of whisky in his hand that the news isn't good.

"They missed her," Abdullah says. "How could they be so incompetent? We gave them a two and a half hour head start."

"So you did, but that was at three in the morning. The sleep deprived desk officer at the embassy first had to wake up Jimmy Davidson, a man notorious for putting five Jack Daniels away before hitting the hay, and by the time Jimmy had banished the cobwebs from his brain and worked out the right person to call in Washington at least forty-five minutes had passed and it was now eight forty-five at night on the East Coast. Who knows where that person might have been? Out to dinner, at a function, screwing his mistress. He wouldn't have been easy to get in touch with, that's for sure. So what, it takes another hour, perhaps even an hour and a half, to track him down, and then he has to work out who to call at JFK. That takes another half hour. They put an alert out and by the time it gets to the immigration officers at their desks the Emirates flight's landed and your girl has slipped through customs."

"They just missed her."

"There you go."

Abdullah collapses onto the couch and lights a cigarette. Ivor notices the swelling on his knuckles. He suspects Charlie Matthew's face came off a lot worse. The plane trundles down the runway and the fasten seat belt light chimes on. Both men ignore it.

"Don't get so depressed," Ivor says. "This is a good thing."

"Ever the American optimist," Abdullah says.

Abdullah slams back the rest of his whisky and presses a call button. A flight attendant appears with a bottle of thirty year old Glenfiddich and refills his glass.

"Think about it, she could have gotten there and applied for asylum. That would have been a fucking shit show. Lawyers, courts, the Princess' story slapped on the cover of the New York Post. Maybe you'd get her back, maybe you wouldn't but one thing's for sure it'd take years and be seriously embarrassing. This way, things can be done discreetly."

"She's disappeared."

"She's a twenty-two year old Afghan who's spent her whole life either in a refugee camp or behind the walls of a palace. She's not going to survive more than a day in New York."

"You really believe that?"

"You did your job, my friend. You got the name she's using. Now let us do ours."

The plane's wheels leave the tarmac, and the plane lumbers into the sky.

***

NOOR ENTERS THE man's apartment. Its wooden floors are

of the deepest, darkest wood. To the left is a tiny kitchen with gleaming aluminum appliances and beyond a spotless living room with a white L-shaped couch and a glass coffee table. Out the corner window, two soaring towers rise above a twinkling cityscape the likes of which she has never seen before. Noor turns. The man leans against the wall.

"This is very kind of you," she says. "The phone?"

"By the couch," he says. "Dial four, one, one. They should be able to get that number for you."

The man continues to stand there.

"Would you mind if I made the call in private?" Noor says.

"Of course not. Need anything I'll be in my room."

He slings his leather bag over his shoulder and enters a bedroom across the way. The door shuts behind him. Noor hurries to the phone and dials four, one, one.

"City and state please," a woman says.

"Excuse me?" Noor says.

"What's the city and state of the number you want?"

"That would be New York."

"New York's an awfully big place."

"Manhattan, I think. The name is Jeremy Matthews."

The woman types away.

"I've got four Jeremy Matthews in Manhattan. Think you could be more specific."

"I'm sorry, I can't."

"Then let me give em to you," the operator says.

Noor realizes she has nothing to write on.

"Would you mind holding while I get a pen?" she says.

The woman sighs.

"Hurry up."

Noor puts her passport down and scans the room looking for a paper and a pen. She sees neither. Then she remembers the tiny kitchen. She runs to it and there beside a block of knives is a pad and pen. She grabs them and runs back past the bedroom door. From within she can hear the sound of a shower running. She picks up the phone.

"Are you still there?" she says.

"Alive and well," the operator says.

"Oh, thank God."

The operator gives Noor the numbers and drops off the line. Noor dials the first. It rings and rings. She hangs up and tries the second. On the fourth ring a man answers.

"Excuse me, but I'm looking for the father of Charlie Matthews."

The line goes dead.

Come on, she tells herself, *keep going.*

She tries the third number and it goes to voicemail. She thinks of leaving a message but decides against it. She can always call back if the fourth number doesn't work out.

Oh Allah, please don't let that be the case.

She dials the fourth number. On the third ring, a woman answers.

"Hello," she says.

In the background, Noor hears a television playing; a late night show with a comedian telling jokes and an audience laughing.

"I do apologize for calling so late," Noor says, "but I'm looking for the father of Charlie Matthews."

The woman says nothing and if it weren't for a burst of applause from the television, Noor would guess she'd hung up.

"Who is this?" the woman says.

"My name is Noor Khan, I'm Charlie's fiancée."

The woman takes another moment to digest this.

"Would you mind calling back tomorrow?" she says. "Jeremy's fast asleep."

"I'm sorry, but it's an emergency. Charlie's life is in danger."

"In Belize?"

"No. In Saudi Arabia."

Once more there is silence.

"Hello?" Noor says.

"Give me a moment," the woman says. "I'll go wake him."

Noor waits. She wonders where Charlie is exactly and what condition he is in. Tears spring in her eyes.

Keep it together, she says to herself. *For his sake.*

"This is Jeremy Matthews," a man says on the other end of the line.

Noor is so relieved she fails to hear the shower turn off.

FORTY

NOOR SCREAMS, HER wrists cuffed to the bars of a hospital bed headrest, her feet in stirrups. The Prince waits between her parted legs, blood splattered all over his thobe. Expressionless doctors and nurses hover around her, but no one intervenes. Noor lets out one final, terrifying wail, and a child slithers into the Prince's waiting hands. A nurse hands the Prince a curved dagger, and he triumphantly cuts the umbilical cord. Noor leans forward, desperate to get a glimpse of her son, but rather than showing the infant to her, the Prince hands him to a nurse. He raises the dagger high over his head. Noor screams but there is nothing she can do. The Prince drives the dagger into her heart.

Charlie startles awake, his right wrist cuffed to the top bar of his cell door. The cuff is bearing the whole weight of his body and has dug deep into his flesh. It feels like his wrist is only moments away from being sliced off. He struggles to his feet and remembers once again why he allowed himself to hang there. The soles of his feet are so sensitive any contact with the floor sends spasms of pain racing up his legs.

He screams out to the guards for water but none come. They never have, even though he can sometimes hear their mumbled conversations down the hallway. He hangs there in the dark. Despite his dehydrated condition, tears stream down his cheeks.

How could I have given in so easily? he thinks. *Why didn't I hold out longer?*

"I'm sorry," he says. "I'm so sorry."

He hears footsteps. He dismisses them as a mind trick. A key unlocks the door, and he swings around as a couple of guards enter. One of them uncuffs his wrist. He's so grateful he wants to get down on his knees and kiss the man's feet. He never gets the chance. The other throws a black bag over his head and together they drag him down the cell block, his feet trailing behind him like bloody pieces of meat. They enter an elevator and he feels it rise. When its door opens, he is hit by a blast of heat.

I'm outside, he thinks.

They drag him through the dirt. Roasting sand particles penetrate the wounds on his feet. He wails in agony. The guards lift him up and throw him onto a cold metal floor. For a moment he thinks he's been placed in a freezer, but then he hears an engine turn.

I'm in a truck.

Lying there in the fetal position, he can't remember when he was last this comfortable. It is so beguiling he doesn't even think to wonder where they are taking him. He drifts off to sleep.

***

NOOR REPLACES THE receiver. There's nothing more she can do. It's now in Charlie's father's hands. She feels her head swoon and looks covetously at the couch.

Perhaps I could lie down a moment, she thinks.

Something inside her tells her it's best not to. She looks toward the bedroom door and trembles.

Get out of here, a voice warns her.

She creeps towards the front door only to realize that she's forgotten her passport. She spots it lying on the arm of the couch. She tiptoes back and retrieves it. The bedroom door opens, and she turns to find the blonde haired man standing there in a white towel. An unmistakable bulge pushes up against its front.

"All good?" he says.

Noor does her best to smile.

"Yes, thank you."

"You should take a shower. Nothing better after a long flight."

"That's very kind of you, but I really need to get going."

"Where you heading?"

"A hotel."

"No need. You can crash here."

"I'd prefer not to."

The man's smile fades.

"That's not very gracious considering I let you use my phone."

"I sincerely appreciate that, really I do."

Noor starts for the front door. The man edges into the center of the room and blocks her path.

"Now the way I see it," he says, "I've been good to you so it's time you were good to me. I promise, you'll enjoy it."

Noor picks up the phone.

"I'll call the police," she says.

"I bet you don't even know the number."

Noor's hand wavers. She doesn't. He smiles.

"You want to do this the easy way or the hard way?" he says.

"Do you promise to let me leave after that?" she says.

"I'll even give you forty bucks for a cab."

Noor nods. She feels her legs wobble.

Keep it together, she tells herself.

"Come on then," he says.

Noor walks into the bedroom. The man closes the door behind her. She can smell the lavender soap he just used. He lets his towel fall to the ground.

"Lie down," Noor says.

"Good girl," he says.

The man lies down on his floor bed. Noor kneels between his legs and takes his penis in her hands. He lets out a long sigh.

"You know you may be the most beautiful woman I've ever laid eyes on. Certainly the most beautiful I've ever shared a cab with."

Noor's hand wanders all the way to his balls. She feels the urge to vomit but instead she cups them and strokes them gently. He closes his eyes. A moan escapes from his lips.

Now.

Noor grips the man's balls and yanks her hand up as if she's lifting a heavy weight off the ground. The man howls. Noor jumps up and runs from the room. She slams the door behind her.

"Fuck, fuck, fuck," the man screams.

Noor sprints for the front door. Behind her she hears the bedroom door fly open.

"You fucking whore."

She reaches the door and scrambles to unlock it. She turns the handle but it won't open. A hand grabs hold of her hair and yanks her backwards. Her passport slips from her hand.

"There's two locks, you stupid bitch."

"Please," Noor screams. "I'm pregnant."

"Then I'm going to fuck that kid right out of you."

Noor tears her hair free and the momentum sends her tumbling onto the floor. The man aims a foot at her belly. Noor twists away and his foot slams into her right buttock.

Noor screams, and scuttles on her hands and knees into the kitchen. The man grabs hold of her hair once again and jerks her back up. She spies the wooden block and grabs the first knife her fingers encounter. He yanks her in the direction of his bedroom and the momentum twists her around. She plunges the knife's six inch blade into his gut. The man lets go of her hair and stares down at its hilt.

"What have you done?' he says.

He pulls the knife out. Blood streams from the wound. He staggers forward. Noor backs up against the counter. He keels over in front of her.

Noor leans against the counter and attempts to regain her breath. Shivering, she edges past his prostrate body and makes for the door. She locates the second lock and yanks the door open. She sprints along the corridor and down ten flights of stairs. She bursts into the lobby. The late night doorman looks up.

"Can I help you?" he says.

Noor shakes her head and runs out into the Manhattan night. It's only when she's four blocks away that she realizes her passport is back at the apartment.

FORTY-ONE

THE TRUCK BRAKES. Its engine turns off. Charlie has no clue where he is or how long he's been asleep. For all he knows the guards could have taken him a mile down the road or five hundred miles across the country.

He hears the doors creak open and two pairs of hands grab his legs. The guards haul him out of the vehicle, and then throw one of his arms over each of their shoulders. Charlie screams, the tendons in his right shoulder as useless as broken strings on a guitar. Like before, they carry him forward, his feet dragging uselessly behind him. They go from the heat of outdoors to the chill of indoors. He hears rustling and whinnying. Strands of straw stick to his bloodied feet.

I'm in a stable, he thinks.

The revelation disorients him.

Why on earth would they take me here?

Once more warm air bathes his body. The men come to a halt and push him down onto his knees. They pull his arms behind him and cuff his wrists. He hears others walking around, the murmurs of hushed conversation, another person being dragged in.

Noor?

His hood is ripped off his head. He finds himself in a flood lit riding paddock. It's enclosed by a circular two story building and has the look of an Elizabethan era theater. Malaya, Noor's Filipino maid, kneels across from him. He is so relieved she isn't Noor that he forgets to sympathize with the predicament she finds herself in.

Perhaps Noor escaped after all.

He can't help but laugh. The ten men who mill about look at him as if he's insane. They're dressed in thobes and ghutras, nine of them Arab, the tenth of African descent. Charlie recognizes him but for the life of him cannot recall from where. He cranes his neck upwards and gazes at the glittering array of stars above.

I must be in the desert, he thinks.

He drops his gaze and sees the African man swing his right arm around and around as if he were a baseball batsman limbering up. He now remembers where he last saw him: Chop-Chop square.

Charlie looks around frantically searching for a way to escape, but what little sense he has left tells him it's useless.

This is the end, Charlie Matthews, he tells himself. *Accept it.*

He starts to shake uncontrollably. Malaya, of all things, smiles at him.

"It's all right," she says, "God is with you."

"I don't believe in God," he says.

"But he believes in you and loves you."

Charlie finds himself nodding. He wonders if that is true. He stares up at the stars and searches out the formations his mother used to take delight in pointing out. The upward curve of Orion's Belt, the plough shaped Big Dipper.

"Are you there, Mom?" he whispers.

He hears a door open and snaps his gaze back down. He recognizes the pudgy man approaching him. The Prince. How many times has he looked at his photo and vowed revenge? The Prince ambles over.

"So you're the one who's brought me so much trouble," he says.

"Please don't do this," Charlie says.

"Nothing can prevent your fate."

"Then at least spare her."

The Prince shakes his head.

"Unfortunately I'm not in a forgiving mood at present."

The Prince turns towards the African executioner.

"Execute the woman," he says.

The African walks over to a table with a white tablecloth spread on top of it and retrieves his curved, shining sword.

Charlie catches Malaya's eye.

"I'm so sorry," he says.

"Don't be," she says. "I'm going home to my Lord and Savior."

The executioner comes up behind Malaya and assumes the wide legged stance that so intrigued Charlie back in Chop Chop Square. Malaya drops her head and closes her eyes.

"Our Father," she says, "who art in heaven hallowed be thy name."

Charlie finds himself reciting the prayer along with her.

"Thy Kingdom come ..."

The executioner brings the sword down and touches the nape of Malaya's neck. Instinctively her neck jerks upwards.

"Thy will be done on earth as it is ..."

In one lightning stroke the executioner whips the sword up and back down. Charlie clenches his eyes and hears the dull thump of Malaya's head hitting the dirt floor. Moments later her body topples over as well. Charlie's heart pounds at a speed he's never experienced before, not even when Abdullah defiled him in the torture room. It's as if his heart is trying to take as many final beats in as it can before it too is put to rest.

"Mr. Matthews."

Charlie opens his eyes and gasps. The Prince is holding Malaya's head. Her eyes are still open, her mouth agape and blood drips from her cleaved neck like rain off a gutterless roof.

"I wanted you to see this," the Prince says. "For this will not only be your fate but Noor's once my son is born."

Charlie stares up at him.

"We caught her," the Prince says. "The moment she stepped off the plane in New York."

"No," Charlie says. "They would never send her back."

"If you think that then you're utterly ignorant of the special relationship our government has with yours."

The Prince tosses Malaya's head on the ground and steps back.

"Execute him," he says.

Charlie twists his head from side to side and locates the executioner cleaning Malaya's blood off his sword with a white cloth. The executioner wanders in his direction. He nods at Charlie as if to indicate that Charlie has his respect and compassion.

Run, a voice screams in Charlie's head, but Charlie finds his legs are utterly paralyzed.

Behind him the executioner's feet shuffle in the dirt. Charlie raises his eyes to the heavens and awaits the touch of the blade to his neck.

"God, please forgive me for all that I've done," he says.

He hears a door burst open, and a man shouts out something in Arabic. Charlie lowers his gaze and sees a man approach the Prince with a satellite phone. The Prince holds it to his ear. A heated conversation ensues. The Prince throws the phone into the dirt and storms away. The executioner walks past Charlie, his sword hanging loosely by his side.

"What happened?" Charlie says.

The executioner turns back.

"The Crown Prince," he says. "He halted execution. But

who knows, maybe, you and me, we meet again soon perhaps."

The executioner strolls away. Charlie collapses onto the ground, and lies there next to Malaya's headless corpse.

FORTY-TWO

IVOR AND ABDULLAH step off the plane. Ivor sees a young, fresh faced agency employee waiting for them in the gangway. Her pant suit is neat and pressed, her hair short of shoulder length. He likes the look of her.

Perhaps I'll bang her if I have time, he thinks.

"Welcome to New York, sir," she says. "My name's Megan Windsor."

Ivor and Abdullah keep walking. Megan hustles to keep up.

"What you got, Windsor?" Ivor says.

"Princess Noor called Charlie Matthews' father at eleven forty-nine last night and informed him of his son's circumstances."

"Let me guess, Daddy's been freaking out ever since."

"He seems to be very well connected. The Under Secretary of State for Near Eastern Affairs called her counterpart in Riyadh a couple hours ago and told him the U.S. government was aware of Charlie Matthews' apprehension."

Ivor stops at the entrance to the private terminal building and catches Abdullah's eye.

"I guess Charlie Matthews exists after all."

Abdullah shows no other reaction than to light a cigarette. Ivor turns back to Megan.

"Where did the target make the call from?" he says.

"A Midtown apartment owned by a certain Stephen Erickson. Deceased."

Ivor raises an eyebrow.

"Sarah McDowell, her alias, is the main suspect in his murder."

***

NOOR SPOTS THE N.Y.P.D. officer strolling down the path and lowers her head. In her imagining every cop in the city is on the look out for her. The officer passes by and she breathes a little easier.

How did it come to this? she thinks. *It's a nightmare that only keeps getting worse.*

For hours after escaping the man's apartment, Noor had roamed the city in a daze. She had stumbled down canyons of impossibly high buildings, meandered through the late night crowds in Times Square, wandered past steaming street vents and garish sex shops outside of which drunken young men would hoot and holler at her. It was as alien an environment as she'd ever been in and as the hour got later it had taken on an almost ghostly quality with only haggard beggars, lonely yellow cabs and the odd police cruiser left for company.

Perhaps this is what purgatory looks like, she'd thought.

Whenever she had seen a police car she would shrink into the shadows of an apartment entrance or scurry behind the nearest phone booth or trash can. She felt like a hunted animal, her pursuers invisible and demonic. And then the sun's rays had begun to leak into the sky and the city had begun to hum again. The morning rush hour had overwhelmed her and it was only by luck she had happened upon Central Park and this pond on which elderly men were sailing model boats. She had collapsed onto this bench, and, for a while, the trees and the water, the chirps of birds and the circuitous routes of the boats had calmed her nerves. The rapidly warming air had enveloped her like a blanket, and she had dozed off only to be jolted out of her slumbers by the incessant flapping of wings. She had opened her eyes to discover an elderly woman with jet black hair sitting beside her. The woman was throwing out bread from a large paper bag into a sea of jostling pigeons.

I have to get out of this city, she tells herself.

Yet she has no idea where to go. Even if she did, she has no way of getting there. Whatever money she had was tucked inside her passport.

I need help, she tells herself.

The only person she knows who might offer it is Charlie's father.

Yet to contact him, I need money.

She turns towards the elderly woman. Noor's stomach rumbles. If it weren't so odd, she would ask for a few pieces of stale bread for herself.

"Excuse me," Noor says.

"This my bench," the woman says in a heavy European accent. "Been coming every day for last ten years."

"No, I didn't mean it like that. I'm happy you're sitting beside me. Truly I am."

The woman stops throwing out bread and screws up her eyes.

"You Indian?" she says.

"Afghan."

The woman nods.

"Jewish, myself. From Soviet Union originally. Terrible shame what happened to your country."

"Yes it is."

"But now you here," she says. "Better times ahead, no?"

The woman pats Noor on the leg.

"I predict a bright future for you and your daughter."

"That's very kind of you," Noor says, "but I'm having a son."

The woman shakes her head.

"No, you carry high. You wait see. You are having girl."

***

"I GUESS, BY now, you're aware of the trouble your son's in," Ivor says.

"Not exactly," Jeremy Matthews says. "My contacts at the State Department are still trying to ascertain what Charlie's been charged with."

"Let me enlighten you."

Ivor takes a sip of his coffee and sizes up Jeremy Matthews. He sits with his left foot perched on the right knee of a four thousand dollar suit, his perfectly put together and decidedly younger wife beside him, her right hand, with its hundred thousand dollar Cartier watch hanging from its wrist, entwined in his. Behind them is a four million dollar view of Central Park basking in the late morning sun.

Fuck I hate bankers, Ivor thinks. *They always act like you're beholden to them.*

He puts his coffee cup down on a book about Tuscan gardens. The wife can't help but wince.

"The first charge is that your son entered Saudi Arabia illegally."

"I'm sure that's something we can clear up with the appropriate authorities," Jeremy Matthews says.

"It carries a mandatory ten year sentence."

Jeremy Matthews tries his best to maintain his composed and serious expression.

"The second charge is that your son ran a drug smuggling operation. A sophisticated one from what I hear. The sentence for that is death by beheading."

Jeremy Matthews blanches. His wife gasps, a little too theatrically for Ivor's liking. He suspects her stepson's death would not grieve her severely.

"That's impossible," Jeremy Matthews says. "He went to Riyadh to save Noor."

"That what she told you, is it?"

"Amongst other things."

Ah, look at you, Ivor thinks. *Trying to pretend you have information that I don't.*

Ivor picks up the manila envelope he brought with him and wanders over to the window. He looks out over the seemingly endless canopy of trees, and can't help but hate Jeremy Matthews even more.

What a pad.

He turns back.

"Did it ever occur to you, Mr. Matthews, that Noor Khan and your son could be knee deep in this little drug smuggling operation together?"

"That makes no sense."

"Why? Because she's from Afghanistan, the world's number one supplier of heroin. Or perhaps because she's the lead suspect in last night's murder of Stephan Erickson."

Ivor pulls an eight by ten photo of Stephen Erickson's bloody corpse from the envelope and tosses it onto the coffee table. The wife gasps. This time it sounds genuine. It pleases Ivor no end.

"I have one piece of good news for you, Mr. Matthews."

Jeremy Matthews looks up in desperate hope.

"The Saudis are more interested in prosecuting this woman than they are your son. If we were able to deliver her to them, my contacts have assured me that the Crown Prince will commute any death sentence your son receives."

Jeremy Matthews swallows.

"What do you need me to do?" he says.

***

NOOR STANDS AT the pay phone with the dead receiver in her hand. She can't believe how little time seventy-five cents had bought her. She castigates herself for not asking the old woman for more money.

It's okay, she tells herself, *you have his address. That's all you need.*

She looks around and sees a hot dog stand next to the park. She walks over and asks the seller for directions to Tribeca.

"You taking the subway?" he says.

"No, I'm going to walk," she says.

He looks at her as if she's insane and points down the street.

"Head down Fifth Avenue," he says. "When it ends ask someone else."

Noor works her way past an endless torrent of pedestrians and can't help but marvel at the women. Here they are dressed in clothes that in Peshawar or Riyadh would stir up a lynch mob. T-shirts and jeans, shorts and tank tops, sleeveless dresses, thigh high skirts, and knee length business skirts. Some women are more conservatively dressed, she even sees a couple wearing abayas, but what strikes her is that it's up to these women what they wear and where they go. Most are unaccompanied with no need for a man to 'protect their honor'. They can go where they wish and do what they want. No restaurant, store or public place is off limits to them, and nor seemingly is any job. There are female businesswomen, bus drivers, store assistants and waitresses; even female cops. Despite the suffocating heat, or partially because of it, she feels giddy.

This is freedom, she thinks.

It takes her an hour to make her way down Fifth Avenue and by the time she reaches the arch at Washington Square Park her clothes are drenched in sweat and her throat is as rough as sandpaper. She spies a fountain at its center in which a multitude of children are playing. She wades into it and drenches her head and neck in its cool waters. She cups its precious liquid into her mouth. A couple of mothers gape at her.

Oh, if only you knew the quality of water we drank in the camps, she thinks.

Noor goes over to one of them and asks directions. That mother becomes only the first of many people she has to ask. No longer are the streets simply numbers that can be easily followed and nor are they laid out in a simple north, south, east, west grid. On a couple of occasions, she's even told that she's walking in totally the wrong direction.

But I'm almost there now, she thinks.

She's on the correct street. She takes shelter from the relentless sun under a convenience store awning and asks its South Asian owner how much further she has to go. He tells her Jeremy Matthew's apartment is only a couple more blocks.

Thank God.

"Are you Pakistani?" the store owner says.

"Afghan," she says, "but I used to live in Peshawar."

The man grins.

"Me too," he says switching to Pashtu. "Until five years ago that was my home."

Noor nods too exhausted to speak.

"Would you like a drink?" he says.

"I couldn't possibly," she says.

"Please, I insist."

The store owner disappears inside, and Noor decides to wait. Without some fluids inside her she's beginning to doubt she'll make the final couple of hundred yards. She stares down the street at the brownstone warehouses. Over half of them seem to be in the process of being renovated. Scaffolding clings to their sides and metal garbage bins dot the street.

The Pakistani store owner returns with an ice cold can of Coke.

"Here," he says.

She rips off the ring pull and guzzles down its contents. Few things have ever tasted so good.

"You're a savior," she says. "I've walked a long way."

"Why? Who are you here to see?"

She notices a group of twenty somethings in baggy jeans exit one of the buildings.

"Do rich people live down here?" she says.

"Not many. Mainly artists, students, those kind of people. The rich live up there."

The man points north, in the direction she's just come.

"How about lawyers?" she says.

"Do you see any?" he grins.

Noor feels queasy and steps further into the shade. That hopeful call she'd had with Charlie's father has taken on a more sinister tone. Now his manner feels too eager, especially when she remembers how brusque he was the previous night. When her money had started running out she had asked for his address, and there had been a significant pause before he gave it to her.

Shouldn't he have been able to rattle it off immediately? she wonders.

Despite the heat, she can't help but shiver.

"Would you mind if I used your phone?" she asks the store owner.

"It would be my honor," he says.

He leads her inside his store and over to the cash register. Beside it is a notary phone and a small television playing CNN.

"Take all the time you need," he says.

He busies himself rearranging a shelf stacked with bags of chips. Noor dials 411. She asks for Jeremy Matthews, but this time she asks for his address as well. The operator says it's on Central Park West.

"Is that near Central Park?" she asks.

"What do you think, honey?" the operator says. "Now do you want me to put you through or not?"

"That's all right thank you."

Noor replaces the receiver.

He set me up, she thinks.

The store owner gives her a friendly smile.

What now? I have no one left.

Noor glances at the television. George H Bush, the American president, is speaking at a United Nations Conference in Rio.

A thought strikes her.

"Excuse me," she says. "How would I get to the United Nations?"

"It is uptown," the store owner says. "On the east side."

"Thank you. Really, thank you for everything."

She heads for the door.

"Miss," the store owner says.

She looks back. He holds out a ten dollar bill.

"You should take the subway. It's much quicker."

"I couldn't," she says, "you've already been too generous."

He opens a fridge and takes out another Coke. He places the can and ten dollar bill in her hands.

"You know, as well as I do, that a Pashtun is honor bound to look after another. Now go and may Allah protect you."

"Thank you," she says. "I'll never forget your generosity."

She walks out of the store and looks in the direction she'd been heading. She shivers and walks the other way.

***

IVOR WANDERS BACK into the vacant living room of the brand new condo. He finds Abdullah looking grimly out the window.

"I told you we should have done this at Matthew's father's apartment," Abdullah says.

"He wouldn't go for it, his kids were on their way home from school."

Abdullah shakes his head as if he would never brook such niceties in Saudi Arabia. Behind him, the couple of toughs he brought with him pack up their restraining gear.

"Something must have spooked her," Ivor says.

"Perhaps she saw your men out front."

"No, she's jittery."

One of the toughs places a long needled syringe back in its leather case.

"Has every reason to be," Ivor says.

Abdullah lights what must be his twentieth cigarette of the last three hours.

"So what now?" he says.

"We wait for her to contact his father again."

"And if she doesn't?"

"She'll pop up sooner or later. She has no one else to turn to."

"Perhaps the N.Y.P.D. could circulate her photo as part of their murder investigation."

Ivor shakes his head.

"Once her photo gets out there, her fate becomes en-twined with the U.S. justice system. No, we're going to do exactly the opposite. Take possession of her passport, say it's a matter of national security."

"Then wait and see."

"Exactly. Wait and see."

"The Prince will be enthralled to learn that's our strategy."

Abdullah drops his cigarette onto the brand new wooden floor and grinds it out.

"Call me if there are any new developments," he says.

He and the toughs leave the apartment. Ivor sighs. He looks at his watch. Five past four.

What now?

He feels horny. Megan Windsor's a no go. A lesbian, he had learned earlier to his chagrin.

Like every bitch at the C.I.A.

He thinks of hiring an escort. Put it down as a miscellaneous cash expense. But then a thought strikes him.

Shit that could be a lot more fun.

FORTY-THREE

CHARLIE STARES AT his battered face in the two way mirror. His nose is puffy and red, the area under his eyes purple. One of his ears is swollen and his cheek has a garish red line zigzagging diagonally down it. It's nothing compared to how he looked a couple of hours earlier.

When he had first gotten here they had wheeled him into the medical wing where a doctor had reset his broken nose, stitched up his lacerated cheek, and placed his useless right arm in a sling. They had then dressed him in a long sleeved white t-shirt and a pair of loose cotton pants and brought him to this interview room. He wonders what sadistic bastard wants to meet him now.

The door opens and a balding man in a wrinkled suit enters. He takes one look at Charlie and winces. A guard closes the door behind him.

"Good evening, Mr. Matthews. My name is Gavin Seaberry. I'm with the consular section of the U.S. Embassy."

Seaberry sits across from Charlie. He opens his briefcase and extracts a pen and a pad of paper.

"It's evening?" Charlie says.

Seaberry glances at his watch.

"It's five past midnight so I suppose technically it's morning."

"On what day?"

"The thirteenth of June, well actually the fourteenth, but that's not important, what is, is the situation you find yourself in right now."

Charlie leans forward.

"There is a woman named Noor Khan," he says. "She flew to the United States from Dubai on an Emirates Airlines flight under the alias, Sarah McDowell. She may still be in the U.S., at J.F.K. to be exact. You need to track her down and protect her before the Saudis return her to this country."

"Mr. Matthews, I have no information regarding this woman."

"Then listen. Go on, write it down. The woman's name is Noor Khan and she is traveling under the alias Sarah McDowell. You need to get back to the embassy and put out an alert. The Saudi are trying to kidnap her, and bring her back here against her will."

"Mr. Matthews—"

"God damn it," Charlie shouts, "put out an alert."

The door swings open, and the guard enters, his hand on his baton.

"It's okay," Seaberry says, "I've got this."

The guard seems unsure.

"Really. I've got this," Seaberry says.

The guard nods and closes the door. Seaberry turns back around.

"Mr. Matthews, I'm sorry but there's nothing I can do for Miss Khan. The particulars of my job are that I'm here to help U.S. citizens in need."

Charlie stares blankly back at him.

It's over. I failed her. Her fate is sealed.

"Now, from what the Saudis tell me," Seaberry says, "your wounds arose when you resisted arrest. Is that correct?"

Charlie looks past Seaberry and into the mirror. He no longer recognizes the man looking back at him.

"Mr. Matthews, are you aware of the charges against you? That you were the mastermind of an extensive drug smuggling operation here in the Kingdom?"

"If they want me to confess, I will," Charlie says.

"I would not advise that, Mr. Matthews. The charges carry the death penalty."

"That's okay."

Seaberry puts down his pen.

"You don't care if you die?" he says.

"No. In fact I'd prefer to."

***

TARIQ SITS ALONE in the Prince's vast reception room. He feels like a shipwrecked man adrift in an ocean. He can't help but remember the better times he's spent here. The evening the Prince told him Noor was pregnant, the time the Prince asked if he would marry his sister.

How close I came to being a part of his family, he thinks.

Tears of frustration rise up. Tariq forces them back down. The last thing he wants is for the Prince to see him crying. No, he needs to appear composed, and, when the Prince offers him the post in Khartoum, he must accept it with appreciation.

As Ivor said, you can recover from this.

The doors swing open and the Prince sweeps in with his retinue. Tariq jumps to his feet and looks for a sign as to the Prince's mood. It's impossible. The Prince's expression is impassive.

"Your Highness," Tariq says.

The Prince carries on past Tariq and slumps into his chair. A servant comes racing over with a glass of water. Tariq stands there paralyzed. He doesn't know whether to sit or remain standing.

"Are you aware of anyone your sister might know in New York other than Charlie Matthew's father?"

"No," Tariq says.

"I'd appreciate it if you gave my question more than a moment's thought."

Tariq wracks his brain. The only thing that comes to mind is that Noor's yet to be found.

How's that possible?

"Well," the Prince snaps.

"I'm sorry," Tariq says.

"Not a family member, a friend from her past perhaps."

"No, not that I can think of."

"Then you're useless to me."

The Prince takes a sip of his water, and Tariq notices the glass shake. Tariq braces himself. The Prince throws the glass across the room and jumps to his feet. He marches up to Tariq and wags his finger in Tariq's face, his own getting redder by the second.

"She has my son," the Prince screams. "My only son, and you stand there like I should accept it."

"You'll find her. I know it."

"That's what everyone says, yet somehow she keeps slipping through my fingers. Tell me, what did I ever do to her to make her hate me so? If I remember rightly I dragged her from a stinking hole and gave her unimaginable riches. She should be on her knees every day thanking Allah for her good fortune."

The Prince waves his hand.

"Go," he says. "I'm done with you."

Tariq scurries as fast as he can for the door.

"Wait," the Prince says.

Tariq freezes.

So this is it, he thinks.

Tariq turns to face the Prince.

"I want you to go to Khartoum," the Prince says. "Not for a visit, but permanently. You will be my eyes and ears over there."

Tariq forces a smile.

"I would be honored, your Highness."

The Prince frowns.

"Nothing's more important to me than the prosecution of the holy jihad," Tariq says.

"For me either," the Prince says. "It's why I thought you'd be pleased."

Tears rise once more in Tariq's eyes, and this time he doesn't fight them back.

"I want you to know, your Highness, how ashamed I am by my sister's actions. How much she has dishonored me. She has acted with nothing but malice. Above all she's wounded someone I respect and love deeply."

Tears well in the Prince's eyes. He begins to sob.

"She has my son, Tariq. My unborn son."

"You will find her, inshallah, I know you will."

The Prince can do no more than nod.

"You have been too kind to me," Tariq says. "I know you considered sending me back to Pakistan, and you had every right to, but I'm going to prove my loyalty to you in Khartoum, I promise."

The Prince reaches out a hand, and Tariq runs over and kneels down to kiss it. The Prince lifts his chin up. Tariq stares into his benefactor's eyes.

"Despite everything," the Prince says, "I don't blame you. You saved my life, not once but on two occasions. I could never send you back to Pakistan."

"Ever?"

"It's never once crossed my mind."

The Prince stands, and Tariq staggers to his feet. The Prince embraces him.

"Have a safe journey, my friend," the Prince says.

The Prince returns to his chair and gestures for one of his retainers to come over. Tariq turns and walks unsteadily down the length of the room. The more his mind clears, the more he realizes Ivor manipulated the Prince into sending him to Khartoum.

But for Ivor, I'd be staying in Saudi Arabia.

At the far end of the room, two servants open the doors. Tariq passes through them into the entry hall. He turns back. The Prince is in deep discussion with a couple of advisors. The doors close, and Tariq finds himself shut out of the Prince's world.

FORTY-FOUR

ELMA LEANS BACK in her chair and casts an eye at the muted television across from her. C.N.N. is doing yet another report on President Bush's speech at the Rio summit. In fact bulletins from the Earth Summit seem to be the only thing C.N.N. has been broadcasting all day; that and footage of some forest fire in Oregon. A perversely appropriate bedfellow, she can't help but think.

I should have gone, Elma tells herself.

It's not like she couldn't have finagled the trip with the slightest bit of effort. Half the building seemed to be there. The networking opportunities alone would have made the eight hour flight worth it. But she hasn't. In fact since coming to New York she hasn't done much of anything, and she knows perfectly well why.

She gets up from her desk and walks to her window. She stares out across the East River at the hulking 59th Street Bridge and the borough of Queens beyond. The river's murky gray surface matches the ominous sky.

What people would give for this view, for my title, for this job, she thinks. *Yet how many would have done what I did to get it?*

At night when she's finally able to fall asleep they visit her. Noor. Charlie. But most of all Aamir Khan. It's strange she

only met him once; that day at the camp when he had been
so eager to impress her and Rod. Yet, she remembers him
like she might a childhood friend, sitting there in his worn
blazer and frayed shalwar kameez. The surprising part is that
he doesn't reproach her for his death. If anything, his kind
eyes offer up forgiveness, and that, in itself, is almost crueler
for she knows she doesn't deserve it. What she deserves is
someone to damn her, the way Charlie had that day he had
stormed into her bedroom.

*But no one will, because no one knows. I'm free to continue my life,
yet somehow I can't.*

She returns to her computer and opens her resignation
letter. She presses print, and her printer whines to life. Elma
pulls out the letter and reads it over. It's short and to the
point. Her boss will accept it. In the last month it's become
clear he regrets ever appointing her, for once you get a job at
the U.N. it's almost impossible to be fired from it. She
wonders if he will smile on reading it. She doesn't care. She
unscrews the top from her fountain pen and signs it with a
flourish. She looks at the clock in the top right corner of her
computer screen. Four forty-five. Time to go. She can hand
the letter to his assistant on the way out. She grabs her purse.

Her phone rings. She stares at it.

Why bother?

She picks it up. Old habits die hard.

"Miss Kuyt, this is security. I have a Noor Khan here. Says
she's here to see you."

Elma doesn't say anything. Someone must be pulling a
practical joke on her, yet she can't fathom who.

"Miss Kuyt?"

"Are you sure?" she says.

"What's your name again?" the security guard says.

"Noor Khan," a woman says.

It's like hearing the voice of a ghost.

"Miss Kuyt?" the security guard says. "Miss Kuyt?"

"I'll be right down," Elma says.

***

ELMA IS UNABLE to hold back her tears for what must be the tenth time since they've been reunited.

"You can't know how sorry I am," she says.

Elma's nose runs. She wipes it with her sleeve.

"After Charlie came by my house, I begged Ivor to intervene. He said it was too late, that you were already on your way to Saudi Arabia, but he did go looking for Charlie. I do believe he saved his life."

"The Quran says that for anyone who saves a life, it's as if they saved the life of all humanity," Noor says.

"But I was responsible for your father's death."

And Mukhtar's, Noor thinks, yet she leaves it unsaid.

Elma's tears continue to fall. Noor sits down beside her on her living room couch. Elma buries her head in Noor's chest and sobs.

"One of the things I've learnt these last few months," Noor says, "is that since you cannot change the past, you need to make the most of the circumstances you are in, even if those circumstances are for the most part miserable."

Noor raises Elma's chin off her breast and gazes into her reddened eyes.

"I forgave you a long time ago, Elma. I know my father up in heaven has also. What we need now is to find me and my child a safe place to live. Somewhere far from New York."

"I could apply for asylum for you through the U.N."

"And allow the Saudis to know my location. No. Never."

Elma nods. She stands up and wanders over to the window as if scanning the whole of the United States for a suitable location.

"There is a place, a small town in the mountains of North Carolina, where I went for a wedding once. We could rent you a house there."

"Won't I stand out?"

"Better that than going somewhere where there are a lot of Pakistanis and Afghans. They'll ask questions whose answers you'll find a lot harder to make up."

"In North Carolina I could pretend to be Indian."

"Exactly. It will be the last place the Saudis will think to look."

North Carolina. It feels almost serendipitous.

All those years Baba had wished he'd taken us there, and now I'm going.

"Let's do it," Noor says.

Elma beams, and for the first time since they were re-united in the lobby of the United Nations, the driven and dynamic Elma, Noor remembers so well, returns.

"What do you think will happen to Charlie?" Noor says.

"Honestly I don't know. What I do know is you've done all you can. Charlie's father is in a far better position to help him than you are."

"His father betrayed me."

"To me that shows the lengths he'll go to save his son."

"So I do nothing?"

"You do what Charlie wants you to do. You find a place to hide."

Noor nods, yet she can't help but feel she's let Charlie down.

There was nothing he wouldn't do for me, she thinks, *yet I've done almost nothing for him.*

"I'm going to freshen up," Elma says. "My make-up's a mess."

Noor does her best to smile. Elma heads for the door only to turn back.

"I forgot to tell you," Elma says. "Before I left Peshawar, I found Wali a job with the Red Crescent; as a manager in their rehabilitation program."

"Have you heard from him since?" Noor says, her spirits lifting.

"Almost too often," Elma laughs. "He writes once a week."

"Would you mind if I read his letters?"

"Of course not. Let me go look them out. In the last one, he wrote that your sister was expecting."

Noor shrieks in delight. Elma smiles.

"I'll be right back," she says.

Elma leaves. Noor allows herself to indulge in a little day dreaming. She thinks of the house that Bushra and Wali must be living in. It will be comfortable; managers at the Red Crescent, even the local ones, make a good living. Bushra will have made it her own, cooking for her beloved husband during the day and lavishing attention on him at night. Noor wonders whether Wali has been able to extract Bushra further from her shell. What he had achieved before she and Bushra had been torn apart was almost miraculous. At times, Noor imagines, Wali making Bushra laugh while at other times he embarrasses her. Bushra will reproach him and with that puppy dog expression he'll promise to never do so again, but of course he will. They will have friends. Wali makes at least two new ones a day, and he will invite them over for hearty feasts. There will be sadness, no doubt. Remembrances of Baba, Noor and Charlie, but if Wali has one quality it's that he doesn't wallow. People must be remembered but one's life still has to be lived. Losing his legs didn't rid him of his *joie de vivre* and losing them won't have either. Their child will be doted on. She suspects Aamir will be his name if he is a boy, and Noor if she is a girl. Her sister's life will be complete.

Noor rubs her belly.

"In Peshawar," she says, "you have a cousin. Someone you'll forever be connected to."

And in that moment Noor resolves to call her unborn son Charlie. In her mind there could be no higher honor.

Noor wanders the short distance to Elma's open kitchen and finds a glass. She still can't get over the fact that in a city so rich, the apartments are so small. Down the hallway she hears a shower running. Elma is clearly doing a little more than freshening up. Noor pours herself a glass of water and is halfway through drinking it when she hears the door bell ring.

She freezes.

In the bathroom the shower keeps running.

The doorbell rings again.

Noor finds herself drawn out of the room and into the foyer. She thinks of shouting out to Elma but then thinks better of it. Elma wouldn't hear her anyway. She puts her eye up against the peephole and gasps. Ivor Gardener stands on the other side.

Elma's betrayed me. Again.

She spins around. Elma is behind her in a bathrobe.

The doorbell rings again, and Noor looks towards the door. The only option she has is to throw it open and run past Ivor.

"Elma, I know you're there," Ivor says. "I saw you at the door."

Noor feels a hand on her arm and whips around.

"Go. Hide," Elma hisses.

She points towards the bathroom door.

"Give me a moment," Elma shouts out. "I just got out of the shower."

Elma gives Noor a gentle push to set her on her way.

"Sure thing," Ivor says, "take your time."

Noor scurries to the bathroom and closes the door behind her. She places her ear to the door. She hears the lock turn, and Ivor enter.

"Hoped I'd find you home," Ivor says.

"How did you know where I live?" Elma says.

"Come on, Elma, I work for the C.I.A. How do you think?"

"Well you've come at a bad time. I'm on my way out."

"Where to?"

"That should be of no interest to you."

"It's of great interest to me. I was hoping to take you out."

"Sorry but someone got there ahead of you."

"So it's a date?"

Elma sighs.

"Yes, Ivor, it's a date."

"Who with?"

"Jesus, Ivor.

"Just a friendly question."

"We're not friends."

"As far as I remember, we were much more than friends."

"Fucking you was the biggest regret of my life ... only exceeded by what you made me do to that poor girl."

"Christ, you still cut up about that?"

"It was very wrong."

Ivor chuckles.

"I forgot you're one of those bleeding hearts. If it's any consolation I hear she's having a ball in Saudi, even has a son on the way, can you believe? Prince's tickled pink and treats her like a princess, which is kinda ironic since that's exactly what she is."

"Bullshit," Elma snaps.

No one says anything. Even from behind the door, Noor can detect a shift in the atmosphere.

"Why? You have better information than I do?" Ivor says.

"No ... no, of course I don't," Elma says, sounding flustered.

Noor searches the tiny bathroom for a weapon. There's nothing deadlier than a tooth brush.

"Sounds to me like you do," Ivor says. "She been in touch with you lately?"

"Of course not," Elma says. "I just know his reputation. Everyone in Peshawar did. For fuck's sake, Ivor, his last wife committed suicide because he beat her so much."

"Men change their spots."

"No, they don't."

"Oh yeah, I forgot, you've never liked men. Not since that teacher of yours banged you up."

"You should leave, Ivor."

"No date then?"

"Get out."

"Let me take a leak and I'll be out of your way."

Ivor heads down the hall.

"Ivor," Elma shouts after him.

"Sorry," Ivor says, "but your boyfriend's gonna have to wait a couple more minutes for his blow job."

Noor twists around and looks for a place to hide. She spies the steamed up shower. Noor pulls the door open and closes it behind her. She drops down on the shower floor. The bathroom door opens. Ivor's shadow appears on the other side of the glass. He pisses with his back to her. Noor stares at the glass in horror. With every passing second the condensation is fading. Ivor pisses against the toilet seat and onto the floor.

"Shit," he says.

He pulls on the toilet roll dispenser and bends down to wipe it up. Noor holds her breath.

Ivor straightens and chucks the toilet paper in the bowl. The toilet flushes and he disappears.

"I'm telling you, we could have a lot of fun," Noor hears him say.

"Goodbye, Ivor," Elma says.

The front door slams shut. Not long after Elma opens the shower door. She collapses on the tiled floor beside Noor, and together the two women sit there, utterly drained.

FORTY-FIVE

CHARLIE'S BEEN HERE before. A nondescript room with two chairs and a formica desk, a ceiling with a metal ring in it and a varnished cement floor. He hears footsteps coming down the hallway. He shivers.

Here we go again, he thinks.

The door opens and a younger interrogator enters with two new muscled goons. Unlike Abdullah, this guy wears Western dress, an open collared white shirt tucked into a pair of tailored suit pants. It reminds Charlie of what the young executives at his father's bank used to wear on casual Fridays. Charlie wonders where Abdullah has gotten to.

Now they've captured Noor, onto bigger and better things, he suspects.

The interrogator grabs a chair and sits behind the desk. He finds a pad of paper and looks at his watch. He writes down the date and time. He might as well be interviewing Charlie for a job. The two goons lean against the wall with practiced nonchalance.

"I am here to take your confession," the interrogator says.

"Okay," Charlie says.

The interrogator's pen hovers above the pad.

"You are going to confess to the crimes you've been charged with?" he says.

"Yes."

"Without reservation?"

"Yes."

The interrogator shakes his head in disbelief. He says something in Arabic. One of the goons strolls over and unlocks Charlie's cuffs.

"Please come, Mr. Matthews," the interrogator says.

Charlie shuffles over to the table. The goon carries his chair behind him. Charlie sits back down.

"What do you want me to say?" Charlie says.

"That you smuggled drugs of course," the interrogator says.

"How did I do that?"

"I don't know. Why don't you tell me."

Charlie gestures at his useless right arm.

"I can only write left-handed. It may take a while."

"I will write. All we need is your signature."

Over the next couple of hours Charlie relates the basics of the plot. How in Pakistan he struck up a friendship with a heroin smuggler; a shadowy figure named Ayub. His plan was to sell the drugs in the United States, but when he returned home he discovered the street price had cratered. He needed to find a place where the mark ups were greater and he fixed upon Saudi Arabia. For understandable reasons, it had the best profit margins in the world. Using a false identity, he secured a job at the hospital and within a month was receiving shipments from Pakistan, the heroin hidden inside imported soccer balls. He used his apartment as his base of operations and soon had a large group of customers. He never asked their names, and they never gave them to him. Before long he had made such a fortune that he closed up shop and was in the process of leaving Saudi Arabia when he was arrested.

"Please sign your name here," the interrogator says.

Charlie does the best approximation he can with his left hand. The interrogator takes the confession and leaves. One of the guards goes out and returns with a Coke and some grilled chicken.

"Eat," he says.

Charlie wolfs the chicken down. It is the first substantial meal he's had since his arrest. Once the meat's gone, he sucks on the bones until they're dry.

An hour later, the interrogator returns.

"We need more details," he says.

Together Charlie and the interrogator come up with an elaborate set of code words Charlie and his clients used. The interrogator becomes fixated with adding a sexual element, and so Charlie develops a storyline about a quartet of Filipino maids who moonlit for him as prostitutes, their clients all sex-starved expats. Saudi men, of course, were too virtuous to ever partake.

Once again the interrogator leaves, and while Charlie waits for him to return, he fantasizes about his own death. He imagines being led out into Chop-Chop square, a crowd of thousands baying for his blood. He will look up into the fiery sun one last time and then the crowd will go quiet as the executioner steps behind him. He will ask not only Noor's forgiveness, but also Malaya's, Aamir Khan's, Mukhtar's, and even Wali's; everyone whose lives he's destroyed by placing himself in theirs. Then he will lower his neck, feel the knick from the sword, and this time his reprieve won't be a distant shout but rather perpetual blackness.

My torment will be over.

The door opens and the interrogator enters. He has the look of a student whose teacher has yet to accept his paper.

"They need the names of your associates," he says.

"How many do they need?" Charlie says.

"Two is sufficient."

Charlie thinks.

"How about Andrew Sanders and Rupert Johnson?"

"These are real people?" the interrogator says.

"Course."

"Where are they?"

"They managed to slip out of the country before I got caught."

The interrogator shakes his head.

"That's not good enough," he says.

"It's the best I got."

"I would like to suggest two other names. Michael Cooper and Jennifer Dubbins."

"Excuse me?" Charlie says.

"They were brought in a couple of hours ago. From what my colleagues tell me, they have already confessed to their roles in your operation."

'That's a lie. They weren't a part of it."

"They confessed."

Charlie stands up. His head throbs horribly.

"You tortured those confessions out of them," he says.

"Mr. Matthews they have clearly implicated you in this drug smuggling operation—"

"I implicated myself."

"And now we need you to implicate these two individuals."

Charlie stares down the interrogator.

"I won't do it," he says.

The interrogator shrugs. He nods at the goons. They extricate themselves from their slovenly poses and make their way towards Charlie.

FORTY-SIX

THE TWO BEARDED men couldn't be more different. One of them barely out of his teens, his wispish beard and clunky spectacles giving him the appearance of an overly intense madrasa student. He looks anything but a mujahid, and it annoys Tariq no end that it's he who, for the most part, has been asking the questions. The second man, on the other hand, is almost a cliché of a mujahid. He is older, with a bushy, graying beard, a worn eye patch, a set of purplish scars down his left cheek, and a hook rather than a hand at the base of his left wrist.

"Are we nearly finished?" Tariq says in Arabic.

"A few more questions," the young one says.

Tariq grimaces. The stagnant air in the tiny, decrepit office is stultifying.

"You wrote on your questionnaire that you have experience with FIM-92s," the young man says. "What are those?"

"They're Stinger missiles," Tariq says. "I used one to shoot down a Communist jet in Afghanistan."

The young man blushes.

"You only have one arm," he says. "How could you accomplish such a feat?"

"Someone else pulled the trigger," Tariq says.

The young man starts writing another treatise.

"Look," Tariq says. "You know who sent me here, don't you?"

The young man looks up.

"You mean the Prince?" he says.

"Exactly. I'm going to be his liaison to bin Laden."

"That's not what we were told. We were merely informed you wished to join the organization."

"Of course but as the Prince's liaison, working at bin Laden's side."

The older man chuckles.

"No one just arrives and begins working at the Emir's side," he says. "You first must prove yourself, show you can be trusted."

"The Prince has vouched for me," Tariq says.

"He has vouched for a number of people."

"I fought in the jihad. I lost my arm, damn it."

The older man scratches his chin with his hook as if to indicate that's not a particularly big deal.

How did I end up here? Tariq asks himself.

The stench. The insufferable heat. The sheer decrepitness of everything. He can't get out of his mind the look of horror on Badia's face when they were first shown their accommodations; a single room in a dilapidated building that overlooked a hill of steaming garbage. Her horror was only exceeded by his own.

He knows the answer, of course.

Ivor Gardener.

The young man finishes writing.

"The emir firmly believes we must be prepared to sacrifice anything, including our lives in the cause of jihad. Are you willing to do that?"

What have you sacrificed? Tariq wants to say.

Instead he just nods.

"Good," the young man says. "Then he'll be heartened to hear of your arrival."

"When do I meet him?" Tariq says.

"When we trust you," the older man says.

"How long does that take?"

"Months, sometimes years. It's different with everyone."

The two men rise and head for the door. Tariq panics.

Years. I can't live like this for years.

"Wait," he says.

The men turn back.

"I know the identity of the C.I.A. station chief in Khartoum," he says.

The two men look at each other. They clearly don't. Tariq's hopes rise.

"He used to visit the Prince back in Peshawar. He was interested in learning about al Qaeda, about bin Laden particularly."

"And you never alerted us?" the young man says.

"We meant to, but events in Afghanistan got in the way."

"Did the Prince tell him anything?"

"Never. He denied al Qaeda even existed, but I know the man's gotten plenty of information anyway."

"How?" the older man says.

"He was in Riyadh last week. He tried to recruit me."

This time the look of shock on the two men's faces is palpable. Tariq knows he's either signed his death warrant or moved four rungs up the organizational ladder.

"What is this man's name?" the older man says.

"Ivor," Tariq replies. "Ivor Gardener."

FORTY-SEVEN

NOOR FEELS SOMEONE shake her. She opens her eyes. It's Elma. She is wearing nothing more than a t-shirt and panties. Noor's heart races.

"Ivor?" she says.

"No. It's Charlie," Elma says.

"Here?" Noor says, now utterly discombobulated.

"No, on TV."

Elma grabs Noor's hand and drags her down the corridor to the living room. They scramble onto the couch. On the television a man plays the guitar and sings the virtues of Taco Bell.

"I don't understand," Noor says.

"Hold on," Elma says, "he's coming."

The commercial ends and a video image of Charlie appears. Over it a female announcer tells of his arrest in Saudi Arabia and his confession to being a drug smuggler.

Drug smuggler, Noor thinks. *It makes no sense.*

"And so this morning, a young American sits in a Saudi jail, facing the prospect of being beheaded in Riyadh's notorious Chop-Chop Square."

The television cuts to a warm set with a woman and man sitting on a couch. Noor is so stunned she hardly hears what they say next.

"Where's Charlie gone?" Noor says.

"Shhh," Elma says. "He's coming."

The television cuts to a reporter in Riyadh. Soon after, the same video image of Charlie appears. This time Noor can not only see him but also hear what he is saying. Noor cries. It's Charlie but it's not him also. His face is drained of color, a barely concealed welt runs down his left cheek and his eyes stare vacantly at the camera. What's worse is his voice. He attests to the crimes he's committed in a low monotone. There is no hint of emotion, no hint of life. Noor knows they have beaten it out of him.

After Charlie, two equally drained and monotone Westerners appear, first a pudgy man and then a disheveled blonde haired woman, before returning to the female host of the show. She sits across from an earnest looking man.

"What do you think the likelihood is of Charlie Matthews being beheaded?" the woman says.

The man clasps his hands together.

"A year ago I wouldn't have said very high."

"We had just won the Gulf War."

"But a year on, the Saudi government is facing fierce criticism from conservative elements for inviting Western forces into the Kingdom."

"Religious fundamentalists consider those lands sacred."

"Exactly. And executing Charlie Matthews, I'm afraid to say, may be a way for the King to placate them."

"Chilling stuff," the woman says. "Now to those wild fires out west ..."

Elma turns off the television.

"I'm sorry," Elma says. "I shouldn't have gotten you up."

"No," Noor says. "I needed to see it."

They sit in silence. Noor sobs.

"I've lost him all over again," she says. "He's going to die all because of me."

Elma wraps Noor in her arms.

Up until now Noor has clung to the tenuous hope that Charlie would somehow be saved, that the Saudis would cave under pressure from the Americans. But there it was, proclaimed on national television.

There's no hope.

Elma allows Noor to sink onto the couch. Curled in the fetal position, Noor falls asleep. When she awakens, she finds Elma, showered and dressed, kneeling beside her.

"How are you doing?" Elma says.

"Surviving," Noor says.

"I'm off to hire a car," Elma says. "There's a Hertz around the corner. Do you think you can be ready in a half hour?"

Noor nods.

"Good. There's a suitcase on your bed with some of my clothes in it. You should choose something that'll make you blend in more."

Elma heads for the door.

"Elma," Noor says.

Elma turns.

"Thank you," Noor says.

Elma shakes her head.

"No, thank you," she says. "You have given me a second chance."

                              ***

IVOR SITS IN the surveillance van and waits. With each passing hour he has become more suspicious. The way Elma had reacted when he brought up Noor Khan was so odd. She had seemed flustered, as if she knew more than she was letting on.

But surely Noor knows Elma betrayed her. Why would she contact her?

He takes a sip from his lukewarm Coke.

Because she had no other option.

He would have sent in a floater last night to bug the apartment, but Elma had never emerged. So much for the date.

"Subject's coming out the entrance," one of the techs says.

Ivor scuttles over to take a look. Elma strides down the street in a simple summer dress. In the morning sun, he can make out the contours of her sweet thighs and delicious ass.

How I wish I coulda tapped that last night.

He watches her disappear around the corner.

"Hold positions," he says.

He'll give it five more minutes. Last thing he wants is for Elma to have left something behind and walk in on them.

***

NOOR HOLDS OUT a pair of Elma's jeans. She remembers Charlie teasing her back in his kitchen in Peshawar. 'It's high time we got you in a pair of figure hugging jeans,' he'd said to her, and in mock anger she had extricated herself from his arms. Oh, how she now wishes she hadn't.

She pulls the jeans on. The heavy fabric rubs up against her legs. They feel so strange and so alien. She slips on the sneakers and a faded New York Yankees baseball cap. She looks in the mirror.

Now you look like an American.

For the first time that day she feels her baby kick. He kicks her a second time and this time it's so hard it takes her breath away.

"All right, all right," she says.

She heads for the door only to catch sight of her dirty

clothes. She throws them into the suitcase that Elma packed for her and heads for the front door. She hears someone in the corridor.

She tiptoes up to the peephole. Outside an elderly neighbor in a prim dress and broad hat walks past with a King Charles spaniel on a leash. Noor takes a moment.

Breathe, breathe.

Noor unlocks the door and creeps into the corridor. She looks both ways. The neighbor's gone. She hears the elevator ding. Noor hurries down the corridor. She comes around the corner and sees the elevator doors closing.

"Hold the doors, please," she says.

The elderly neighbor makes no attempt, and the doors slam shut.

Damn.

Noor looks up at the floor dial. The elevator seems to be stopping at every floor. Behind her she spies the door for the stairs. She heads for it.

***

THE ELEVATOR DOORS ding open, and the elderly woman steps off with her King Charles spaniel. The dog yaps at Ivor and the tech. There's nothing Ivor would like to do more than kick the little shit across the lobby. The woman and her dog pass, and Ivor and the tech step on the elevator. Ivor presses the button for the eighth floor and fingers the capped syringe in his right pocket. He wonders how much of a struggle Noor will put up.

Once this is inside her it won't matter, he thinks.

The elevator doors creak open, and they make their way down the corridor towards Elma's apartment. The tech crouches in front of the lock. It offers no more than a couple of seconds of resistance. Ivor steps inside, hoping Noor will shout out thinking Elma's home. The tech closes the door behind him. Ivor waits. Nothing. Ivor wanders through the foyer and points towards the living room. The tech nods. Ivor takes a quick look around the bathroom. He opens the shower door before heading down the corridor into Elma's bedroom. He stands utterly still. He gets down on his knees and looks under the bed. No one. He clambers to his feet and slides open the closet door. He parts the rack of shirts, jackets and dresses.

Perhaps you were imagining things, he thinks.

He closes the door and goes over to Elma's armoire. He looks through the drawers. T-shirts, sweaters, socks, panties, a couple of vibrators, some very expensive lingerie. He shuts his eyes and remembers how Elma had peeled it off in Peshawar while he watched from the bed. Never before or since had he experienced such a delectable sight.

"All done," the tech says.

Ivor turns. The tech leans against the bedroom door.

"Any signs?" Ivor says.

"None that I can see."

The tech sets to work installing a device in Elma's bedside lamp. Ivor makes his way to the living room. He scans for evidence that two people were here; perhaps two dirty coffee mugs or bowls of cereal. There's none.

You were imagining things, he says to himself. *If Noor Khan spent the night she would've left with Elma or be here now.*

The tech pops his head in.

"All done," he says.

Ivor nods. If there's any recompense for chasing this red herring it will be some decent audio of Elma having sex or using one of those vibrators.

That'll help while away some lonely nights back in Khartoum.

He follows the tech out and heads for the front door.

***

NOOR REACHES THE second floor and drops the suitcase.
She takes a moment to catch her breath.

I should have taken the lift, she thinks.

She picks up the suitcase and struggles down the final set
of stairs. She sees a door in front of her. On the other side,
the elevator dings as if to taunt her. She pushes the door
open.

"Morning," she hears a man say.

She recognizes the voice immediately.

Ivor Gardener.

She steps backwards and twists out of view. The door
slams shut. She spins around and sees another door to her
left. She pushes it open and finds herself in a dimly lit
corridor. She sprints down it. From back in the stairwell, she
hears the door to the lobby bang open. She comes to another
door with an exit sign above it. Noor shoves the door open
and steps into the cacophony of the Upper West Side. Noor
looks around. Everyone seems like a potential C.I.A. opera-
tive: the FedEx delivery man unloading boxes at the curb, the
newspaper vendor across the street, the mother pushing a
child in a stroller.

Keep going, she tells herself.

Noor bundles her way down the sidewalk, her suitcase a
dead weight in her right hand. She looks over her shoulder
and sees Ivor fly out of the back entrance of the apartment
building. She tumbles into a man in front of her.

"Hey, watch it," he shouts.

The pedestrians ahead of her have stopped at a crosswalk.
She knows she can't afford to wait.

She prepares to run across the street when she sees Elma
at the wheel of a white compact car, stuck in the interminable
traffic. The traffic starts up. Noor rushes in front of Elma's

car. Elma brakes and stares wide-eyed at Noor through the windshield. Horns blare. In a crouch, Noor works her way around the other side of Elma's car. She flings the passenger door open and jumps in.

"Go, go, go," Noor shouts as she shuts the door behind her.

Elma steps on the accelerator. Noor lies flat on the seat. She doesn't dare look up.

"What's going on?" Elma says.

Noor turns back in her seat.

"It's Ivor," Noor says.

Elma stares back at Noor in horror.

"He was in your apartment."

***

IVOR STANDS ON the sidewalk, out of breath. He looks about. All he can see are a mass of pedestrians and cars caught up in a clamor of horns and construction noise.

You're going crazy, you know that? he says to himself.

When he'd seen that door open and close without anyone coming out, he'd been convinced it was Noor. But now, he's less sure. In the stairwell, he had sent the tech up the stairs while he had taken the door to the left.

Maybe he found her.

He doubts it.

But if it wasn't her, who was it? A custodian? A resident perhaps?

It doesn't make any sense.

Surely I'd have caught up with them.

His pager vibrates. He retrieves it from his jacket. It's for a Sudanese number. He doesn't recognize it.

Tariq? It's gotta be.

Ivor takes one last sweep of the street.

Fuck this, he thinks.

He heads back in. Tariq's much more important.

FORTY-EIGHT

"I HEAR YOU'RE leaving," Abdullah says.

"I've things I got to take care of in Khartoum," Ivor says.

More than just things, Ivor thinks.

He still can't quite believe Tariq has been in touch so soon. Tariq had said he had his hands on something so important they needed to meet face to face. Ivor jiggers his leg under the table. He wishes he could be there right now. Abdullah lights a cigarette. He is considerate enough to blow the smoke away from Ivor.

"You really think bin Laden is a bad egg, don't you?" Abdullah says.

"You guys obviously do," Ivor says. "You banished him from the Kingdom."

"He's nothing more than a poseur."

Ivor shoves a chunk of rare filet mignon in his mouth.

"I wish I could be as laid back as you," Ivor says. "But personally I think he wants your King's head on a platter and American blood on his hands."

"From what I hear Sudan has tempered his spirit."

"One way or another I'll find out."

"You have an agent in al Qaeda?"

"You don't?"

Abdullah laughs.

"You never change, Ivor. You can't help but answer a question with a question."

Ivor points his steak knife at Abdullah.

"I was taught by the craftiest of Arabs."

Abdullah smiles. Ivor leans back and takes in the ridiculous caricatures of the rich and famous plastered all over the Palm's walls.

"It's funny," he says, "all these people so desperate for recognition when that's the last thing you and I want."

"It's an affliction," Abdullah says.

"One that Prince of yours suffers from."

Abdullah shrugs.

"I don't get why you guys go to such trouble for him," Ivor says.

"He is a distinguished member of the royal family."

"A distinguished member who's tight with bin Laden and wouldn't blink if he had a chance to take out the King and every single one of his relatives."

"But he won't, and he never will."

Abdullah takes a sip of his wine and dabs his mouth with his napkin.

"Our governments may be friends, Ivor, but we have fundamentally different approaches to how we treat our political opponents. You lot always seek to destroy each other. Democrats versus Republicans. Right versus Left."

"And what? You guys treat each other with compassion?"

"Courtesy."

"I think Charlie Matthews would disagree."

"Oh come on, he's not an opponent. He's a cockroach and cockroaches must be crushed. But your political opponents, your equals so to speak, we've learnt that the more honorably you treat them, the more likely their fevered ambitions will cool. On the other hand, if you take them head on, well then you create resentment and bitterness, two qualities that only worsen with age."

"So you do everything in your power to find this Khan girl in the hope the Prince mellows."

"During, what you in the West like to refer to as, the Third Crusade, there was a battle where Saladin saw King Richard's horse cut from underneath him. All of a sudden this mighty warrior, whom even the bravest Muslim warriors feared, was vulnerable. Do you know what Saladin did? Instead of ordering all his forces to charge the King, he sent his brother with his best stallion so Richard might ride away."

"Sounds like he missed a golden opportunity to kill the bastard."

"Or he took the opportunity to make a friend. Six months later, he and Richard made peace and the Holy Land remained in Muslim hands for the next seven hundred years."

Ivor stabs his fork into his last remaining morsel of steak.

"Working from your theory, let me give you a piece of advice. I wouldn't execute this Charlie Matthews if I were you."

"It sounds as if you have a soft spot for the man."

Ivor chuckles.

"Shit, perhaps I do. But there's another reason."

"Enlighten me."

"You may think of him as a cockroach, but the American people won't, whatever crimes you dream up for him. Think about it, here's a good looking, white Desert Storm vet getting his head chopped off by some big, burly dark skinned dude in a square filled with turban wearers yelling 'Down with U.S.A.'. That's sure as hell going to stir up a whole load of resentment, especially since we just saved your collective asses."

"The King is aware, but the Prince–"

"Needs to be reminded the more shit he stirs up, the more our journalists will dig, and in this country they get to publish whatever they want. Does he really want the true facts of this case to come out?"

"I severely doubt it."

"Then advise him to lock the guy up and throw away the key; people over here will soon forget about Matthews, hell they might even think he got what he deserved. Besides, you never know. At some point he might be useful when it comes to finding this girl."

Abdullah swirls the remnants of his wine around his glass.

"This girl, this girl. She's proving to be much wilier than anyone foresaw," Abdullah says.

"Shit, maybe the Prince should treat his next wife better."

Abdullah smiles.

"I fear that is as likely as finding water in the desert."

Ivor looks at his watch.

"Hate to do this to you, but I got a flight to catch."

Ivor squeezes out of the booth.

"Please keep me abreast of any information you learn from Tariq Khan," Abdullah says.

Ivor stares Abdullah down. He bursts out laughing.

"You really are a wily bastard," Ivor says. "You and that Khan girl are a good match."

"I agree," Abdullah says. "She is definitely a worthy opponent."

FORTY-NINE

THEY HAVE DRIVEN for ten hours now. The only stop they made was to fill the car with gas. Noor looks over at Elma. Every so often her eyelids droop before she forces them back up. Noor spots a road sign. A couple of motels are a mile ahead.

"We should call it a day," she says.

"We're only a couple hours away," Elma says.

"Not if we crash."

Elma sighs and guides the car towards the right lane. A horn blares, and Elma jerks the steering wheel back. A truck blasts past them.

"Sorry," Elma says.

This time Elma checks her blind spot, and they make their way off the freeway. Half a mile down the road they come upon a drab two story building with a red tile roof and an even redder sky behind it. Elma pulls into its parking lot. Inside, she gives the desk clerk a false name and pays in cash. Their second floor bedroom has two queen beds with ugly floral bedspreads and a scuffed wooden desk. Elma locks the door and goes to the window. She pulls back a blind and peers down into the floodlit parking lot.

"Don't you think they would have snatched us by now?" Noor says.

"It's not their style to create a scene," Elma says.

Noor can't quite believe it, but Elma is more paranoid than she is. She joins her by the window. Outside a black S.U.V. pulls in, and a couple of burly guys in red plaid shirts get out. Noor instinctively steps back.

"We should sleep in the bathroom," Noor says.

Elma nods. They take a pillow from each of the beds and retrieve some blankets from the closet. In the bathroom they eat the remainder of the snacks Elma bought at the gas station; Pringles chips, a couple of bananas and a Snickers bar. Afterward Elma sits on the toilet so Noor can perform her prayers. On completing them, Noor turns off the light and they lie down next to each other on the tile floor, a blanket each for warmth. Elma keeps shifting her position in a futile attempt to get comfortable.

"This sucks," she says.

"I've slept in worse places," Noor says.

"Sorry, of course you have."

From down the corridor, Noor hears heavy footsteps approach. Elma tenses. For a moment the footsteps seem to stop in front of their bedroom door. They carry on.

"Do you think that was them?" Elma hisses.

"I really don't believe they followed us," Noor says.

"If only I shared your confidence."

If only I did too, Noor thinks.

After everything she's been through she's confident of nothing anymore.

Nothing but Charlie's love.

Noor reaches out her right hand and takes Elma's in hers.

"What do we do when we get there?" she says.

"Find a place for you. I took out more than enough money to pay your deposit and the first month's rent."

"Will you stay?"

"No, but I'll come back in a couple of weeks with a fake Social Security card and a birth certificate for you. With those you can get a job, have your child's birth registered."

"Then I need a name."

"Do you have any ideas?"

"One of Baba's favorite writers was V.S. Naipaul."

"So that's your surname."

"And though it was sacrilege to say so back in Pakistan, Indira Gandhi was always a hero of mine."

"Indira Naipaul, I like it."

Noor smiles.

Baba would too.

"Will you visit me often?" Noor says.

"I don't think that would be wise. I'll open a post office box back in Manhattan under a fake name. If you ever need anything, and I mean anything, you can write to me there."

Noor's eyes glisten.

"I'll be on my own," she says.

Elma squeezes her hand.

"You'll be free," she says.

Free, Noor thinks. *What a concept.*

Down the way, Noor hears more footsteps approach. Elma's squeeze transforms into a fearsome grip.

Please, Allah, Noor prays. *Please afford me the chance for that to be true.*

FIFTY

THE GUARDS SHAKE Charlie awake and hand him a set of clean Western clothes.

"Put on," the burlier of them says.

Charlie does the best he can. His body is so bruised that even the slightest movement creates ripples of pain. When it comes to putting on his sneakers he finds it impossible. His feet have swollen to twice their normal size.

"I can't," he says.

The burly guard bends down and tries to shove one on. Charlie howls in pain and soon after the guard gives up. His compatriot takes out a pocket knife and slices open the back and tongue.

"Now try," he says.

It is not aesthetically pleasing but it is a solution. The burly guard cuffs Charlie's wrists while the thinner one places a blindfold over his eyes.

"Where are you taking me?" Charlie says.

Neither man replies. They lead him outside into a van. As soon as the back doors close, the van drives away.

Perhaps this is it, Charlie thinks.

He feels a certain peace. His life hasn't turned out the way he expected.

But no one's does, he thinks. *And for all of us it must eventually end.*

Some time later the van creaks to a halt, and the back doors open. An unseen hand rips off his blindfold, and he is yanked outside into the blistering heat. His eyes adjust. They are on the edge of Chop Chop Square. Despite his professed calm, his heart can't help but race.

This really is it.

The burly guard grabs Charlie's arm, and Charlie finds himself being escorted through a side door into what looks like a red brick fort. They enter an anteroom where his interrogator waits. It's devoid of any furniture and on its pale green walls hang framed quotes from the Quran.

"You are at the Palace of Justice," the interrogator says. "All you must do is confirm your confession."

So this is my trial, Charlie thinks.

He wonders whether he'll be executed afterwards. It would make sense.

"Do you understand, Mr. Matthews?" the interrogator says.

Charlie nods.

"Then let's go."

The guards escort Charlie into a courtroom. Charlie is taken aback. For some reason he had expected it to have a more medieval feel. Instead it's not much different to those back in the States. In the public seats there is a smattering of Westerners. The only one he recognizes is Seaberry. Charlie is escorted to the defendants' table and from an opposing door Mike and Jenny are led out. They show no emotion whatsoever, not even when they see him. Charlie's heart breaks. He knows only the most vicious torture could have elicited such passivity. They are made to stand next to him.

Three elderly and long bearded judges enter and sit before them on a raised dais. The interrogator proceeds to read out their confessions in Arabic. An interpreter translates the confessions into English. Charlie looks in Mike and Jenny's direction when he hears the part where he implicated them in his drug smuggling scheme. If nothing else he wants to mouth how sorry he is. The two of them don't offer him an opportunity. They stare resolutely at the floor. The interrogator finishes reading the confessions and looks at Charlie.

"Do you confirm your statement confessing to these crimes?" he says.

Charlie remembers the many and varied tortures the interrogator took delight in inflicting upon him. His left arm shakes uncontrollably. He can't imagine enduring another minute of such pain.

But you must.

"Well," says the interrogator.

"I confirm my statements regarding my own crimes," Charlie says, "but not those I made about Mike Cooper and Jenny Dubbins."

Whispers course through the courtroom. The interrogator's eyes burn into Charlie as the judges lean forward and listen to a translation. Every capillary in the chief judge's face seems to burst. He wheels on Charlie and screams at him. Even the interrogator seems shaken by the outburst.

"Answer yes or no," the interrogator says.

Charlie looks directly at the judges.

"Mike Cooper and Jenny Dubbins were in no way connected to my crimes. My written statements are nothing but lies extracted through torture."

The interrogator pales. The chief judge demands to know what Charlie said and in a quavering voice the interrogator tells him. This produces an even longer outburst from the chief judge. Charlie can't help but smile. For the first time in a long while, he has regained a measure of independence. A set of guards grab a hold of Mike and Jenny and hustle them out of the courtroom. The chief judge calms down enough to gulp down a glass of water. With his rheumy gaze fixed upon

Charlie, he begins to harangue him in Arabic. This time the interpreter doesn't bother to translate. A collective gasp goes up in the public gallery.

That's it, Charlie thinks. *I've been sentenced to death.*

The judges stand and shuffle from the courtroom. Charlie's guards grab him. Seaberry pushes his way up to the rail.

"Don't worry," Seaberry says, "we'll appeal your sentence."

"It's okay," Charlie says. "I'm happy to die."

"But you're not going to. They sentenced you to life in prison."

The guards yank Charlie into the anteroom and slam the door shut. The interrogator is there. Charlie is too thrown by his sentence to react to his presence.

"You fool," the interrogator says. "They were going to send you to Al Ha'ir prison where all the foreigners go. But now you're off to Buraidah instead."

The interrogator shakes his head more in pity than in anger.

"I would wish you luck but it would be pointless. After all no one would say such a thing to a man on his way to hell, now would they?"

FIFTY-ONE

IVOR SITS AT the back of the dim cafe and waits. Tariq is already fifteen minutes late. He sucks down his Coke and taps the table. He wonders what Tariq's information is.

Could bin Laden be preparing an attack? In the Middle East perhaps? Europe even?

Ivor peers through the dense smoke. Every man in the place smokes tobacco from a shish, the water pipe every Sudanese man is addicted to. Ivor has to credit Tariq for his spy craft. It's almost impossible to see anyone in here and thus almost impossible to be seen. He spots a one armed man winding his way past the tables and smiles.

Finally.

Tariq emerges from the haze. He carries a briefcase.

"Sorry I'm late," he says. "I had to make sure I wasn't being followed."

Beads of sweat dapple his forehead. He places the briefcase at his feet and wipes his brow with his sleeve.

"I don't know how you can stand this heat," Tariq says.

"You should try Luanda," Ivor smiles. "Makes this shithole feel positively chilly."

Tariq stares back at Ivor stony faced.

Guy's never had a sense of humor, Ivor thinks.

A waiter comes over. Tariq orders a chai.

"So what's so urgent?" Ivor says.

"I was able to get my hands on a list," Tariq says.

Tariq looks around to make sure no one is watching then bends down and fiddles with the latch on his case. He pulls out a crumpled document. Ivor sees it's written in Arabic script. He wonders if Tariq knows he can read Arabic.

Probably not.

"It's of every al Qaeda member in Sudan," Tariq says.

Ivor's heart beats appreciatively harder.

"I need you to make a copy and get this back to me," Tariq says.

"Course," Ivor says.

All he wants to do is reach out and grab the document from Tariq's hands.

"You promise?" Tariq says.

"Jesus, Tariq, stop cockteasing me."

Tariq hands it over. Ivor feels the weight of it.

Jesus, it must be thirty pages long.

"Is there a bathroom around here?" Tariq says.

"Think I saw one near the front," Ivor says

"Be right back."

Tariq gets up out of his chair. Ivor hardly notices. He is already fixated on the list's first two names.

أسامة بن محمد بن عوض بن لادن

أيمن محمد ربيع الظواهري

Usamah bin Muhammad bin Awad bin Laden and Ayman Mohammed Rabie al-Zawahiri. The leaders of al Qaeda.

Ivor scans the first page. He doesn't recognize any other name. The list does, however, give the men's ages and their countries of birth. Jordan, Egypt, Algeria, Saudi Arabia,

Yemen. He grins. This is a gold mine. With a little help from his friends in other foreign intelligence services, he'll soon know who all of them are.

He flips to the next page and runs his eye down it. He recognizes no names there either.

Strange, he thinks. *I should know a few.*

The next page is the same and then on the next page the names start repeating themselves.

What the fuck?

He looks through the haze for Tariq. He's nowhere to be seen.

Ivor's gaze comes to rest on the briefcase. It sits innocently next to Tariq's empty chair. Ivor's stomach drops.

No.

He jumps up and slams into the waiter returning with Tariq's chai. The cup goes flying.

Ivor stumbles past a table of astonished shisha smokers, beyond a tea stand manned by an obese man with a booming laugh.

You can make it.

He sees the light bleaching through the entrance. Of all things, it reminds him of the entryway to heaven.

Time seems to slow, the faces of those around him appear frozen as if someone has just taken a photo.

He feels intense heat on the back of his neck, sees a flash so bright it almost blinds him, and finds himself flying through the air accompanied by everyone and everything around him.

Fuck, he thinks.

Then everything goes black.

FIFTY-TWO

THE TWO GUARDS drive Charlie through an endless desert.
The needle never dips below a hundred.

It's as if they can't wait to be rid of me, Charlie thinks.

They hadn't bothered with a prison van. Instead they're
ensconced in a white Lincoln Continental. Its backseat is the
most comfortable thing Charlie has sat on in days.

Most likely the most comfortable thing I'll ever sit on again, he
thinks.

Charlie gazes out at the desert. But for scrubby bushes and
the odd isolated palm tree nothing grows out here. In some
areas the desert is as flat as a football field, in others great,
rippling dunes rise up and throw off ominous shadows. From
time to time, they pass a gas station and the odd dilapidated
fort, but apart from them and other cars and trucks that's it
for humanity.

Finally the monotony of it all sends Charlie to sleep. He
doesn't wake up until he senses the car come to a halt.

"We here," one of the guards says.

Charlie opens his eyes and spies the mud walls of Buraidah
Prison looming over him. If it weren't for the barbed wire, it
could be a fort straight out of medieval times.

The prison's giant metal gates creak open and the Lincoln rolls into a courtyard in which hundreds of bare headed prisoners in grimy, threadbare thobes mill about. They turn their heads in the Lincoln's direction. A low rumble of voices gradually turns into a searing cacophony of yells. The inmates approach on all sides, their eyes glinting, their baying mouths revealing sets of crooked yellowed teeth. The khaki wearing prison guards do their best to hold them back, their six foot canes slicing through the air. One catches an inmate across the forehead and he goes down, blood gushing so profusely that it seems like his head's been carved in two.

I'm a lamb about to be thrown to the wolves, Charlie thinks.

Yet to his surprise, he feels no fear. Death is something only people who value their lives fear.

The car inches through the crowd and makes its way to a cordoned off receiving area. A phalanx of guards waits, their necks crooked as each of them tries to get a glimpse of their first ever Western prisoner.

The car comes to a halt. The back door is thrown open and a rush of hot air invades the ice cold interior.

"I love you, Noor," Charlie says, and steps out into the unknown.

FIFTY-THREE

NOOR JOGS UP the path, the dense woods encroaching on either side of her. Her lungs burn. It's been a long time since she ran this far. The gradient mellows, and before long she is hurtling down a tunnel of rhododendron bushes, their deep green foliage ablaze with bright pink flowers. The tunnel peters out, and she comes upon a wooden bridge standing astride a crystal clear stream. Her feet thump across it. The path curves to the left and she emerges beside a small lake with round lily pads near its shores and a quilt of trees around its edges. On the hill above sits a lone white mansion, the one time residence of a textile baron she had read. On the lake's circular path she can make out in the dim light the occasional person walking their dog or jogging like herself.

Being free, she thinks.

She continues around the lake and can't help but reflect on the last three days; the sleepless night at the motel with imagined C.I.A. operatives passing their door every twenty minutes; the drive up into the Blue Ridge Mountains, she is ashamed to say, she missed due to exhaustion; the incredibly easy house rental process with a landlord so trusting she feared for the woman's well being; the trip to the supermarket with the inevitable stares from the all white clientele; and then the final goodbye with Elma, tears streaming down their cheeks as they clung to each other.

"We did it," Elma had said.

And so they had.

Noor reaches a small parking lot and carries on up a steep asphalt road. By the time she gets to the top, her legs are slabs of jelly and her pounding heart is begging Noor to stop. Yet, Noor continues on as if this run is a small part of her penance for being in a place like this while Charlie languishes in a Saudi prison.

After they had left the motel at dawn, Elma had turned on the radio. Charlie's sentencing had been the third story on the news, and when Noor had heard his sentence, she hadn't known whether to laugh or cry. He was going to live but the sheer injustice of it all was overwhelming.

"The main thing is he's safe," Elma had said. "Who knows what the future will bring."

At the time, Elma's words hadn't stifled Noor's tears, but now, as Noor plods along a two lane highway, she knows Elma was right.

Only Allah knows what the future will bring.

Noor reaches the outskirts of town, though to call them the outskirts is somewhat of a misnomer. The town is barely more than a one stoplight street bordered on either side by brick buildings of various hues. For the most part they house quaint stores and restaurants that Noor has already learned are inundated by tourists during these summer months. Even at this early hour a few have made it into town, and are either enjoying a coffee and a ham biscuit at Sonny's Grill or window shopping in the yet-to-be-open arts and crafts stores.

Noor comes to a cross street and bounds across it only to hear the whoop of a police siren. She halts in her tracks and sees a police cruiser inches away from her. She edges over to the sidewalk and the cruiser pulls up beside her. A chiseled young officer in a short sleeve shirt rolls down the window.

"You all right, ma'am?" the officer says.

"I'm sorry about that," Noor gasps, still trying to catch her breath.

The officer grins.

"I'm the one who'd been sorry if I'd run you over."

Noor begins to breathe normally.

"You're the girl who's renting Sally Evan's lodge, aren't you?"

Noor once more feels a creeping fear invade her body.

"How do you know?" she says.

"Heard she rented her place to an Indian girl, and, to be honest, we don't get many people of Indian heritage round these parts. Least not Indian Indians, if you know what I mean."

Noor nods. The officer blushes as if he's wondering whether he's gone too far.

"Don't worry," he says, "folks around here are the welcoming type. I'm Gavin Spencer, by the way."

"Indira Naipaul."

Gavin's eyes flit to Noor's round belly.

"Will your husband be joining you soon, Indira?" he says.

"No," Noor says. "I'm single."

For a second time, Gavin can't help but blush.

"You have any problems," he says, "don't hesitate to call the station."

"I won't."

Gavin gives her a clumsy wave and carries on down the street. Noor thinks about running the rest of the way home but her legs refuse to countenance such a suggestion. Main Street soon peters out. She walks on past a cluster of picturesque churches and up a steep road until she arrives at her house. It is tiny but perfect. Made from white clapboard, it has a gray shingle roof, and two bay windows on either side of a heavy, black door.

She unlocks the door and enters the hallway. To the right is her bathroom and to the left her bedroom. She drops her keys in a bowl and carries on down the hallway into her living room. It is simply furnished with a worn couch and a couple of wicker chairs. Sally, the landlord, had been renting it on a weekly basis but, as Sally had put it, the constant cleaning had started to get the best of her. When Elma and Noor had offered to rent it on a long term basis she had jumped at the opportunity.

The kitchen is small and separated from the living room by a long counter. It has a sink, a fridge and a microwave oven. It's all Noor needs. She pours herself a glass of water and opens the double doors at the back. A small lawn, enwrapped on all three sides by towering trees, faces her. Noor drains her glass and her gaze comes to rest on a chestnut oak. It reminds her of the one in Charlie's garden back in Peshawar. She walks under it and stares up its trunk.

You can do this, a voice inside her says.

Little Charlie gives her a kick. It's impossible to tell whether her unborn child is egging her on or warning her.

"This is stupid," she says.

She heads toward the house only to feel him kick again. She stops.

Don't do it, she thinks.

Yet she can't help herself. Noor turns back and is soon shinnying up its bare lower trunk. She groans. Her recent run and her pregnant condition don't make it easy. Breathing heavily, she arrives at its first limb. She pulls herself on to it.

That's enough, she tells herself.

Yet she keeps going up, beyond its second and third limbs, until she reaches its fourth. She looks back down and sways. The leaf strewn ground is forty feet below. She reaches out a hand and steadies herself.

You're a fool, she thinks.

Through the tree's uppermost foliage she catches sight of

the view. Noor gasps, for as far as her eye can see, stretches a series of undulating mountains of differing shades of blue. Wisps of mist hover between them, the sky in the west bleached white as it awaits the rise of the sun in the east.

This truly is paradise, she tells herself.

Noor sits down on the limb. Tears well in her eyes. The last time she was up a tree, Charlie had proposed to her. She smiles as she remembers him on one wobbly knee demanding a yes before he would sit back down.

And, of course, you gave it to him.

Noor reaches out a hand as if Charlie's right beside her.

"I will always be yours," she says. "In this life and that to come."

She knows all of this, this view, her ability to go on a run, her very freedom is Charlie's gift to her, and, in that moment, she knows it's her duty to make the most of it.

"I love you, Charlie," she says as if hoping her words will travel around the world and into his ears.

Noor rises and makes her way back down to the ground.

END OF BOOK TWO

ACKNOWLEDGEMENTS

With any second book in a series, you don't wish your acknowledgements to be merely a laundry list of those you acknowledged in the first book. So to all those I acknowledged then, please know I am still eternally grateful.

However, it would be remiss of me, if I didn't acknowledge Clarke, Harry and Frankie again for the love and joy they bring into my life: it is the fuel that allows me to keep on writing.

I would also like to credit Heather Frary, a new early reader, with some great suggestions I ended up incorporating into the final chapter of the book.

And, of course, I would like to acknowledge my parents, to whom this book is dedicated, my mother, especially, who has championed *Refuge* and encouraged me like no other. In a different life I am certain she would have been one of London or Auckland's top P.R. consultants.

And, finally, I would like to acknowledge all those readers who read the first book, and those who sent me such wonderful emails. Nearly every day another email would pop in my inbox, often when I was having grave doubts as to whether I could get the second book done. To know the first book touched so many people has been the greatest gift I could have ever received.

N.G.O

http://www.facebook.com/Refugenovel

http://www.ngosborne.com